Advance Praise For Derrick Credito's
Lost In The Surf

"Derrick Credito returns to the ocean, anchoring a moving story of fatherhood and transformation. A powerful follow-up to *The Year Of The Tsunami,* this novel expands upon Wes Levine's journey into a layered exploration of fatherhood, identity, and new beginnings where the ocean connects a father's past to a son's future. Ultimately, *Lost In The Surf* is about family, forgiveness, and learning how to move forward without forgetting where you've been."

—ALISSA ARFORD, author of *Welcome To Seagull Street*

"Set in two very different homelands, Amsterdam and Los Angeles, Derrick Credito's *Lost In The Surf* pops and sizzles with action on every page…Vivid and illuminating."

—MARY KENDALL, author of *The Accidental Heiress*

Lost In The Surf

Lost In The Surf

DERRICK CREDITO

WANDERING BOHEMIAN
PRESS

Wandering Bohemian Press
Columbia, Maryland, United States of America

For information about special discounts for bulk purchases, or for public appearances, please contact wanderingbohemianpress@gmail.com.

Set in Baskerville

Editor: Ray Lewis III (Los Angeles)
Author Photograph: Scott Homebrew (Baltimore)
Cover Layout & Design: Rick Schroeppel (Nashville)
LCCN: 2025928105
Paperback ISBN: 979-8-9866419-2-8
E-book ISBN: 979-8-9866419-3-5

Wandering Bohemian Press, First U.S. Edition, May 2026
Wandering Bohemian Press Imprint Design by Jon Malfi

For my daughters, Jacqui and Zoey

"Be the ocean, not the wave."

-Unknown

1

Wes Levine pushes an olivewood bread basket into the open kitchen of Sub Dude, his fast and casual sandwich counter in Central Amsterdam. The wheeled cart brims with Italian torpedo rolls. Today's bread order is perfect, but for one pointy fragment baked into a shape closer to a surfboard than a sub roll. Lost in thought, Wes holds the light golden-brown slab over his shoulder like an American football. It slips from his hands, dropping to the kitchen floor.

It's a quiet slice of the day at this longtime fixture in Amsterdam's crowded food scene. At least for now, no one is approaching the front counter to ask about the short-order menu, or lingering at the curbside to eyeball the candied Belgian waffles in the window display. From behind the cash register, Wes looks outside through the glass case, where frosted pastries faintly perspire under white-hot display lights. On the other side of the glass is Amsterdam, the city his grandparents almost didn't escape in 1940. For Wes, playing catch with the misshapen slab of bread is a diversion from the specter of tragic histories he can't and won't forget.

Wes is a survivor of the 2004 Indian Ocean tsunami. After spending the previous night alone in a ramshackle beachfront bungalow, Wes stayed alive by staying in bed, thus avoiding the fast-moving, seismic waves that would consume his father,

Stanley Levine, a Baltimore pizza carryout owner turned deadbeat dad who'd reinvented himself as a globetrotting scuba diver. Just three days before catastrophe struck South Asia and a quarter million people died, Stanley had resurfaced in Wes's life. From behind their scuba masks, on Christmas Day they saw the bottom of the Andaman, a colorful and majestic basin in Southern Thailand. The following morning, Stanley went diving alone. Wes was planning to join his dad on the beach, but the dead battery on his cell phone saved his life. By 2024, that ordeal is a twenty-year-old memory. Though he lives and breathes surfer chic, Wes hasn't touched a beach in decades.

Formerly a coffee and pastry walkup called Sofia's Croissanterie, Sub Dude is now a full-service kitchen where tubular sandwiches are served Philadelphia style to a local public accustomed to daintier pleasures like croissants and bite-sized French cookies. From chocolate-glazed pastries to overstuffed pastrami grinders, everything about Sub Dude is big. As a teenager, Wes got his start in the restaurant business at his dad's pizza joint, an enterprise that tanked with the senior Levine's mounting gambling debts.

Welcoming a moment of levity, Wes goes long and launches the board-like roll over his shoulder, throwing a perfect spiral to Faisal Ahmed. Neither Wes nor Faisal have any siblings, but their years of working together have turned them into something like family. In the table area, they play catch until Faisal's dad Omar comes bustling into the café.

Faisal catches the roll and holds it behind his back, secretly dropping it into the wastebin when Omar looks the other way. Having grown up in rural Egypt, Omar knew chronic poverty, and says he can still feel those sharp hunger pangs that drove him to wake before dawn and pilfer milk from village cows.

After Jummah prayers, Omar returns to the café in a loose black thobe covering him to his ankles. In the stairwell to the loft, Omar changes into a chef's coat. As his father replaces him at the grill, Faisal rolls up his apron and tosses it into a laundry bin, fist-bumping Wes on the way out. Omar scrubs the grill with a brush wand; sometimes he does that even when the surface is spotless. Now in his mid-sixties, Omar qualifies for a pension but says his work is what keeps him going.

"Since I've been here so long," Omar solemnly tells Wes. "I can't imagine doing anything else."

"I guess this is like our little piece of the city," Wes adds. "Sub Dude is without a doubt one of the most successful second acts Amsterdam's ever seen."

Before Sub Dude, the old Sofia's Croissanterie had teetered on the brink of collapse. At Sofia's, Omar and Faisal worked for Evo, a Bulgarian businessman and money launderer who always had surly-looking men in suits coming in to talk to him. After a close brush with some local gangsters, Evo became a born-again Christian. He swore off his old ways and set out to make an honest living solely off espresso shots and cream puffs, even closing the shop on Sundays. With the financial muscle of his wealthy financier Harry Jarsdel, Wes bought the space from Evo, expanding operations to include subs, paninis, and all-day breakfast. Every month, another restaurant or café in Central Amsterdam starts losing money and ultimately shutters its doors. But somehow, Sub Dude outlives them all.

"Did I tell you what happened to Evo?" Omar asks Wes. "They found him dead in a field."

"Damn," Wes replies. "Did he owe someone money?"

Omar shrugs. "I just heard it happened last week over in Kolenkit. Maybe he crossed someone in a gang?"

"Don't know," Wes says, staring through the window at a woman parking a motorcycle on the sidewalk.

Jen Souza slips off her helmet, shaking her long dark curls loose. After a month of dating, she's coming to see Wes where he works. At the front counter, Jen steps to the touchscreen wearing a black medical facemask.

"Feeling better?" Wes asks from behind the cash register.

"A little," she replies, lowering her mask for a moment. "It's not COVID or anything. I'm just getting over a nasty cold."

"I can make you anything you want," Wes says as the ordering screen freezes on an error message. "It's on the house today."

Jen scrolls into a note on her phone and orders a full-length sub, speaking from under the mask. "I'll have a cheesesteak with chicken, not steak. Can that be made with avocado, sriracha sauce, lettuce and tomato but no onion?"

"Sure thing," Wes returns, jotting the order on a green guest check. "That's the Spicy Californian, my personal favorite. What kind of cheese do you like?"

"I'm picking this up for someone," she says bluntly. "Provolone's fine. Once I'm over this cold, I'd love to get together with you again. Soon, my mom's leaving to take care of my grandmother in Indonesia. Lately our home life has been upside down. I need to be there for her, so let's have coffee at my place in Kolenkit."

"Coffee sounds good," Wes agrees. "I'm off next Tuesday."

"Great," Jen says as Wes hands her the sub. "Then it's a date."

"The Van Gogh Museum was fun," Wes adds. "On Facebook, I almost posted the selfies we took in front of those sunflower paintings. But I wanted to ask you first."

"Sure, tag me if you want. Maybe next time we can check out Rembrandt."

"From what I've heard, Rembrandt's more intense than Van Gogh," Wes says, tapping the pen on the register as another customer walks into the café. "Duty calls. I'll ring you soon."

Jen lowers her facemask. "You better," she playfully replies, bouncing her voluminous hair back into the helmet.

Jen tucks the paper-wrapped sub into a small backpack and accelerates on her motorcycle to the other side of the train station. A forty-year resident of Amsterdam, Omar tells Wes what he knows about Kolenkit, and none of it is good.

"Hey buddy?" Wes approaches Omar at the grill. "You think she's bringing that sub to another guy?"

Omar waves off the question, clanging his spatulas to mince up some mushrooms and onions. "Listen to yourself, Wes. You've been seeing her for three weeks. Don't drive yourself crazy with those thoughts."

"The thing is, I really like her," Wes confesses.

"How did you two meet, anyway?" Omar asks.

"Long story. When I first came to Amsterdam twenty years ago, we got together once. Our paths didn't cross again until I ran into her in the cheese aisle at Albert Heijn."

"What kind of cheese did she buy?" Omar probes, suddenly curious. "If it's cheddar or mozzarella, you'd better run. But if she likes Swiss or cottage, that girl is a keeper."

Wes thinks hard on it. "I honestly can't remember. Would it be okay if she likes brie?"

Omar pauses. A split second later, the first dinner rush swarms through the front door. In front of the register, Wes tapes an OUT OF ORDER sign on the malfunctioning touchscreen. Before Omar can turn around to look, ten more green guest checks are hanging over the grill.

On Tuesday afternoon, Wes types Jen's address into Google Maps, pedaling his old Dutch bike on the loop around a trail. While cycling past waterbirds and tulips along the glistening recreational lake, two other loops are circling in his head: Omar keeps reminding Wes that Kolenkit is a dumpy, despairing part of town, and Evo's killers and their accomplices are from that no-good northwestern corner of Amsterdam.

Wes finds his way through unfamiliar streets, following the route as the dot on Maps blinks away from the lake. In Kolenkit, the old apartment units are drab, brown slabs of concrete, a gloomy departure from Central Amsterdam's historic and cosmopolitan charm. Garden beds outside the residential building are overflowing with weeds. When Wes finally passes a playground, it's all post-Chernobyl vibes: empty swing set, empty sandbox, and no children or parents milling around the rusty sliding board. On a street corner, a divided gang of men in leather jackets shout into each other's faces. Two of the guys put up their fists, but cooler heads prevail when someone steps between them.

Finally, Wes finds Jen's apartment community. He quickly pulls his phone off the handlebar clamp. On the screen, he verifies the address and slips the device into his pocket. No one in Kolenkit is smiling, at least not on the street. Outside Jen's door, Wes chains his bike to an iron grate by the stairwell.

A much older looking woman slowly opens up, and immediately Wes apologizes for knocking on the wrong door. She's tiny and Asian, with haunching shoulders that make her look even older and smaller. It's Jen's mom. She lightly bows her head, moving in slow feathery steps, not uttering one word to reveal what language she speaks. Like everyone else in Kolenkit, Jen's mom doesn't smile either. But with gracious finesse, she lifts a hand to point Wes inside. When she closes the door, the handle slips off and crashes to the floor. Wes picks it up and offers to assist, but she takes the lever handle and easily snaps it back into place.

Jen's sitting on the sofa in black jeans and black tee shirt, her tight and revealing heavy metal chic clashing with mom's beige jersey hijab. Wes comes to the sofa and Jen quickly covers the spotty cushions with a purple throw blanket. Jen's mom turns her back, walking a slow, creaky path into another room. Once that door shuts, Wes and Jen finally hug.

"Your mom's nice," Wes politely starts the conversation.

"Mom's second husband died and left her in fairly good shape financially," Jen reflects. "She's been a big help ever since I had to move out of Centrum."

"So, who's the surfer in the family?" Wes asks curiously, glimpsing a golden surfboard standing upright in the corner.

Jen hesitates, pursing her lips. "Well, it isn't me," she replies jovially. "That board hasn't seen much action in a while."

"Me neither," Wes admits. "I mean, I surfed a little in California when I was young, but have never even been to a beach in the Netherlands."

"Well, let me put it like this," Jen says, rolling her eyes in exasperation. "Bloemendaal is for rich, smart people who love nature. Everyone knows Kolenkit is on the wrong side of the tracks. When in Bloemendaal, I just say that I'm from Amsterdam."

"No judgement from me," Wes responds as Jen springs for the beeping coffeemaker. "I live in the loft above Sub Dude. It's in a great location, but my living quarters aren't exactly glamorous."

"Centrum's gotten so expensive," Jen adds. "Nowadays

housing is out of control. Living outside the city makes more sense when you're on a fixed income."

"Where are you working these days?" Wes asks.

"I work from home as a medical transcriptionist," Jen cuts in. "Just so you know, I haven't been back to the Red Light District since that one time we got together."

Wes smiles wistfully. "Hard to believe it's been twenty years."

"Do you have any children, Wes?" Jen asks him.

Wes shakes his head. Since falling into a life of international travel in his twenties, Wes had never felt settled enough to seriously consider starting a family, to become for a child what his parents had been for him. That, however, is a complicated picture. In the late seventies, Wes was born from an unplanned pregnancy to parents who'd wait a few more years before marrying. Though Wes never doubted his parents loved him, Dad deserted the family when Wes was sixteen, setting Mom back many years on her long and tormented road to peace and prosperity.

"I'm in the middle of my forties," Wes concedes. "Even if I became a parent next year, I'd still be going to my kid's graduation as a pensioner."

"You know, that's why I'm glad I had my son young," Jen discloses. "I wouldn't want to start taking care of a child at my age, either."

"Oh, you have a kid?" Wes asks, a little startled. "That's cool, I guess. How old is he?"

"Zen just turned nineteen," Jen answers. "Today he went to the beach to go surfing with his friends. Sorry I didn't tell you sooner."

"It's okay," Wes begins. "The thing is, I've always loved the idea of having a family. But at some point, I guess I figured that ship had already sailed."

Jen sets her coffee on the tray, slinking closer to Wes on the blanketed sofa cushions. As she cozies closer and runs a hand across his chest, they start to kiss. "You're such a nice guy, Wes. I've always gotten such good vibes from you."

Keeping quiet, Wes looks downward. "Oh, Jen," he says,

bringing caution into a moment of sexual tension. "Isn't your mom in the other room?"

"There's something I want to tell you," Jen whispers into Wes's ear.

"Go ahead. Tell me anything you want."

"Are you sure?" she asks, turning to face him closely. "Okay, here goes. Zen is your son."

"What?" Wes replies in disbelief. "Are you sure? I mean, how?"

Jen takes Wes back to that day in 2004, when he became her final client in the Red Light District. For hours after their encounter, Jen stared into the trashcan at a gaping hole in the gooey condom, nauseous with indecision but sure that she didn't want to go through another abortion. From the start, Jen admits, she found sex work too risky for her liking, and the busted rubber was the final straw.

"Any chance that someone else could be the father?" Wes asks, suddenly fast and feverish. "I should probably get a blood test to be sure. Would that be okay with you? How old did you say Zen is, anyway?"

"I told you already. He turned nineteen on the twenty-third of July," Jen confirms, counting on her fingers. "Exactly nine months from that October day in 2004 when you and I got together."

"But, but," Wes stammers. "Didn't you see anyone after that? Or maybe before?"

"Nope," Jen shoots back. "Like I said, I quit and turned in my sex workers' union card that same day. I know my body. It may have been twenty years ago, but I still remember everything."

Wes covers his mouth as though afraid of what he might say next. "I just can't believe I have an adult son who's never even met his father. How does Zen feel about all of this?"

Jen rests a hand on Wes's shoulder. "Don't be so nervous, dear. This is not like America, or that Jerry Springer Show. No one in Europe makes jokes about single moms or absent dads."

"If Zen is my son, I want to play an active role in his life. But I've never even made one child support payment."

"I chose to have this child," Jen reminds him. "And since I didn't run that by you first, I'm not asking you for *alimentatie*."

Wes sighs. "How about a DNA test, just to be sure?"

"I'll talk to Zen, and we can set something up at a clinic, if that makes you feel better," Jen offers.

Wes nods acceptingly. "When do I get to meet Zen?"

The front door opens, and in walks a young man carrying a longboard still crusted with sand. Dumbstruck, Wes stands up from the sofa. They're almost equal height. Wes and Zen have the same deep-set brown eyes, the same thatch of dark chestnut hair, the same weathered but slender hands.

"You're back early," Jen quietly calls across the room to Zen. "Catch any waves today?"

"None, *niets, nada*," Zen replies flatly, setting his board upright in a corner.

"Zen," Jen approaches her son, touching the side of his hand. "This is Wes. He's the owner of Sub Dude."

"Oh, the cheesesteak guy?" Zen asks. "You make a killer sandwich, dude."

Wes winces at Zen. "Omar was on grill that day. I'll let him know you liked it."

"Mom?" Zen asks. "What's with the funeral vibes?"

Jen turns to Wes, clearing her throat to invite him to respond.

"It's been many years," Wes fumbles for the right words. "Back when we were in our twenties, your mom and I knew each other for a short time. A very short time. Then a month ago, we ran into each other at Albert Heijn. Since then, we've been dating. And today, she told me that I'm your father."

"So, you're that guy she's been talking about?" Zen asks.

"Guess I'm heading into some unchartered waters here. Can I give you a hug?"

"Um, okay. Do your thing," Zen answers indifferently.

As his sudden, unforeseen foray into fatherhood begins, Wes is fighting back tears. "This is unreal," Wes utters. "I have a son. You're my son."

"It's okay, man," Zen says, wiggling out of the tight embrace. "Go easy on yourself. I'm not mad at you."

"You're practically my twin," Wes replies, his voice cracking with emotion.

"Hey Wes?" Jen asks from across the room. "Do you still think we should set up an appointment?"

"No, I don't," Wes responds to Zen, who reluctantly leans closer and hugs him back. "I've never been so sure of anything in my life."

Amsterdam, October 2004

In the heart of town, a church bell tolls on the hour. It's always loudest around Oude Kerk, the old church, Amsterdam's oldest building. A full-circle tower bell strikes a low desolate tone. Every time I hear that melancholic chime echoing across the Canal Ring like a death knell, I'm less impressed, less subdued, and less attuned to the resonant gong or whatever it is supposed to signal.

I live in a very modern city, where I'm a throwback in a yarmulke and prayer shawl who spends all day with a quill in my hand. In a room without windows, I dip my quill into bitter-smelling ink again and again. When the ink fumes become unbearable, I step outside for fresh air. Sometimes what I need is a break from being an anachronism, and to remind myself that despite my temporary commitments as a Hebrew scribe, an ancient profession with dwindling staying power in this emerging digital age, I'm as modern and relevant as I've ever been. That is, as modern and relevant as one can be while cloaked in the archaic modesty of a black suit and a wide-brimmed hat.

Sometimes smoking a potent joint at a coffeeshop does the trick, which today leads me to a heavy, spicy lunch in Chinatown. Before I know it, I'm walking up and down the rose-tinged alleys in De Wallen, dazed like a space cadet when I follow a trail of neon light down another sultry side street. I'm thinking about sex, though not necessarily because of any urge from within. At every corner, they seduce me from behind the soft allure of red velvet curtains. Some of the women standing in those rosy, luminous windows press their barely-clothed bodies against the glass. A forceful knock startles me. I turn around, and the banging from inside is a wide-eyed blonde with a broken smile and blackened gumline. She looks bony and brittle in her thigh-high stockings and skimpy bra. Staring straight into my face, she flails her stick-thin arms against the glass door.

"Why don't you come in and fuck me?" she insists. "Fifty euro."

I balk at her straightforward entreaty with a polite smile and walk on. Looking through another doorway, I feel more drawn to a woman with long dark hair and a healthy glow that puts my mind at ease. She's so pretty that I nearly trip between stones on the cobbled sidewalk.

From outside the door, I peer into the small room, a boxy hole in the wall with a cot and sink. She looks up from her cell phone, her alluring dark almond-shaped eyes drawing me closer. A playful grin reveals braces running across her teeth. She cracks open the door, just enough to reach out and wave me in. Sooner than I can form a thought in my head, I'm indoors on the other side of bright red lamplight and she's puckering her full, luscious lips all over my face.

"Three kisses for Holland," she says, leaning closer. "What's your name, dear?"

"I'm Wes," I reply, following her up a narrow staircase. At the top, she opens the door to a room more spacious than her ground-level shoebox.

"Hi Wes," she greets me with an uncommon, gracious sass. "I'm Jennifer. You American?"

"Yeah," I say absently, my mind still replaying a sensual loop of those kisses of a moment ago. "You must be Dutch."

"My grandfather was from Utrecht, but I'm all mixed up," Jennifer says as she sways to the window and turns the red curtains shut. "I'm also Indonesian, Moroccan, Brazilian, and Lebanese."

My Jewish grandfather was born in Utrecht, too. I smile and nod, without volunteering pieces of myself that might kill the mood: part Dutch means I'm too hip to local traps. Part Italian might come across as too proud. Part Irish and German, too white. I'm also Jewish, and very possibly considered an enemy across the pastiche of Jennifer's ethnicities.

Jennifer edges closer, lightly touching the back of my hand. "So, what's your story, Wes?"

"*My* story?" I ask, snapping out of a daydream. "Jennifer, not even my fantasies are as pretty as you. You're beautiful."

"Thanks baby," Jennifer responds and kisses me again, this time on the lips. "You seem like a real gem."

She takes my hand and asks me in straightforward Dutch to get undressed, *kleding uit.* I unbutton my shirt and slither out of my black frock coat, feeling like a snake shedding its skin. We sit at the bedside and Jennifer lays down some ground rules, which I understand is standard procedure. I nod respectfully as I slip her a fifty and await an experience unfathomable to me a moment ago.

I hardly have a moment to look at her bare-naked body before we're bouncing on the mattress. Jennifer mounts me, letting the softness of her breasts brush against my chest, down to my navel, and further still. She pops a condom into her mouth and slides it on me. We glide together. Jennifer holds me close while I clutch the mattress. Afterwards, I catch my breath and she holds me close. Her long, curly hair feels like home to me.

"I'm getting good vibes from you," Jennifer says, rolling the lace panties up her legs.

"This is exactly what I needed today," I thank her. "Guess I'm kind of new to this."

"You're a sweet guy," Jennifer says on the way downstairs.

"Can I see you again sometime?" I ask.

She gives me a beaming smile, all lips and no braces. "Come see me whenever you like," Jennifer answers, leaning closer to kiss me again. "One for Holland, one for me, and one for you."

2

In their first awkward moment together as father and son, Zen comes at Wes with questions. Each one hits him like a gut punch. *Who are you? Why now? Why not twenty years ago?* Wes doesn't have a single answer. He has an apology. Again and again, Wes apologizes for not being around all those years while he was busy building a brand as Amsterdam's top cheesesteak slinger.

"You don't have to be sorry for everything," Zen tells him. "Where are we, Canada?"

Wes grins without grasping the comment. "Have you been to Canada?"

"Twice. Some of my cousins live in Montreal," Zen says as Jen hands him a coffee cup. "I'll pass, Mom. Coffee's boring."

Zen turns around and dashes to the refrigerator for a can of Red Bull. Finding nothing, he scans the kitchen countertop for loose coins, announcing that he's heading out to the convenience store. "Need anything from the Quick Mart?"

"Energy drinks aren't good for your heart," Wes says to Zen. "My grandparents lived into their nineties, but heart disease is what got them both."

Zen freezes up and slowly closes the front door, turning around to listen closely. "What about your parents? Are they still alive?"

14

Wes shakes his head. "My dad was a scuba diver, and he died in a tsunami. Back in 2020, Mom came down with COVID."

"So, my grandparents are dead," Zen says distantly. "Dude, where the hell were you when it was just me and mom?"

"You know, Zen, I really wish we'd met sooner. My own dad disappeared from my life when I was sixteen, so I know the feeling."

Zen backs away, giving Wes a cold glare. "No, you don't. At least you had a dad until you were sixteen. I'm nineteen and never even had one."

"I know this must seem like it's coming out of nowhere," Wes assures him. "But I would've rather been with you from the day you were born. I really mean that."

"So, for twenty years you couldn't bother looking up Jennifer Souza on Facebook?"

"I only knew her first name," Wes states the utter truth. "We didn't know each other well. Before our paths finally crossed at the supermarket, I didn't even know your mom was still in Amsterdam."

"Zen, dear," Jen says, pointing to the porcelain wares on the bamboo tray. "You don't have to drink all the coffee. But let's be Dutchies for a while and connect over a cup, hmm?"

Zen rolls his eyes and shrugs. From the kitchen countertop, he holds a cup under the Keurig machine, pressing buttons until the house blend trickles out. Cup in hand, Zen returns to the sofa to find out more about the biological father now sipping hot coffee in the living room. "Do you know how to surf, Wes?"

Zen's question startles Wes, making him feel exposed and embarrassed at how long ago that was. Wes always loved the idea of being a surfer. From deep within, he longed since an early age to taste the risk and rush of dancing his way out of a steep vertical wall. But in reality, Wes can count on one hand how many times he's stood on a surfboard. When he caught his first tube, a gentle barrel wave in Seal Beach, Wes chalked it up as beginner's luck. A couple years later, he flew into San Diego for his cousin Evan's bar mitzvah. At the celebration,

Evan's parents gifted he and Wes with a week of surfing lessons in Oceanside. Evan shredded wave after wave while Wes, then twenty-two, couldn't keep up with his precocious thirteen-year-old cousin. On his next trip to Laguna, Wes wiped out on a few choppy swells at Doheny State Beach and spent the rest of the week bicycling up and down the Venice Beach boardwalk. A few years later in Southern Thailand, Wes went scuba diving with his dad in Phuket's Andaman Sea on the day before the tsunami. He hasn't felt drawn to an ocean ever since.

"It's been a while since my last time on a board. I'm a little rusty," Wes admits. "Guess I've always been a decent swimmer. That's half the battle, isn't it?"

Zen smirks, the closest he's come to cracking a smile since meeting his father. "Where are you from, anyway?"

"I haven't been back to the states in twenty-one years," Wes responds. "But I was born in Baltimore, and grew up in a quiet, leafy suburb out in the county."

"Baltimore?" Zen asks quizzically. "Is that the West Coast?"

"No," Wes answers, laughing lightly. "East Coast."

"You seem more like you're from California," Zen remarks, and Wes can't tell if it's a compliment or a diss.

"I went to California a few times before moving abroad and relocating to Amsterdam permanently," Wes shares. "But enough about me, Zen. I want to know what your life has been like. What have you been up to lately?"

"I just graduated secondary, and I'm taking a year off school to figure out what's next. Me, Mom and my *nenek* went to Jakarta last summer for my great-grandmother's one hundredth birthday."

"Mazel tov," Wes replies. "That whole part of the world is fascinating. Before you were born, I spent a year bouncing between Thailand and New Zealand."

At that, Zen's expression doesn't change, and Wes tries to engage him again. "Is there anything you want to ask me?"

Zen looks straight into his father's eyes. "I want to know how you met my mom."

"Well," Wes comes back slowly. "Your mom and me…"

"You don't have to bullshit me," Zen interrupts. "My mom

and I are Dutch. We're open like that."

"Well, we saw each other just once and, like I said, we didn't meet again until a month ago," Wes replies carefully. "All those years, we've been like two ships passing in the night."

"I'm not talking about those years," Zen says impatiently. "I want to know more about how it went down on the day you got together."

"Normally condoms are very safe and effective," Jen tells her teenage son. "But the condom broke, which almost never happens in that line of work."

"So, I guess that makes me a miracle baby," Zen fires back, a little bitter. "This is just me, but if I got a girl pregnant in my twenties, I'd seriously hope she'd get an abortion."

Jen turns to Zen, her eyes radiating steely determination. "I chose that once. You know the story. I was barely twenty myself. It was with some guy I met at a bar. I wasn't going to let an impulsive one-night stand change my life forever. But in my pregnancy with you, Zen, I got a totally different feeling. I knew that you'd be a gift of love. You're the greatest gift of my lifetime. If Wes and I never met, we wouldn't be here now."

"So, Mom, you're saying you would do it all over again if you could?"

"I wouldn't change a thing," Jen replies, calm and firm. "All this time, you and I have been like Zennifer. Just the two of us. But now if it's not too late, we have a chance to be a family."

"I'd really like that," Wes says, turning to Zen. "I want to be in your life. Just like any good father would."

"Go easy on yourself," Zen reassures Wes, patting him on the arm. "I understand the situation better than you think."

"Next time I have a day off, I'd love to go surfing with you," Wes returns, his face suddenly beaming with hope. "Can you tell me where I can buy a wetsuit?"

"You'll probably want to order it online," Zen answers quickly, heading back to the front door. "That reminds me, I left mine hanging outside to dry."

Zen heads outside, giving Wes and Jen a moment alone to process what just transpired. Wes looks into Jen's eyes and tells her he loves Zen already. They start to kiss. After a hot moment of light making out, they quickly pull apart and sit up straight as Jen's mom creaks out of her room. She walks to the sofa, her steps slow and intentional. Jen's mom smiles warmly at Wes and says something in Indonesian that brings mother and daughter into a heartfelt embrace, a brief moment of joy cut short when Zen returns to the living room empty-handed.

"It happened again," Zen says, clenching his fists. "My wetsuit's been stolen off the guardrail."

Omar is working up a sweat behind the stovetop, experimenting with a new recipe he's been pitching to Wes for the Fall menu. Over a bubbling clay pot, Omar strains the sour milk to make *ayib*, an Ethiopian cottage cheese he spreads inside the sub roll. He adds spicy cubed tenderloin *tibs* and a drizzle of lemon and garlic tahini dressing. Omar slices the sub to go halves with Wes, who takes one bite and decides the Ethiopian is the newest cheesesteak on Sub Dude's menu.

"You've caught me at good time," Wes says. "I just found out Jen's son is mine. His name is Zen. What a good-looking kid. He's as sharp as they come."

"Congratulations, dad," Omar replies, setting down his half of the sub to nudge Wes's shoulder.

"Last week, Jen bought that sub for Zen. You made it. He said he liked it."

"So, is Zen going to university?" Omar asks presumptively.

"He's figuring things out at the moment. Zen wants to become a professional surfer."

Omar purses his lips. "How do you do that in the Netherlands?"

"I don't know. I really don't know," Wes goes on. "Wouldn't it be easier to pursue a career like that in California?"

Omar squints, slipping into a moment of deep thought. "Easier, yes. But also, more competitive."

"And it could also be a big step up for Zen and his mom," Wes adds. "They're living in Kolenkit. I've got to say, it doesn't feel much like Amsterdam over there. Not a very happy place."

"You have a responsibility now," Omar says with a quiet

seriousness. "A man who doesn't teach his son a skill might as well teach him to be a thief."

"He's not going to be a thief. And to your point, Omar, I have a legit question. How am I supposed to teach Zen anything about surfing, when he's light years ahead of me?"

Omar doesn't respond. He looks away and returns to his work, focusing his full attention on the pots and pans in front of him. Omar pours the mesh strainer full of tangy Ethiopian cottage cheese into glass Tupperware. Wes stands outside the walk-in refrigerator, where Omar carries the container to a shelf.

"That's a fair question, Omar," Wes returns. "I'm asking what you think I should do."

"First, make sure your son and his mother aren't hungry," Omar says from inside the refrigerator, where he sets the *ayib* next to a block of cheese. "You should move with your family to where there is safety and also opportunity to build a life together. And we both know that is not in Kolenkit."

"They could move upstairs with me," Wes suggests. "It's small, but with some privacy curtains we could turn the space into two bedrooms. Just a thought."

Omar's thoughts are on the *ayib*. Counting in his native Arabic, he waits a moment before removing another strainer from the heat.

"Where did you learn to make Ethiopian cheese?" Wes asks.

"When I was a teenager, I took a bus from the countryside and tried to find work as a cook in Cairo. But when that didn't happen, I ended up in a refugee shelter. I stayed there with some Ethiopians. All of us had been dealing with the same thing. No one wanted to give a job to a poor country boy. And most Egyptians avoided the Ethiopians, thinking they wanted to steal our share of the Nile River. They couldn't find work, either. Do you want to know what else we had in common, Wes? I saw hundreds of people come and go from that shelter, and not one of them had a father to help them find their way into the world."

Wes plucks his buzzing phone from the breast pocket of his chef coat. "Check it out. Zen's calling me!"

"Hey," Zen begins. "I ordered a new wetsuit, and they sent me two by mistake. We're the same size, and so I was thinking maybe we could check out the beach together?"

"I'd like that," Wes responds quickly. "How's tomorrow?"

"In the morning, Mom and I have to take *nenek* to the airport. But today, I'm not really doing anything."

"Let me see if I can get someone to cover for me at work. I'll call you again in a minute, okay?"

Omar's back at the grill frying up little hills of sliced white onions and mushrooms. The lunch rush is coming any minute now, and a dozen sub rolls are already toasting in the wood-fired brick oven.

"Enjoy the day with Zen," Omar says, sooner than Wes can ask.

"I don't want to abandon the grill and leave you in a tough spot," Wes replies. "Can you hold down the front of the house until tonight?"

"We've got this," Omar says. "Adil's on his way, and Faisal comes in at three."

"So, do you need me to…"

Omar shoos Wes away from the kitchen. "Go, go!" Omar says, insistent and sincere. "Go be with your son, family man."

It's low tide at Bloemendaal, and though the waves are slow and gentle, the crests are higher than what Wes had been expecting on the tranquil train ride to the North Sea coast. Wes and Zen step out of the changing room in matching wetsuits, looking like twin black seals about to storm the beach with surfboards. They walk on a downward slope to the shore, and Zen rushes ahead to splash himself in the shallow water.

"How far in do you want to go?" Wes asks a little timidly.

"I like to paddle out until everyone on the beach looks like ants," Zen replies, pointing to the line where the water ends.

"Just because it's low tide doesn't make it totally safe," Wes cautions, his eyes on the vacant lifeguard chair. "Why don't we take our time and get to know the ocean floor. Let's wait until there's a lifeguard on duty."

"It's nothing to worry about," Zen says, pointing to a few

swimmers already far into the water. "I know we just met and all, but I'll make a deal with you. I'll be your lifeguard, and you can be mine."

Wes steps into the water to hug Zen around his shoulders. "Okay, Zen. We can do that."

Feeling for rocks with his feet, Wes tests out the seabed. He hasn't seen a beach since Phuket. Whenever his friends share summery photos on Facebook of their holidays at the ocean, Wes usually looks away and keeps scrolling. Even twenty years after the tsunami, he still cringes at tiny capillary waves on an uneventful afternoon in Bloomendaal. Wes turns away, his gaze trailing off to the dune grass, where their land clothes sit in a small locker room built into a poolside espresso bar.

"Can we wait a while?" Wes calls to Zen, who's already wading in the barrel waves. "I need a cup of coffee."

From the breaker zone, Zen walks through the shallow water. Wes is standing still on the wet sand, as small children on boogie boards cruise gently to their moms and dads at the shoreline. "Are you okay?" Zen asks.

Wes covers his eyes, feeling the burn of tears and sweat. "The ocean still freaks me out."

Zen leans closer. "I guess that tsunami was pretty brutal."

"Check out the break, Zen," Wes says, taking a seat on the sand. "Does it feel like those waves are coming at us from a diagonal angle?"

Zen twists out a bewildered frown. "From what kind of angle?"

"It might not mean anything," Wes resigns. "What do I know? I haven't seen an ocean in twenty years."

With sadness and pity, Zen stares into his father's eyes. "You mean, like, no beach at all?"

"I've been running Sub Dude nonstop. I guess that's what keeps me from thinking about things that happened in the past."

"Mom told me she lost a cousin in Indonesia that day," Zen shares. "I wasn't even born yet."

"Don't worry about me, Zen. Sorry I couldn't go in the water today. I'm just experiencing post-traumatic stress."

"I get it," Zen says, sitting beside his father on the sand. "Just listen to your intuition. If something doesn't feel right, you don't have to apologize for not doing it."

Wes turns to looks at Zen, his eyes full of pride and wonderment. "You're pretty amazing, Zen. I'm really proud of you."

"Proud of me for what?" Zen asks, curiously suspicious.

"For being the kind and understanding young man that you are," Wes says. "You know, I was really looking forward to surfing with you. But what I didn't expect was that all those horrible memories from a lifetime ago would come flooding back."

"So, where do you swim for exercise?"

"It depends on the time of year. This summer, I've been taking up space in the swimming lanes at *Marineterrein*. You ever been?"

Zen balks at the idea of swimming in an urban basin. "You mean the canal pool? I don't know. I've heard that water can get nasty. I swim laps at an indoor community pool."

"That's what I do in winter," Wes says. "*Marineterrein* isn't like the canals in Centrum. If you like it, I'll buy you a monthly pass and we can swim until they close for the year."

"Okay, cool," Zen says, plucking his upright surfboard out of the sand. *"Marineterrein* awaits!"

In the locker area, they change back into their land clothes. Surfboards and wetsuits in tow, they hop a train. Their first stop is Kolenkit, where Jen is on her laptop working from home when they drop off the boards. From there, Wes and Zen catch two more trains to Waterlooplein. Beyond the underground metro station, a flower market is in full force, with vendors peddling trinkets at shaded tables. Wes steps to the canal lane in swimming trunks, while Zen still wears his full-body wetsuit, and he has his reasons.

"After graduation, me and my mates went out on a pub crawl in De Wallen. We got a little sloppy and a few of us fell into the canal."

"Were you okay?" Wes asks, a little alarmed. "Did anyone get hurt?"

"I was okay, but one of my mates twisted his ankle and had to get carried out the water by a fire brigade."

Wes gives Zen a once-over. "Thank the stars you were okay. It must've been one hell of a shock."

"What shocked me was the fishy, piss-smelling canal. This water seems a lot cleaner, but for now, I'll keep my wetsuit on."

"I hope we can try the beach again some time," Wes says, pointing in the distance at a three-masted ship slowly drifting to the docks. "Let's see who can get there first."

"Okay. You're on," Zen tags Wes on the back, plunging into the canal water on a race to the distant vessel. "See you on the other side!"

The following afternoon, Wes is back on his bicycle, pedaling to Kolenkit with love on his mind. He's going there to see Jen, cutting short yet another shift at Sub Dude. They finally can spend time together, alone, with Zen back at the beach and his grandmother now on a plane to Jakarta. And once again, Wes is leaving more work for Omar, who says he understands and respects Wes's shifting priorities. In a text to Omar, Wes swears up and down that he'll be back in Centrum early enough to help him close the kitchen.

At the apartment complex, Wes hops off his bike and drags it up a flight of steps. A man with his bare ass out is pissing on the stairwell wall. Wes sidesteps the smelly trickle, gulping air as he sets his bike in the vestibule. He knocks on the door and Jen opens up almost immediately. She pulls Wes into a close, warm hug before he can even take a good look at her. They hold hands on the way to the sofa. The low, soft lights in the living room make Wes feel right at home.

"We took mom to the airport this morning," Jen hints to Wes, her fingers dancing lightly on his chest. "Zen's out catching waves with his surf buddies."

"Yeah, earlier he texted to say he was going back to Bloemendaal with his mates."

"He really likes you, Wes. Yesterday when Zen came home, he was so happy you spent the day together. Mom's happy, too. She's very traditional, but she understands our situation."

"I don't see it as a situation," Wes says. "We can be a family. You don't have to be Zennifer anymore."

Jen smiles, touching Wes on the arm. They move close, their lips locking in a pulse-racing kiss. As they touch each other under their clothes, the kissing turns intense and heavy breathing begins. The dimly-lit living room transports Wes back to that brothel cabin encounter in the Red Light District. Twenty years later, the kisses are slower but deeper. The touching and grinding turns into full-blown intimacy, and Wes asks Jen a question he immediately regrets.

"What should we do about birth control?"

Jen slips out of Wes's arms. "Wes, I'm forty-four. And just so you know, I've been sterile since Zen was a baby."

"Sorry for asking, I just want to…"

"Yeah, I get it. You don't want to make another mistake."

"It's not like that at all, Jen. Look, how can I prove that I'm all in for you and Zen?"

Jen looks at Wes with eyes that could cut glass. "If you really feel that way, I need to know I'm more to you than just an easy lay."

"I think the world of you," Wes returns. "Just give me a chance to show you how important you and Zen are to me."

"Okay, then," she says with an eager smile, reaching for his belt buckle. "We can still do it, you know."

Afterwards, they cuddle in the nude and drift asleep, sweaty and satiated on the sofa. A key jiggles in the front door, startling Jen. She springs from Wes's chest. In one swoop, Jen gathers her clothes from the floor, balling them up as she scurries to the bathroom. The dead bolt tumbles and Wes jumps into his pants. He's still buttoning his shirt when the door opens and Zen busts in with a surfboard under his arm.

"Hey Wes, where's my mom?" Zen asks.

"Um, the other room," Wes replies, swiping his socks from the living room floor.

Zen returns his longboard to the corner, trying to suppress a chuckle. "Hope I'm not interrupting anything."

Wes doesn't respond. He swipes the throw blanket to cover up the sofa cushions, checking the time on his phone. "It's already seven-thirty. I need to get back to work," he says, blushing and embarrassed.

"How did you get here today?" Zen asks. "Did you ride your bike?"

"Yeah, I did."

"There's no bike here."

Outside the door, Wes scans the iron grate railings from one end to the other. "I forgot to lock it."

"Bummer," Zen says. "I'm sure you know by now this neighborhood is a pretty troubled place. We have to keep our doors locked and our windows shut."

"I guess Uber or Lyft is the fastest way back," Wes says, typing into the app. "How are the rideshare services in this area?"

"It usually takes them a while to get here, so text your co-workers," Zen suggests. "Let them know you might be running late."

"At least now, I can hang out a little longer," Wes says to Jen, who steps out of the bathroom with loose upswept curls framing her heart-shaped face. "You look as stunning as you did on the day we met."

"Aww, thank you," Jen replies, tucking a loose strand of silken black hair behind her ear. "Sorry about your bike. Around here, you either lock it or lose it."

"That's how it goes for bikes anywhere in Amsterdam," Wes says, checking his phone for an update. "The nearest driver's forty minutes away. Does that give me enough time to help Omar close the kitchen by ten o'clock?"

"You should be fine," Jen says. "Text me when you get back."

At ten forty-five, the driver double parks at the curb outside the Central Station. Wes hurries out, stepping into a Saturday night in Amsterdam, when storefronts shutter their doors for the evening and the foot traffic is flowing south to the Red Light District, the heart of it all. Wes sprints across the street to Prins Hendrikkade. He works up a sweat as hotel signs and traffic lights swirl in the corner of his eye.

Wes dashes through the crosswalk to Sub Dude, where the

lights are out. Keychain in hand, Omar is locking the front door, slumping down the front stoop with a tired sadness in his eyes. He's cradling a foil-wrapped sub. Whenever Omar takes his dinner home, it's usually after working straight through his shift. Wes is a little winded when he greets Omar, whose pitted complexion looks dull and sallow. After pulling double shifts for three straight days, Omar's eyes are bleary and bloodshot.

"Hey buddy," Wes calls to Omar, his voice weak with concern. "I'm really sorry. My bike got stolen and Uber took forever. You weren't kidding about Kolenkit. Every day, it's something else."

"I'm glad you're making time for your family," Omar says. "But tomorrow, I'm taking the day off."

"Of course, buddy. You got it," Wes answers straight away. "I'll stay on grill the whole day if I have to."

Omar holds the rolled-up sub to his nose. "Before closing the grill, I made myself an Ethiopian with *ayib*. I haven't eaten all day."

Wes smiles at Omar with a mix of pride and sympathy. "The Ethiopian's going to be a hit when our new menu drops."

Wes turns to check the windowfront, glimpsing sweet and savory trays of colorful Belgian waffles and giant sausage rolls still basking under the display lights. "Looks like you missed the window," Wes mentions to Omar, digging into his pocket for the keys. "I'll be back in a minute."

Wes reaches into the refrigerated pastry case to shut off the lights. Through the window, he sees shadows looming large on the sidewalk. A pair of younger men are cornering Omar, throwing down wild hand gestures. One of them spits in Omar's direction. The taller guy is leather clad in a black captain hat and knee-high combat boots. He strikes Omar's shoulder, while the denim-wearing sidekick puts up his fists. Wes bangs on the window, shouting through the glass. Losing his balance, Omar drops his dinner. Leather Punk laughs as Blue Jean Billy spits on the sub that Omar waited all day to eat, kicking it into the cobblestone pavement.

Wes rushes outside to confront them. "You're way out of line, guys. This man's worked hard all day. And now I have to open the grill again so he doesn't go home hungry. Between the two of you, there'd better be twenty euro, because you're paying for it."

"What the hell is he on?" Leather Punk snarls to Blue Jean Billy.

"Tell me boys," Wes says, eyeing the smashed remains of Omar's dinner. "Why do you blame a hard-working man for your troubles?"

"Fuck all Pakis!" Blue Jean Billy yells in a meek nasal voice incongruous with his bigoted, tough-talking vitriol.

Wes backhands his phone to Omar, whispering for him to capture everything on video. "My man here is not from Pakistan. He's Egyptian. So, it looks like you've got the wrong one, pal."

"He looks like his mother bred him in a mud pit, so I say we got the right one," Leather Punk spews, waving his arm in a spiteful salute from the tip of his leather hat. In the streetlight glare, Wes spots a tiny steel swastika pendant dangling at the brim.

"Nice hat, asshole," Wes says, slapping it off Leather Punk's half-shaved head.

Leather Punk breathes fast and heavy. "I got a knife."

"Okay," Wes replies too easily. "Go ahead and show us your knife."

Leather Punk pats the front and back pockets of his black leather pants, coming up with nothing.

"Well?" Wes asks, stepping close enough to smell the liquor on the punk's breath. "Did you leave your knife at home?"

Leather Punk reaches behind his back again. "Why don't you go back inside and make your little sand rat another sammie."

"Scumbag," Wes says as they break into fisticuffs. "Let's do this."

Leather Punk lands a cheekbone punch and Wes bursts out laughing. Taking lower body shots, Wes tries to get the punk winded instead of knocking him out in one punch. On the ground, Leather Punk holds his stomach and catches his breath. He reaches below the groin and from behind his belt pulls up a bone knife handle.

While Omar is capturing the fight on video, Blue Jean Billy knocks Wes's phone from his hands. The screen shatters, but before Wes can think about that, Leather Punk hobbles closer and takes a swing, landing another shot to the face. With one eye open, Wes charges back at Leather Punk, who leans cockily against the pastry display, and smashes him with a lightning-fast upper cut. The back of his head craters into the glass case, which shatters over a rack of éclairs and jumbo donuts. Glass shards rain on the cracked assortment of whipped cream wonders and king-sized pizza slices. Blood spurts from Leather Punk's head and he can't afford to move a muscle without worsening his deep, gaping wounds.

"Hold the foil on him to stop the bleeding," Wes tells Blue Jean Billy, unwrapping the smashed sub. "Call an ambulance. You already fucked up my phone, so use yours."

On this frenetic Saturday night, everyone with a smartphone is thirsty for something scandalous. Many of them take pictures and videos, spicing up their social media newsfeeds with a bleeding man in leather pants groaning inside a smashed-in window. He's still not moving, but his eyes twitch just enough to assure stunned onlookers he's not dead.

Amsterdam's little corner of Instagram instantly lights up with hashtags like #welcometoamsterdam and #bluntsbitchesandbrawls. Debauched faces with cell phones stop outside the bloodied café window to feed their cameras with shocking snapshots. Wes keeps both hands in his pockets. His knuckles are scraped, his eye puffy and swollen. But next to the pastry case bloodbath, they're superficial scratches he won't remember in a week.

An ambulance whirls from Central Amsterdam's busiest intersection to park on the sidewalk. The two medics take one look at the blood-soaked windowfront and immediately call for backup. Inside Sub Dude, Wes turns on the lights to reopen the kitchen. On the other side of the counter, Omar slumps in exhaustion at a table. From outside, the medics can't safely move Leather Punk, who's fixed as firmly into the window as the frame. One of the medics rushes into the café, reaching into the pastry case with large gauze pads. By now, a road barrier is redirecting traffic away from Prins Hendrikkade, where police cars line the street and tourists trickle into Amsterdam's main artery. Camera phones surround the medics, who lift Leather Punk on a stretcher. Travel feeds on Instagram, TikTok, and Facebook are blowing up globally.

"No more photos!" shouts an elder police officer at passers snapping pictures on their phones.

At the stovetop, Wes fires up a skillet to warm some *tibs*, mixing the beef cubes with sauteed tomato and onion. Holding an icepack to his bruised eye, Wes scoops a white lump of *ayib* cottage cheese into a bowl for a few seconds in the microwave, heating it just enough to spread across the sub roll.

He's pulling out all the stops for Omar. Mixed together, the spicy meat and tangy cheese steam up the lightly toasted roll. Wes adds a diced-up spread of lettuce and tomato. After plating the Ethiopian sub, Wes serves it to Omar in the café, where a few police officers are questioning him.

"I understand the man in leather struck you first," an officer confirms with Wes.

"He sure did," Wes says. "Before that, they pushed Omar and spat on his dinner. That's clearly assault."

The second officer turns to Omar. "Were there any other witnesses?"

"I witnessed it all through that window," Wes rushes to respond. "Look, officers, Omar's had quite a day. So, if you have any more questions, I can talk to you."

"Well, there's nothing more to discuss, Mister Levine," replies the officer at the table where Omar is digging into his dinner. "Thank you for doing our job for us."

"I think everyone on Instagram can see I didn't intend to smash his head through the window," Wes says to the police. "He had a knife and a Nazi pendant on his little leather hat."

"That's true," another officer chimes in. "We didn't find a knife anywhere, but his leathery little swastika cap is being taken to the station as evidence. Like the saying goes, the only good Nazi..."

"Is a dead one," the other cop concludes, turning to

acknowledge Wes with an approving smile. "You've done Amsterdam a service today."

"I've been living in this city for twenty years now," Wes says with a cool shrug. "Is that long enough to get elected mayor?"

The officers chuckle in the doorway. "Have a good night, Mister Levine."

"Wait, officers?" Wes calls across the café. "This might be a rookie question. But who do I need to call to fix the window?"

Wes points to the pastry case, that messy smattering of toppled pizza slices and *poffertjes.*

"Someone with the city will send a glass setter tomorrow morning," the officer says, plugging a memo into his cell phone. "For now, we'll seal it off with yellow tape. Thanks again for doing all the heavy lifting tonight."

Wes pulls a N-95 mask over his nose and mouth. With latex-gloved hands, he carefully plucks the larger shards of glass and loads the spoiled pastry trays into trash liners. While Wes cleans up, a group of teenagers on the sidewalk snap selfies in front of the busted, bloodied window. Wes sweeps up the glass and runs a bleach mop across the blood-stained floor around the display case. In the aftermath of the Saturday night fist fight, Wes thinks back to the last time he'd gotten physical with someone, when he had no choice but to use his hands in self-defense. Twenty years ago, Wes had a run-in with a burly, incomprehensible man who'd broken into the synagogue with a chisel, a hammer, and a few cans of red paint. Masada-trained Wes escaped a headlock, grabbing the hammer and putting the baldheaded lout to sleep. A cop on the scene threatened Wes with an assault charge, the synagogue walls still dripping with hateful words painted large.

That won't happen again, Wes tells himself on a walk to the tram with Omar, who heads home to his apartment in Haarlem. After all, Wes always offers cops on the beat a generous public service discount. Back at Sub Dude, Wes locks the door and heads upstairs to rest. But he isn't quite ready to sleep, not on this greatest day of his life. Nothing would change that: not the stolen bike, the blemishes on his hands, the bruised eye, the busted phone screen, or the broken window.

I have a successful brand that's stood the test of time. I've been working with the same great people for twenty years. And now I have a family, Wes counts his blessings, watching from his bedside at the train station lights twinkling in the still of night. *I'm the luckiest guy in the world.*

I walk alone through dusty streets with no signs, eventually finding my way. The shallow, muddy river I follow to the island's interior soon runs dry. In water-weary Phuket, I'll take whatever path I can get to a safe haven somewhere off the shores of this blessed, cursed island.

A honking taxi horn lets me know that now, I'm back in the world, one week out from whatever just happened. The driver stops and asks if I need a ride. Without turning on his meter, he cruises along the first paved road I've seen in weeks and points me to a gamer cafe with Internet access.

"You call your family. Let them know you okay," the smiling, sweet-faced driver tells me. In a room full of computers, a Thai teenager in a loosely buttoned white *Mattayom* shirt stands up venerably and bows his head as I drag myself to the table area. Internet access at last. He pulls out a chair and signs me into the desktop. When I reach into my pocket for money I don't have, he waves away my hand.

"Mai tong," he says. "You don't have to."

Scrapes and gashes on my face reflect off the computer screen. I cringe at the raised, swollen welts on my neck and arms. As I log into my e-mail account, the young café worker returns with a plastic bag of sliced pineapple and a bottle of Oishi green tea. He sets them next to the keyboard and I give him a smile, the only thing I have left to give.

After I send a message to Harry, we soon connect face-to-face on a Skype call. Harry's a crying mess from the moment he sees me on the screen looking so battered, my face soiled by the storm of a thousand lifetimes.

Harry insists that I need medical attention and commissions a helicopter to airlift me out of Phuket and into Bangkok's best private hospital. With sooty fingers I pick pineapple pieces from the plastic bag and guzzle the cold tea in a hurry, because now there's a long line of stranded tsunami survivors hovering outside the door. My mind is falling apart after a week of sleeping under an open-air tent. Though I'm sitting down, the room is spinning. I'm so exhausted that I nod off behind the computer screen.

I wake up in the hospital, at first clueless as to how I got there. A doctor and a nurse restrain me from pulling the needle off the crook of my arm. It's my first day back in Bangkok. But this time around, I'm not Teacher Wes. Now I'm Patient Levine. Realizing where I am, I start to recall flashing glimpses of the loud helicopter ride, when I drifted in and out. It takes a minute for me to come to terms with the IV fluid bag that's pumping electrolytes into my bloodstream. A young woman nurse brings to the bedside a tray of sliced mangos, fried rice, and red Jello squares. Before I can taste anything, it's all gone and I fall back asleep. I wake up and a smiley male nursing assistant, a young-looking face with black emo bangs sweeping over one of his eyes, is sponging the scrapes on my feet in a soapy medical basin.

On the second day, different nurses come to take my vitals. Their stethoscopes descend on the bedside all at once, making me worry something is seriously wrong. Yesterday, only one nurse at a time had checked on me, a predictable rotation of slim women in the same crisp, body-hugging white uniform.

"Why do I need this?" I ask the lead nurse, a woman around my age.

"We have to make sure your blood pressure is stable," she says, injecting yet another needle into my arm. "You've been through a lot, Mister Wes."

The tsunami is the only thing on TV. From bed, I flip the channels and everything is wall-to-wall coverage of water and washed-out beach towns along the Andaman coast. On CNN, I'm reminded that George W. Bush and Dick Cheney are heading into their second inauguration. The next news story is told by reporter from another devastated beach somewhere in the Indian Ocean, which makes me feel even worse. It's like an entirely different planet from those calm waters and stunning coral reefs I'd experienced underwater. Just me and my dad and our oxygen tanks on Christmas morning. Being Jewish, it was our first Shabbat together in over ten years. I never imagined it would be our last.

When the doctor asks, I try piecing together what happened before and after the world around me turned into a flood zone. What I remember most vividly comes back in flashes: a pretty blonde British woman calling me "Love" the moment before a giant wave sweeps her and dozens more off the hotel deck, or Dad saying *I love you* five or ten times in two days. I don't doubt that he did, but maybe Dad was just making up for the ten years he'd been completely out of touch. The tsunami made me forget about every other time I'd been blindsided, including when Dad left home and disappeared into Mexico.

But the doctors in white coats can't — or don't want to — answer the questions I have about my memory. Like why I remember what I saw happening to others, but so little about what happened to me when 100-mile-an-hour waves hammered the shore. They bring in a casually dressed man with dyed silver hair and furry black brows. He introduces himself as a professor of psychiatry at Chulalongkorn, Thailand's top university. The shrink is around my parents' age, and his expression doesn't change when I mention losing my dad in the tsunami. Instead of asking questions, he leans closely to shine a pocket flashlight into my eyes. I follow his finger, looking away from the bright light. The shrink sighs in resignation.

"Most likely," he says with the other doctors looking over his shoulder. "The sensory overload has left your memory understandably hazy. This last week has been an especially traumatic time for you."

"To be honest, Doc," I say. "I don't remember much. I should have more memories of what happened in Phuket, you know?"

"You may benefit from counseling. But all of your vital signs are in the normal range."

"So, um, like," I stutter. "Is that a good thing?"

"A very good thing," the shrink says with a smile so big it unsettles my nerves. "Sound body, and sound mind. You'll be discharged this afternoon."

I welcome this news, a clean bill of health to close out my hospital stay. The only problem is that I don't have anywhere to live. But soon after the silver-haired shrink leaves my room, Harry knocks on the hinge of the open door in board shorts and a pink tank top.

"Hey handsome," Harry says melodically.

"So glad to see you again," I tell him with my arms reached out.

"I wanted to tell you something, Wes. Last year, I'm sorry if I pushed you too hard to apply for a second citizenship."

I wave off Harry's apology. "Come on, you saved my life. Besides, I think I'd give my first-born son to be back in Amsterdam."

"What sort of work would you do in the Netherlands?"

"I used to love those little walk-up cafes. You know, the ones with big, creamy pastries in the windows? Maybe I could open one in Centrum and put a grill behind the counter."

Harry breathes through his nose and sighs. "So, are you a cook or a baker? Do you have a specialty?"

I don't respond right away. "My dad used to have a pizza place back in Baltimore. I make killer cheesesteaks."

Without saying a word, Harry looks out the window and already I know that he'd make a different choice. Last year, I lived there for three months, and Amsterdam had the most eclectic food scene. From any cobblestone sidewalk in the city, you could stumble into almost every sort of comfort food but usually not the cheesy, melty American inventions. Harry's frown suggests he thinks my idea isn't a very good one, and that maybe Chef Wes should take another stab on a different cutting board.

"There are plenty of spaces near Central Station with a windowfront and small kitchen," Harry returns. "But on a landing visa, you only get to stay in Europe for ninety days out of every hundred and eighty."

"So?" I ask. "Can't you pull some strings at the embassy?"

"I can get you back into the Netherlands on a special scheme known as DAFT, or the Dutch-American Friendship Treaty. Once you have your visa, I'll set you up with an account, and you'll just be required to keep the original deposit in the bank. You can apply for permanent residence after five years, if of course you decide to stay."

"Anyway," I change the subject, springing from the hospital bed. "I'm still not sure if my father made it or not. He might still be alive."

Harry leans closer to the bedside and holds me in a sad, somber gaze. "Wes, I know you've…"

"Yeah, I've been through a lot," I cut into his sentence. "All the doctors here have said that much. But my dad wanted to go to Amsterdam. In the event that he's still alive, I'd like to think that maybe we'd work together again. Just like old times."

Harry looks away, again. He's on the brink of tears, which makes me feel bad for bringing up the tsunami again.

"I'm glad you and your dad got to have a happy reunion in Phuket," Harry slowly gets the words out. "So far, in the media outlets, Stanley Levine's name has not come up on any list of survivors."

"Are they even making lists?" I ask him, defiant in my doubt. "I haven't seen one."

"Wes, from what you've shared, your dad texted you his plans right before going out on the water. You can take comfort in the fact that he died doing…"

"He died doing what he loved," I interrupt Harry again to mock what feels like a cruel cliché. "Look, I watched one fucking wave completely wipe out a hundred people at a hotel pool. Right before my phone died, Dad said he was planning to go scuba diving and invited me to join him. I stayed alive because I stayed in bed, Harry. And for all I know, he could've still been in bed at his girlfriend's place with a dead cell phone battery of his own."

Harry winces. "I know you're hoping for the best, mate. Has anyone picked up your dad's phone?"

I shake my head. "At the end of the day, I haven't seen a body or a death certificate. So, until someone tells me otherwise, I'll hold on to hope that he's still alive."

"Okay," Harry agrees, his voice hollow and hesitant.

"Okay?" I ask. "What are you saying okay to?"

"To Amsterdam," Harry says. "I know a space near Central Station where I can set you up. To cut down on your expenses,

I recommend that you consider living upstairs in the loft above the kitchen."

"Did they ever find my passport?" I ask, slipping out of the medical gown and into the only pair of clothes I own, the tattered cargo shorts and Bob Marley tee I'd been wearing since the morning of the tsunami. "I don't have a Thai baht to my name."

Harry nods and hands me a red envelope. "To start, here's six thousand British pounds. Your lost passport has been returned to the American Embassy in Bangkok."

"Hey, Harry?" I ask, looking into the envelope at the colorful stream of currency. "Can I kiss you?"

Harry lowers an eyebrow, taking a half step back. "Come on, Wes. Are you thinking clearly?"

"Never been clearer," I reply.

"But you're straight."

"And a kiss doesn't have to lead to sex," I remind him.

"I always found you lovely and attractive," Harry confesses. "But I think you already know that."

"You've shown me the meaning of love so many times, and we haven't even known each other for a year. That's worth a kiss."

Harry looks me up and down. "Really?"

"Yes," I assure him as I move closer and tilt my head.

"Okay," Harry says, and I plant my lips.

"What in the hell was that?" Harry asks.

I don't know if he's dumbfounded or disappointed until his mouth lands on mine. And before I know it, our lips are opening and closing together. In the corner of my eye, a Thai nurse in mint green scrubs covers her mouth and giggles with other hospital staff outside my door.

"Thanks for saving my ass," I whisper in his ear, squeezing Harry's arm while my other hand grips the money. "Again."

3

On Sunday morning, Wes springs awake at seven-thirty when a pounding knock on the café door shakes the upstairs floor of the boarder loft. First, he reaches for the nightstand to check for facial bruises on his phone camera, but the screen is a giant web of tiny cracks. From bed, Wes jumps into the first clothes he can swipe from his cluttered footboard shelf. Loud, forceful knocking persists. Wes makes his way downstairs to open the door for the glass setters, three hard hats in royal blue industrial overalls. One of the glass setters holds out an iPad to show Wes the invoice for the new window, the new frame, and the new refrigerator display case.

"Does insurance cover it?" Wes asks, half-awake and groggy with a bruise under his eye.

"I can't answer that, but your insurer can. We're municipal contractors," one of the workers replies. "Your restaurant must remain closed until an inspector approves the repairs."

Wes looks up from the screen and groans. "Why did you replace the frame when it's just a glass repair?"

"The frame was badly damaged. We're all quite astonished that the man whose head went through the window last night has survived."

"Well, thanks for coming quickly," Wes says, looking down at his shattered phone screen. "Here's one more thing to fix."

Wes walks through gabled brick neighborhoods in search for a phone repair shop. Instead, he finds townhouse windows with wide-open curtains of living rooms projecting quaint, candid snapshots of Dutch home life. It's too early on Sunday for shops to lift their shutters. His phone screen is so deeply cracked that searching on Google Maps is a nonstarter. Finally, Wes arrives at a phone accessory shop next to a bicycle rental garage. Behind the counter, the tech with full tattoo sleeves takes a quick look at Wes's phone and says it's a two-hour job. While waiting for the repair, Wes rents a bike. The late July sun warms his back as he rides beyond the city center to glimpse windmills, tulip gardens, and tiny detached houses with red roof tiles.

Back in town, the tattooed tech hands Wes his fixed-up phone with a pristine new screen. Straight away, Wes goes to his feeds on Instagram and Facebook. Videos of the bloody scene at Sub Dude are going viral. Expecting the comments to vindicate him, Wes scrolls through reactions and comments that mostly favor Leather Punk. One reply to a violent video post sends a chill down Wes's spine, **what was he trying to do, kill the guy?**

After returning the rental bike, Wes hops a tram in De Pijp. In five minutes, he's outside the train station by the café. With a chef knife bag strapped on his shoulder, Adil is standing outside the locked door to Sub Dude.

"Sorry I couldn't call to let you know," Wes tells Adil, a halal butcher who sometimes picks up grill shifts. "I'll pay you for today's hours, but we've got to stay closed until an inspector can approve the repairs."

"What happened to the window?" Adil asks. "And your eye. Are you okay?"

"I'm fine," Wes replies swiftly. "A couple hooligans attacked Omar. The one whose head went into the window pulled a switchblade on me."

"Oh wow," Adil says, unchaining his bicycle from the rack. "Glad you're both okay. Should I come in tomorrow?"

"The inspection should be done by then. Just text me in the morning to make sure we're open."

On his calculator app, Wes is running the numbers: five-thousand euro will cover the major repairs, which insurance might reimburse partly, if at all. Replacing his phone screen has set him back two hundred euro, and Wes decides his next bike must cost less than that. Riding around town on a shiny new model with all the bells and whistles is like begging every bicycle thief in Amsterdam to help themselves.

Wes burns an hour on the phone, dialing every municipal number in his contacts. He connects with someone at the Netherlands Food and Consumer Product Safety Authority, and they pass along phone numbers of authorized building inspectors. None of the city inspectors pick up the phone, but finally, a private company takes his call. Within the hour, a building inspector turns up at the café, looks quickly at the windowfront and signs off on it. The whole job takes no more than sixty seconds, but it's another five hundred euro, which also comes out of Wes's pocket. Behind the front counter, Wes cuts the check and the inspector emails him a certificate to allow Sub Dude to reopen their doors for business. The sun is already settling over the westward canals nearby. Wes decides to turn in for the night instead of slinging subs in the hour before closing time.

At six o'clock on Monday morning, Wes is getting all the stations up and running two hours ahead of schedule. First, he flushes out the steel coffee baskets at the espresso bar, and then greases up the breakfast grill. Wes tears into boxes of fresh deliveries to align trays of éclairs and iced waffles into layered, eye-popping dessert shelves in the sparkling new display case. On the glass cover, Wes sees a reflection of the purplish bruise under his eye. The bottom line is kicking his ass, too. The average pastry in the case goes for around five euro a plate. And so, with five-thousand euro in losses from the weekend, Wes sets a goal: one thousand pastries in a week. From the grill, he greets the guests in the doorway and takes their order. Wes single-handedly whips up cheese omelets, cappuccinos, and brick oven-warmed pizza slices. While Wes serves the table, Faisal comes in to start his shift.

"How's it going, brother?" Faisal approaches Wes at the

grill, leaning in with a side hug. "Your eye's all swollen. Are you okay?"

"It's just a scratch," Wes replies. "Believe me, the other guy looked a lot worse."

Faisal smiles back. "I really appreciate you standing up for my dad."

"The guy got a couple hits on me. Then before I knew it, his head looked like a ketchup dispenser. I won't lie, but when I saw him bleeding all over the pastries, I thought he might be a goner," Wes confesses. "His little sidekick smashed my phone and I spent half the next day getting the screen fixed. We're in the hole, bro. Let's try to move more pastries to make up the difference."

"I'll tell my homeboys on grill to keep the new display case stocked and neat," Faisal says dutifully.

Martin Leeuwenhoek enters the café. He's out of uniform in blue jeans and a checkered flannel shirt, no badge or gun belt. Instead of placing an order, the off-duty Amsterdam police officer sits at a table. Wes hands Faisal a grill spatula and crosses the counter, pen and green guest check pad in hand. Over the years, Leeuwenhoek's diet has zigged and zagged, and Wes never knows what the sandy-haired, hulking, twenty five-year police department veteran is going to order for lunch. A few years back, while Leeuwenhoek recovered from a heart attack, Wes sent cooked meals to his wife and kids every day and catered a welcome back party for him at the city's police headquarters.

"So, what's it going to be today, Martin? Plant-based or paleo?" Wes asks cheerily. "Lately I've been putting a new twist on the bacon cheddar. Do you like fried onion sprouts?"

Leeuwenhoek shakes his head, looking dismally downward. "Not hungry, thanks. I'm here today not as a police officer, but as a friend. Do you have a minute?"

Wes drops the guest check pad on the front counter. "Sure, what's going on with you?"

Leeuwenhoek frowns with folded hands held solemnly against his chest. "They're likely to press charges."

"Charges for what?" Wes asks, swiping a damp terry cloth

from the front counter. "Did something happen to you?"

"Public Prosecution is about to press charges for the Saturday night incident," Leeuwenhoek states, holding a stoic, by-the-books facial expression.

"Great," Wes returns, wiping off the tabletops. "So, they'll charge the guys who hit me and Omar?"

"The young man you punched into the window is recovering from surgery," Leeuwenhoek begins. "It took doctors hours to rinse the glass out of his scalp and stitch him up. He's looking at a skin graft, a concussion, and a long recovery ahead of him."

"I'm not proud of what I did. But that guy pulled a knife."

Leeuwenhoek shakes his head. "A knife wasn't found anywhere on the scene."

"He shoved Omar and called him a sand rat," Wes says.

"What a horrible thing to say," Leeuwenhoek replies. "It's a shame anyone would behave like that."

"Tell me, Martin. Over the years, how many times have we been through this? Someone comes into my place of business and harasses my business partners over their religion or their skin color. It's a crime, but no one's ever held accountable."

"Every time, those bigots have been wrong," Leeuwenhoek says sympathetically. "But they're not the ones facing charges."

"Okay," Wes responds. "Then who is?"

Leeuwenhoek eyes Wes with a calm, pitiable gaze. "The victim's family is pressuring prosecutors in the OM to charge you with attempted murder. Under Dutch law, that's a Category 5 crime, the second most serious."

In that moment, Wes forgets to breathe. "Attempted murder? What are you talking about?" Wes answers, scrolling through the videos on his phone. "I had no choice but to fight back. The guy threw the first punch and whipped out a switchblade. It's not like I was trying to murder him!"

"The victim's family sees it differently," Leeuwenhoek says, somberly. "According to the family, by the time he'd gotten to the hospital, he lost so much blood that life support measures were taken to keep him alive."

"I wouldn't purposely punch someone through the window

of my own business," Wes says, handing his phone to Leeuwenhoek. "I'm a trained martial artist. I don't fight dirty."

Leeuwenhoek cracks a strange smile Wes can't quite decipher. "Down at the station, we've been reviewing all the online clips we can find. So far, nothing has shown him throwing the first punch or holding any kind of weapon."

Wes reaches across the table to hand over his cell phone. "Just watch the video Omar took, please."

The video looks unsteady, wavy at times. At the start, Wes is laying into Leather Punk with a barrage of body blows. By that point, as Wes recalls it, the knife had slipped from the punk's hands, disappearing from the curb to somewhere in the car lane. Leather Punk whimpers and squirms away as the short clip ends.

Leeuwenhoek gives Wes a look of resignation and returns the phone. "You should erase that video immediately. Between you and me, the department is investigating everything on social media. We don't have enough to clear you, but we aren't giving up. Your best hope is that someone on Instagram has posted a clip that shows him with his knife. That would rule out attempted murder. But even then, the victim's family is expected to press civil charges of their own. If that happens, you could lose the business."

"That's an easy one," Wes replies. "I can turn the title over to Faisal, since he was off that day."

"You might want to leave Europe until all this blows over," Leeuwenhoek suggests.

"That doesn't seem fair," Wes objects. "My grandparents fled this city to escape the Nazis. Now, I'm going to lose my business of twenty years to a Nazi?"

"At this point, Wes, we can only assume that charges against you are imminent," Leeuwenhoek tells him.

Wes stands up from the table. "How can I fight this? I need to talk to a lawyer."

"No charges have been filed yet," Leeuwenhoek explains. "Hiring a lawyer in advance would only make you look guilty. I'm going to keep pressuring the department to scour the Internet until we find something that tells the whole story.

Today, Internal Affairs is seeking authorization to access video clips posted on social media with private settings."

"This is too much. Is there a way I can avoid the charges?"

On his phone, Officer Martin Leeuwenhoek looks something up on Google. "Like I said, this might be a good time for you to enjoy some travel outside the European Union. If you're not here to stand trial, so as long as the charges are relatively minor, they won't stick."

Wes sighs. "I just don't get it. On Saturday night, when police arrived on the scene, they actually thanked me for doing their job. They didn't arrest anyone. Am I going to get arrested now?"

"I'll do everything I can to prevent that from happening," Leeuwenhoek replies. "I believe your side of the story, Wes. But the victim's family is expected to make a case against you. With whatever pull I might have in the department, I can stall an arrest warrant for another forty-eight hours."

"This is tough for me," Wes says, rubbing his temples. "When I was sixteen, my father got himself into a jackpot and fled the country, leaving me and my mom on our own. Now I've just found out that I have a teenage son here in Amsterdam. If I leave, how do I keep him in my life?"

"Take him with you to America," Leeuwenhoek says, heading for the door. "Reach out on my personal number if you need anything."

"Wait. You're saying I've got two days to leave the Netherlands?" Wes asks.

Leeuwenhoek turns around and shakes his head. "Two days to leave the European Union."

As Leeuwenhoek walks out, Wes locks the entrance and flips the plastic door sign to the closed side. Under the bureau in his bedroom, he retrieves an accordion folder. Thumbing through the files, Wes pulls up the deed to the restaurant and prints out a title transfer document. He promises to explain later and signs over the ownership of Sub Dude to Faisal. Having no interest in frittering away his minutes to celebrate or elaborate, Wes checks his phone for the time. Now forty-seven hours remain.

With his legal fate hinging on whatever videos of the Saturday night brawl might exist on Facebook and Instagram, Wes dives into the bundle deals on Expedia. He burns another hour scoping out his social media feeds with all the relevant hashtags he can think of: #amsterdamfight, #centralstationbrawl, #foodfightinthedam. Just one video with a knife would clear Wes's name. Finding nothing new in the clips online, he plucks his American passport from the nightstand and books a one-way flight to Los Angeles.

Wes scoops up his belongings, hastily zipping them into two suitcases. Each time he dials Jen's number, the call goes straight to her voicemail. He texts Zen, **hey, can you call me as soon as you can?** and to Jen, **sorry I missed your calls. It's kind of urgent. Can we talk?**

Soon Jen's name and avatar pop on his screen, and Wes rushes into the call. "Hey! So anyway, an unusual situation has unfolded at work, and I'd rather talk about it in person. Can I come over?"

"Fine," Jen says, numb and distant.

"Is everything okay?" Wes asks.

"You haven't called since Saturday," Jen replies, her disappointment palpable.

"I wanted to call you, but my phone was completely out of commission. That night, my screen got smashed in a fight outside the restaurant," Wes goes on. "I'm sorry for not reaching out sooner, but I've been dealing with a world of shit. If it's okay, can I tell you what happened when I see you?"

"Sure, whatever you want," Jen replies tepidly, warm enough to spur Wes into ordering an Uber with enough room for suitcases.

When Wes shows up at Jen's apartment with all his luggage and rings the bell, she takes a long minute to answer. Jen opens the door with a mixed drink and cigarette in hand, her eyes looking tired and glassy. "We just had sex three days ago, and you waited until today to call me?"

Wes holds out his arms. "Please hear me out. I couldn't get my phone fixed until Sunday afternoon. Soon as I got back into town, these two guys attacked Omar when he was closing all by himself. I got in caught in the middle of it. One of them smashed my phone."

Jen blows out a smoke ring, looking him over. "Did he smash your eye too?"

"He got the first hit. But even though I was attacked, I'm the one facing charges."

"What's with the suitcases?" Jen asks suspiciously. "I can't have you moving in or anything. We don't have the space."

"That's not my intention," Wes replies, feeling his heart sink. It's not like they don't have the room, since Jen and Zen until recently had shared their small apartment with her mom.

"I've got to leave Europe before any charges are pressed against me, and I'm flying to Los Angeles tomorrow at noon."

Jen downs the rest of her drink, dropping half a cigarette into the glass.

"And what about your restaurant?" she asks.

"Today I transferred the deed to Faisal, Omar's son. According to my cop friend, I could be looking at civil or criminal charges. Maybe both. But at least now that my name is no longer on Sub Dude's papers, no one can come after the business since technically I no longer own it."

"I took Zen to California when he was five," Jen shares as they walk inside. "We went to Disneyland, the Walk of Fame in Hollywood, and the David Letterman show. Oh wait, that was on our trip to New York. We saw Jay Leno in Burbank."

Wes smiles understandingly. "Are your passports ready?"

"Yeah," Jen answers evasively. "Okay, so here's the story. A while back, I was in a relationship with an American woman named Abby. We lived a double life and pretended to be roommates so my mom wouldn't know. While we were together, Abby helped Zen and I get green cards. Our plan was to quietly make it official and move to New York City, but then Abby ran off to Dubai and married a billionaire."

"It's okay, Jen. Everyone has a past, but I'm thinking about the future. How much time do you and Zen have left on your green cards?"

"About two years," Jen says. "But are you saying we should drop everything and move with you to America? We hardly know you, Wes."

"Two years is a lot better than two days," Wes says as a matter of fact. "That's what I'm looking at."

Jen cracks a half-smile and sighs. "Okay. I guess you can count me in."

"Do you think Zen is going to go for it?"

"Go for what?" Zen boisterously asks from his bedroom.

"Hi Zen," Wes greets his son with awe and reverence. "I've got myself into some trouble here in Amsterdam, so tomorrow I'm flying to L.A. Would you and your mom like to..."

"Hell yeah, dude!" Zen cuts in. "Come on Mom, this is the chance of a lifetime. In California, I could surf and you can finish the screenplay and quit your job!"

Wes casts a beaming, charming smile at Jen. "Zen has a point. If you want to write for the movies, where else but L.A.?"

Jen touches Wes on the hand. "Do you know where we're going to stay?"

"Probably a hotel at first," Wes answers. "Money's not an issue. Since starting Sub Dude twenty years ago, I've been sending most of the profits home to the states. Come on, Jen. Let's go be family."

"Let's go for it!" Zen echoes, his energy infectious. "Can I check my surfboards as luggage?"

"That shouldn't be a problem, dear," Jen says, turning to Wes. "I'll ask our neighbor Emil to take us to the airport in his hearse. Emil drives for a funeral home. This will make it easier for us to leave without being noticed."

"We should go as soon as possible," Wes suggests, dialing in two more flights on his Expedia app. "Once we get to the airport, I'll be in the clear."

"Wes, you're lucky I hate living in Kolenkit so much," Jen says, equally scathing and truthful. "As a lifelong Amsterdammer, I'm a sucker for sunny weather. Let's go to California. Maybe that's where we can finally be a family."

"Consider it done," Wes says, plugging in their seat selections. "Good news. There's still plenty of room on the flight. My seat's going to be just a couple aisles away from yours."

A black Cadillac hearse slowly parks in front of the apartment unit. Jen steps out in all-black, from the headscarf to the high-heeled boots covered by a long dress. Hiding her dark, searching eyes behind thick black sunglasses, she greets Emil, a sixty-something Dutch-Spaniard with a healthy olive suntan and a tufty white beard. They load luggage into the long funeral wagon, setting their suitcases around an open wood coffin. Zen stacks his surfboards over the coffin, leaving Wes and Jen to sit between pieces of luggage. Space is tight, but it's only fifteen-minutes from Kolenkit to Schiphol International Airport.

Emil puts on a peaked, shiny chauffeur hat and steers the hearse with slow, deliberate dignity. Once they pass the highway ramp for Rotterdam and Utrecht, Wes checks his messages and a text from Leeuwenhoek dings on the screen: **Good news Wes. We've found a video clearly showing a knife in his hands. An American tourist posted it privately on Facebook. Now any claims of attempted murder will never hold up.**

"Guess I've got that going for me," Wes says to himself as he texts back. **En route to airport ATM. Glad you found that video. Now everyone can see what really happened. Thanks for having my back. You're a real friend.**

As the hearse crosses a bridge, Zen peeks through the white curtain in the rear window. "There's a cop behind us."

"Don't touch the curtains," Wes tells Zen, a second police car now trailing closely behind the first. "Let's not make any sudden moves. It's only a problem if there are sirens."

Sure enough, blue lights flash in the rearview. Emil slows to a stop, ordering Wes to situate himself inside the coffin. The sirens wail too loudly to hear anything else. The hinged lid is too heavy for Jen and Zen to lift and shut. Wes crawls into the coffin, the safest place in the hearse.

"Cover him with your boards," Jen whispers to Zen while a slow-stepping officer approaches the driver side.

"We're looking for an American national who has committed grievous bodily harm against a Dutch citizen. Who is riding in your vehicle?"

"These are my neighbors," Emil responds to the officer. "They're traveling for a funeral."

"That's a lot of luggage for a funeral," the officer comments, pointing to the heaps of suitcases.

"Most of it is not theirs," Emil states formally, prompting the officers to turn their attention to the rear window. Jen cracks open the back door.

"Good afternoon, officers," she says. "My son and I are on our way to the airport."

The officer stares suspiciously at the wooden coffin, shining the light upon the makeshift lid. Through a tiny crack between Zen's surfboards, Wes sees the flashlight glare as he lay still and silent in the coffin bed.

"I'm sorry for your loss, *mevrouw*. Travel safe," the officer says, nodding at the other policemen who return to their cars and drive off.

"Wes?" Emil asks from the driver's seat. "You okay back there?"

"Doing fine," Wes replies, his voice muffled by two fiberglass surfboards still concealing him inside the coffin. "I'll stay put for now. Let me know when we get to the airport."

"We should spend the night in a hotel," Jen suggests. "Our flight is sixteen hours from now. That's too much exposure if we hang around the airport that long."

"We want to avoid any more contact with police," Wes says from the coffin bed. "I'm definitely going to give my buddy Martin Leeuwenhoek a piece of my mind before we fly out."

"So, where am I taking you now?" Emil asks.

Wes pushes the surfboards aside, his head popping out of the coffin like a dead man springing back to life. "Let's hold off on the airport. I have a running account with a hotel near Schiphol."

In the morning, they roll their luggage to the lobby and check out of the room. Zen and Jen follow Wes outside the hotel to the shuttle bus, their suitcases and surfboards held closely. The shuttle drops them off at the international gate.

The three of them move through the checkpoints like any other family, showing their passports together and helping each other hand off their bags to the airline check-in agents. They empty their pockets, pass through the metal detector, and collect their carry-ons on the other side.

"We're an hour from takeoff," Wes says, waving Jen and Zen to the escalator. "Let's find our boarding gate."

Once they settle into the plane, Wes texts Leeuwenhoek. **Whatever happened to forty-eight hours, buddy? Yesterday we almost didn't make it to the airport with five cop cars on my ass.**

Three dots flash on the message thread as Leeuwenhoek responds immediately. **The video evidence on social media is in your favor. At this point, they probably won't even charge you with simple assault.**

A tall blonde flight attendant approaches Wes, where he's still thumbing a reply by text. "Sir, it's time for all mobile devices to go on airplane mode."

"Of course," Wes says, buckled up and focusing on the message to Leeuwenhoek. "I just need a moment."

Simple assault? Really, Martin? I just signed over my business of twenty years for a misdemeanor?

Wes sends the text, getting an immediate response. **You're going to California, man. Why don't you lighten up? Would it hurt to show a little appreciation?**

"Sir," the steely-eyed flight attendant interrupts Wes again. "We're taking off now."

Thanks for nothing. Wes sends one final text to Officer Martin Leeuwenhoek before shutting off his phone. **Nice to know you.**

Amsterdam, March 2005

And, just like that, I'm open for business in the Netherlands.

Welcome to Sub Dude, one of the first food walkups outside the gates of Amsterdam's central train station. In this high-traffic location, our prices are a little higher than other fast and casual joints throughout the city. Our rent is higher, too, but our ingredients are better. For anyone who lands in Amsterdam and takes the direct train from Schiphol, Sub Dude is an early point of contact. Before the museums or Dam Square or even an incandescent glimpse of neon lamplight in Red Light District, a visitor to Amsterdam first sees Sub Dude. It all begins with a window display of Chantilly-topped Belgian waffles with Twix bars sticking out of the cream, and it doesn't stop there.

Our specialty is a proud product of the U.S. East Coast. At Sub Dude, our cheesesteaks are served Philly style with a brick oven finish to melt the cheese into an overflowing Amoroso roll. As an alternative, we also make a more delicate-looking European panini press — half the meat for twice the price. I'm convinced that customers prefer the paninis for the fancy-looking grill marks, with our surfer silhouette logo seared into the bread.

I make a lot more money off those cheesesteaks than I ever did as a teacher or scribe. But in truth, without Harry Jarsdel's heart of gold and financial muscle, I'd still be sleeping with one eye open under a tent shelter in tsunami-battered Southern Thailand.

The unmistakable Sub Dude logo hangs above the door on a metal blade sign: an outline of a skinny surfer in a tank top toting a longboard and a hoagie roll. If I could have it my way, we'd focus solely on cheesesteaks and ditch the breakfast menu, the espresso bar, and the puffy pastries in the window display. Usually when we talk on the phone, Harry reminds me to keep the menu consistent with what it was when the walkup had been known more for coffee and croissants.

"Don't fix what isn't broke," Harry tells me, and I don't

disagree. After all, he's the one keeping our lights on. Sub Dude is more than just another Amsterdam café with candy bar-topped croissants to tempt passersby at the hazy corner display window. It's a place where anyone gallivanting through Amsterdam can enjoy a hearty meal before or after cycling on bike lanes or trekking through cobblestone sidewalks sometimes leading to canal-front chaos.

My new upstairs living space is always warm, thanks to the heat rising from the brick oven. Harry says that in summer the loft will become a sauna, but while it's on the chilly side for most of the year, I'll have free heating. I'm still not comfortable with the idea of bringing a date back to my place. The low ceiling and the slim, hidden staircase bring to my mind Anne Frank, who'd sheltered with her family in an attic only a few streets away from where I live and work. Enclosed and hidden, that space was all Anne and her family had, until they didn't.

I can't complain because a couple months ago, I was sleeping under a giant tent with hundreds of destitute tsunami survivors, nothing but a dead cell phone and a pair of broken sunglasses in my otherwise empty pockets. Fast forward two months, and from my bedroom window, I can see one end of Amsterdam's majestic central train station to the other. Looking back, my trip to Phuket now seems like a dream gone terribly wrong. And here I am, feeling like a million bucks on the other side of a nightmare in which many died, including my fearless thrill-seeking father Stanley Levine, and millions more are still without homes.

Somehow, I always land on my feet. That's what Dad used to say at Ocean City when eight-year-old me would try standing on a flimsy boogie board. Years later when Dad was out of the picture, I discovered the gloriously rugged coastlines west of Los Angeles. I've always been drawn to the Golden State for the obvious perks like surf and sun, but also to the wit and wisdom of California-style double entendre. Innuendo is not so common in straight-talking Netherlands. But even here, they're catching on.

"Sub Dude?" a Dutch hipster once asked me. "So, you're looking for a dom chick?"

One of my regulars once blurted out what has become my signature pitch, "get subdued…at Sub Dude."

Inside the display case, I consolidate creampuffs and croissants on a single tray. As I set aside the last remaining strawberry-glazed donut for my upcoming break, a group of five clean-cut men drag their luggage into the table area. They're dressed for Business Class, and their accents are clearly American: upbeat, energetic, and assertive. Assuming I don't speak English, one of the tie-wearing guys approaches the front counter in a slow, drawn-out voice.

"Three Phill-ies with ev-ery-thing, a Cal-i-for-nian with chick-en but no a-vo-cado."

In a more natural-sounding voice, the guy next to him asks for the vegetarian sub, which requires me to open a second, smaller grill that no animal product can touch.

"No lett-uce, and no to-ma-to," the leader of the pack enunciates.

"Hey, man. I'm as American as you are," I counter the customer's condescending tone.

"Oh great," he replies, suddenly peppy and positive. "It's nice to find someone who speaks perfect English."

As I scribble the orders on a green guest ticket, I overhear the guys in line chatting about an upcoming wedding. One of them is gushing over a two-year-old daughter at home with his pregnant wife. The meekest-looking dude in the group says he's amped to chase broads in the Red Light District, and I'm sure he's not the only one with *that* on his mind.

Omar and Faisal return from the market with bags of fresh vegetables. I'm forever grateful for their network of reliable Halal butchers. To keep up with demand, we order enough fresh cuts of ribeye to last three weekdays. Sometimes we sell out in the middle of a Saturday or Sunday. A quick phone call later, and one of their local butchers comes through, usually on a motorbike with a cool box built into the bumper. In the two months we've been working together, the Egyptian father and son have become two of my closest friends.

"Sabaho," I greet them in Arabic, immediately sensing tension as a couple guys at the counter start to fidget. *"As salamu*

From the register, I pick up on the disturbed rumblings of throats clearing at the sound of Arabic, a language I've been learning with surprising ease since coming back to Amsterdam. Standing in the doorway, Omar balances a brimming tomato bag. He stumbles and a few tomatoes spill to the ground. One of the Americans smirks and points straight at Omar.

"I promised Leanne and little Kayleigh I'd make it home from this trip in one piece," says the biggest guy in the pack. "I see you've got terrorists working here. I'd like to ask you to make our subs, my friend. I won't eat anything touched by shit skin."

"Okay, you can get the fuck out of here right now," I fire back without a moment of thought. Just one of the guys turns around and wheels his suitcase to the door. "Sorry," he says from the doorway. "Cancel the California cheesesteak."

"Who do you think you are, taking up for these sleeper cell agents?" the angry customer asks, stepping so close I catch a whiff of his rancid coffee breath.

I drop my steel spatula, letting it clang to the floor. Two more guys in the group scoop up their luggage and head for the exit. "No vegetarian," one of them says. "Forget about one of the Phillies."

"You're a disgrace," I say to the two guys still standing at the front counter. "We're not serving you, and if you don't leave now, we can call the police."

"Hey man, I don't want trouble," the shorter, quieter American says to me.

"So, I see you have a voice," I react. "Your friend is offensive, so what does that make you?"

Before he can answer, a pair of policemen in bright neon vests step into the queue. Without another word, the two American guys turn around and calmly leave like nothing on the menu had tickled their fancy.

"Good afternoon, officers," I say to the Dutch cops. "What can we get for you today? Bacon and cheddar, the usual?"

"Ha, that was funny the first five times," Officer Martin Leeuwenhoek quips. "My wife has me on a low-fat diet again.

I'll take a California chicken sub. White meat if you have it."

"Excellent choice," I reply, scribbling CALI WM on the green guest check. "And for you?"

Officer Jan Kenning orders a cappuccino, and asks for the last strawberry glazed donut that I'd been craving since my shift began.

"So," I make small talk while slicing open the Amoroso roll with a long bread knife. "How's the crime in Amsterdam today?"

"Mostly parking tickets," Kenning says nonchalantly as Omar whips up his cappuccino. "There's nowhere left to park in this city as it is."

"Well, if you have a moment," I say, dropping a slab of chicken to let it sizzle on the grill. "Can you trail those Americans to their hotel? I heard them say they're staying at the Crowne Plaza."

"Okay," Leeuwenhoek responds indifferently. "What did they do?"

"We just experienced a racist verbal assault. I only want good vibes in this joint, officers."

Without saying anything, the police officers turn inward as if to confer telepathically.

"We're sorry to hear about that," Kenning finally says.

"Truly sorry," Leeuwenhoek adds. "But I wouldn't advise trying to charge a tourist over a verbal slight. Just let it go."

"It wasn't just a verbal slight," I clarify for the officers. "What he said about my employee was hate speech. It was so vile that his friends walked out on him. Workplace discrimination is a crime, and I'm asking you to enforce the law. Now Martin, do you want avocado on that California chicken sub, or does your wife want you to cut down on natural fats too?"

"Look, I'll send someone over there to talk to them," replies Officer Martin Leeuwenhoek, pointing his walkie-talkie antenna at the windowfront pastry case. "Avocado is fine."

4

They touch ground in Los Angeles around ten o'clock at night and wait for a shuttle in the heat haze outside the terminal. With a tear welling in his eye, Wes walks on American soil for the first time in over twenty years, recalling the polluted air he'd battled every day as a young man in Bangkok. Soon, a Hertz vehicle saves Wes, Jen, and Zen from the airport's localized soot and smog, shuttling the travelers and their luggage on a short drive through a glitzy boulevard of hotels and restaurants near the airport. When they arrive at the rental counter with their suitcases, travel bags, and Zen's three surfboards, the agent suggests upgrading from an economy car to a more spacious SUV.

"It's your lucky night," the agent says, his eyes sparkling as he swipes Wes's credit card. "Someone brought a Ford Bronco back early."

From the car lot, Wes follows the freeway signs south to Manhattan Beach, where a small hotel room on Sepulveda Boulevard awaits them. They haul their bags into the tight space, transforming the hardwood floor into a sea of suitcases. Between the two twin beds and TV stand, no one can step in any direction without bumping into something.

"There's a Taco Shell next door. I'm gonna hit it up," Zen says, nearly tripping over his backpack on the way to the door.

"Seriously?" Jen asks, checking the bedside clock. "It's two in the morning."

"Nothing else is open and I'm like famished, bro," Zen says, standing in the doorway. "Later on!"

In the twin bed, Wes slips closer to Jen, holding her from behind. "First day in L.A., and already Zen's talking like a California surfer," she whispers.

"Though I've only known Zen for a short time," Wes reflects aloud. "Somehow I think that's just who he is."

Jen clears her throat, turning out of the embrace to face Wes directly. "I want him to go to university. People look at you differently when you don't have an education. Have you noticed that?"

"I got a college degree. Back in the nineties, practically everyone went to college. But at the end of the day, what are we supposed to do with all that knowledge we've absorbed?"

"I went to the Amsterdam Film School for a year," Jen admits. "But I had to quit because I ran out of money."

"Are you working on a screenplay now?" Wes asks.

"Kind of," Jen says hesitantly. "Writing only happens with whatever time I can carve out of the day. Maybe things would be different if I'd finished my degree."

"At the intersection of school and surfing, I'm sure there's something for Zen to discover here in California," Wes suggests. "Now that he's in a surfing epicenter, give him a chance to live his dream."

Jen smiles softly. "I'm so glad I found you, Wes."

"And finally," Wes whispers back, wrapping his arms around her. "It's just us."

"I'm really tired," she responds from her pillow, gently squeezing his arm. "Maybe in the morning."

Wes opens his eyes to the sound of traffic chugging along Sepulveda outside the street-facing window. At the foot of the bed, he sees Jen standing between two piles of luggage. When she pulls apart the curtains too fast, they slip from the rod, falling to the floor. Sunlight spills into the room. On the other side of the bare window is a deserted swimming pool with dead leaves floating on the surface.

"Zen didn't come home from the taco place," Jen says shakily.

"Does he usually stay out all night?" Wes asks.

"Sure, with his friends back in Amsterdam. But he doesn't know anyone here!"

Wes points to Zen's wallet and passport on the small desk next to the bathroom. In the corner of the cramped suite, one of Zen's surfboards is missing. "He probably didn't go far."

Wes grabs his phone and dashes next door to the Taco Shell. He cuts through the queue to show the cashier a photo of Zen. "My nineteen-year-old son didn't come back to our room last night. Around two a.m., Zen said he was getting something to eat. Has anyone seen him?"

Introduced by her name tag as Gabi, the pretty cashier with sleepy eyes steps away from the register while Julio, a skinny-mustached manager in a skinny striped tie looking old enough to be her father, takes the next customer's breakfast order. Wes pulls up his screensaver, a selfie from his one and only day with Zen at the beach in the Netherlands. Gabi holds the phone closely to zoom in on Zen. Her soft pink lipstick and blue winged eyeliner brighten her serene, angelic face. Smiling faintly, she looks up from the screen.

"Yeah, he was here with his board when my shift started. But that was eight hours ago."

"Any idea where he went after that?" Wes asks. "We just got here from Europe. We're really worried because he hasn't even texted me or his mom."

Gabi smiles knowingly. "Didn't you unlock your phones before the trip?"

"What do you mean, unlock?" Wes asks.

"Whenever I visit my mom in Mexico, I unlock my phone so I can still use it."

"Good to know. Which way to the beach?" Wes asks.

Gabi looks through the wide dine-in area window, pointing to an uphill path of houses and palm trees. "My shift's almost over. I can walk with you to the Strand."

"The Strand?" Wes asks anxiously. "Where's that?"

"The shops, the restaurants, everything close to the ocean," she answers with a kind, sympathetic wink. "Downtown Manhattan Beach, sweetie. It's expensive as hell, but don't worry. The shops aren't open yet and trust me, it's chill. I'm sure that's where Zen went with his surfboard."

"Thanks a million, Gabi, I'd love it if you could show me the way. Sorry, everyone," Wes says to the people lining up for their breakfast.

"Good luck *amigo,*" says a chunky construction worker in an orange vest who sends Wes a supportive fist bump.

Morning rush hour on Sepulveda is one big bustle of honking horns, the cars speeding up and slowing down with wavelike, oceanic rhythm. But off the boulevard, it's tranquil and breezy on a quiet street of big Mediterranean homes with front-facing terraces. On the other end of a steep hill, the ocean comes into view. Once they're in Downtown Manhattan Beach, they've already seen everything from brand new mansions to older, beachy cottages still standing the test of time.

"Where in Europe are you from?" Gabi asks politely. "Your accent's American."

"Originally I'm from Baltimore, but I've been living in Amsterdam for twenty years."

Gabi pulls off her silky bright headdress, letting her thick brown curls bounce over her shoulders.

"Baltimore's got a vibrant Jewish community," she says cheerfully.

Reluctant to reply, Wes shrinks back. "I guess it's home."

"So, is Zen a pro-surfer?" she asks, smiling curiously.

"I think he'll go pro," Wes answers quickly. "He's all about surfing. I can tell it's what he really wants to do."

"Zen is very lucky to have such a supportive dad."

Wes returns Gabi's smile with a fleeting grin, grimacing as he stretches his legs, all those tense lower-body muscles still tight after fifteen hours sitting on a plane. His loose necklace pendant slips from under his shirt. Wes clenches it quickly as if hoping Gabi didn't see it.

"The Magen David!" she says reverently. "You're Jewish?"

"Yeah, I'm not religious anymore," Wes quickly tells her. "Back in the Netherlands, I own a restaurant with a father and son from Egypt. Bringing together Amsterdam's Muslim and Jewish communities has always been the secret to our success."

"That's beautiful," Gabi says. "Some of my Jewish family lives in L.A. Now I stay with my Uncle Ilan in Torrance."

"I used to be a scribe," Wes mentions offhandedly. "But that part of my life is over."

"Were you more drawn to restaurant work?" Gabi asks with genuine interest.

"I don't know," Wes gradually opens up to her. "Back in Amsterdam, my therapist always said I was meant for more than a career in food service. Maybe it was just my way of holding on to memories of my dad, who had a pizza place in Baltimore. He died in a tsunami. December 2004, Thailand."

Gabi looks Wes over and touches his arm, her eyes warm with concern. "I'm sorry you've been through so much loss. Hope your best days are still ahead of you."

"Thank you. You're very kind," Wes says. "Zen's mom is probably worried sick. None of our phones are working. I should get back to her soon."

"Okay," Gabi replies, a little distant. "So, I can show you to the pier. But you'll be on your own after that."

"I really appreciate you walking with me this morning," Wes thanks her again.

Gabi focuses on her phone. "It's okay. An Uber's on the way. I got to get home and sleep before my next shift."

"At the Taco Shell?"

She shakes her head and pulls a business card from the back pocket of her striped black work pants. "Bring in your phones and we'll get you and your family in a California area code. I also work at a phone store in the L.B.C."

"That's Long Beach?" Wes confirms as they stroll past a mural of a beachgoing family nestling on a picnic blanket.

Gabi points to an approaching car with a purple beacon shining through the windshield. "My ride's here."

"Thanks a ton, Gabi," he says. As Wes takes the business card, he holds out the other hand with the Star of David necklace coiling in his palm. "Here, you can have this."

Gabi's eyes widen in disbelief. "Really? Are you sure? Thank you so much."

"Please don't mention it," Wes replies. "I just thought it might mean more to you."

"I've always wanted to have one like that. Would you help me put it on?"

Standing behind Gabi, Wes thumbs the clasp open to latch the chain around her neck. *"L'chaim,"* Wes says as Gabi laughs lightly, turning to face him. "May life always be kind."

Gabi leans in and hugs Wes, her ruby red lips colliding with his cheek. "Thanks, Wes," Gabi says, tapping the pendant on her neck as she looks with longing at the mural of a happy family's day at the beach. "I'll always treasure it."

Gabi settles into the backseat and waves once more to Wes, who stands curbside at a tiny boho-chic jewelry store on Manhattan Beach Boulevard. He lingers for a moment to watch Gabi's ride fade into sun-drenched uphill traffic. A familiar voice calls to him from behind.

"Hey," Zen makes his presence known. "Who was that?"

Wes turns around to face Zen, who sits at an outdoor café table with a blonde surfer girl in a loose white shirt over a bikini top exposing her glistening, sun-kissed skin. Their surfboards stand upright against the storefront window at Peet's Coffee.

"Come on, now," the young woman says to Wes, playful but semi-serious. "The truth will set you free."

"Gabi works at the Taco Shell next to the hotel, and she saw Zen grabbing a bite last night," Wes says. "She was nice enough to walk with me to the beach."

"Was she?" Zen asks skeptically, pulling a napkin from a dispenser. "You might want to clean up before Mom sees."

With his phone camera, Wes checks his face and dabs away the faint lipstick mark. "Could you at least let us know when you stay out all night?"

"When I came back to the room for my board, and you and Mom were conked out. I texted to let you know where I was going."

"None of our phones are working because they're still on a

Dutch network," Wes points out. "Those texts didn't come through."

"Anyway, this is Ava. We met on the beach early this morning."

"Nice to meet you, Ava. I'm Wes. You can probably see who's who. Catch any waves?"

"We did," Ava responds, tilting her phone Wes's way. "Zen slayed some killer tubes before the first daylight. This clip we filmed is already going viral on Instagram and YouTube."

On Ava's phone, Wes watches the clip of Zen cutting through the hollow core of a long wave. Pointing forward on his board, Zen twists and turns to match the rhythm of the ocean until the wave curls and breaks. Zen charges forward to balance his way through the foamy swash. The camera pans to the horizon, where the water ends at a tangerine-purple sky illuminating the ocean.

"That's incredible," Wes responds, stunned at the exploding metrics on Instagram. "Four-thousand likes, a hundred shares, and the day is barely getting started. The camera angles are out of this world. How do you do it?"

"The camera's waterproof," Ava says, calm and casual.

"Ava's studying film," Zen puts in. "At U.C.L.A."

"Film, Television, and Digital Media," Ava clarifies. "This Fall is my last semester. Surfing's my real passion, but let's face it. That's still a man's world."

"You shouldn't let anything stop you from doing what you love," Wes tells her. "Hopefully Zen took some videos of you surfing, too."

"I wouldn't know how to work a fancy camera like that," Zen bashfully admits.

"I came for the sunrise. And we both just happened to be out on dawn patrol," Ava says. "Let's do this again, Zen."

"Yes," Zen replies as they swipe their boards and head to the pier parking lot. "I'll message you on Insta and call once my phone works again."

"Sorry Ava?" Wes hesitates to ask. "The hills here could give San Francisco's a run for their money. If it's not out of the way, would you drive us back to our hotel on Sepulveda?"

"Sure," Ava agrees. "I'm in Laurel Canyon."

"Nice. So, you're out in the Hills," Wes replies. "What's the commute like?"

Ava pulls up a map, sharing her phone screen with Zen. "About an hour on the 405. Two or three in rush hour."

"I appreciate you giving us a lift," Wes says as they load their surfboards on the roof rack of Ava's boxy, chocolate brown vintage Volkswagen. "And most of all, thanks for finding Zen."

Jen's still in bed when Wes turns the door open. From the entrance, the hotel room looks more like a storage unit, all their travel bags stacked half way to the ceiling. Wes and Zen try to tread lightly around the suitcases. With a winsome smile, wetsuit-wearing Zen leans on his sandy surfboard.

Jen springs from bed, relieved and appalled. "We were worried sick! Why didn't you text us?"

"I did," Zen replies innocently. "But I had no idea that our European phones don't working here."

"We've got to unlock them," Wes recommends. "Gabi from the Taco Shell also sells cell phone plans in Long Beach, a short drive south on the 405."

"Whoa!" Zen cuts in. "Ava's house is north on the 405."

"First of all," Jen asks firmly. "Who's Gabi from the Taco Shell, and who's Ava?"

"Gabi helped me find Zen at the Strand in Downtown Manhattan Beach," Wes responds forthrightly.

"And Ava," Zen begins. "She's a super kind surfer girl who I met on the beach this morning. Ava posted a video of me cutting a killer tube. It's already going viral!"

Jen sighs, giving Zen an accepting smile. "How did she get your video so many views?"

"Ava studies social media at U.C.L.A. She's really smart. I wish my phone was connected to the Internet so I could see that video blowing up!"

"Which reminds me," Wes says. "Gabi gave me her business card. She can help us with our phones later today."

Wes goes to the hotel front desk, an office behind a glass

window facing the constant whir of cars on Sepulveda. On a courtesy phone, he dials the number on Gabi's card. After a few minutes of automation in English and Spanish, Wes connects to a live human. He asks for an appointment with Gabi and takes the earliest option. With a couple hours to spare for lunch, Wes returns to the room and invites Zen and Jen out to eat.

"How about some Taco Shell?" Zen suggests.

Wes shrugs indifferently. "Didn't you just have Taco Shell?"

"Yo, that shit's good!" Zen raves, patting his washboard stomach. "I'm gettin' hungry just thinkin' about it."

"Come on, Zen. This is California, the world's dinner table. With all the options here, why don't we eat somewhere authentically Mexican?"

"Okay, Mister California," Jen says to Wes, winking slyly. "You lead the way."

They climb into the Bronco, snaking their way down a winding hill and eventually finding a parking lot by the pier. Not far away, they happen upon a Mexican restaurant with outdoor seating and a Mariachi trio trailing the servers. The big sombreros, big mustaches, and big guitars drift from the sides of tables with melancholy melodies that make diners smile between bites of nachos and salsa. Wes speaks a little Spanish to the waiter, who brings fish tacos and a round of cool gazpacho, sizzling steak fajitas for the main course, and some creamy tres leches cake slices for dessert.

"You know, I think this is the first meal we've had together as a family," Wes says when the bill comes to the table.

"Dad, I'm never going back to the Taco Shell again," Zen remarks with a satisfied sneer, gnawing on a wooden toothpick. "This is so much better."

"The Taco what?" Wes jokes, handing off the leather presenter to their server. "Never heard of it."

After lunch, freeway traffic is touch and go. Wes steers the bulky Bronco into the fast lane, looking further ahead at cars grinding to a halt. Two police cruisers cut through the shoulder with sirens ablaze. Wes changes lanes to get out of the backup, eventually taking the North Bellflower exit. Soon, the boulevard opens into a long drag of shops and plazas. From across the parking lot, the bright red phone company logo shines in the storefront window.

"Hi," Wes says sunnily to the store employees standing quietly behind the counter. "We have an appointment with Gabi. Sorry we're late. Heavy traffic on the 405."

"Something happened," softly responds the sales associate, a Black woman with side-swept blonde hair. "Gabi is not with us anymore."

"Are you sure?" Wes asks, digging into his pockets for Gabi's business card. "She told me she was working today."

"Didn't you see the news on Facebook?"

"I haven't been on Facebook. We're from Amsterdam, so none of our devices work here. Gabi offered to connect our phones to a local network."

"Earlier today," she slowly continues, clutching the gold cross around her neck. "There was a shooting near Torrance."

Wes covers his mouth. "Oh no. A shooting?"

"Gabi was on her way home when the car got sprayed with bullets."

"Please tell me she's okay," Wes begs. "Was Gabi hurt?"

Gazing blankly ahead, the sales associate with teary eyes answers affirmatively. "Gabi died this morning in the emergency room."

5

With a new smartphone and an aching heart, Wes returns with his family to the hotel on Sepulveda Boulevard. Next door, a line at the Taco Shell is stretching out the door. Wes glimpses the bustle for dollar ninety-nine burritos and wonders if Gabi's co-workers even know what happened. On the ride back from the phone store, Zen had let it slip out. Now Jen knows about Downtown Manhattan Beach, the necklace, and the lipstick smear.

"Who does that?" Jen asks, pushing Wes's arm away when he reaches across the center console.

Wes takes a deep breath before responding. "Please hear me out. All I did was give her a religious pendant I no longer wanted. Gabi was discovering her Jewish roots, and it meant a lot to her. Come on, Jen. In her final living moments, she helped locate our son. I thanked her and she thanked me."

"You never wear that necklace over your shirt. From what you've shared with me, you don't believe in God," Jen pries further. "How did Gabi see your star pendant?"

"The chain slipped off my neck on the walk down a steep hill," Wes explains to Jen as she climbs out of the Bronco. "Look, that poor young woman is dead. And it's all because she took time out of her busy day to show me to the beach. A simple act of kindness cost Gabi her life."

Jen heads back to the room alone. From the parking lot, Zen waves to Wes, who rolls down the window but at first stays silent, trying really hard to not feel the sting of betrayal.

"I get it," Wes says without looking up. "But Gabi and I did nothing inappropriate. You know, I would've found you without anyone's help. And now, Gabi's dead."

"Huh?" Zen mumbles, dazed and oblivious. "What are you talking about?"

"If it's not too much to ask," Wes says, twisting out enough of a smile to let Zen know he's not angry with him. "I'd just like to be by myself for a minute."

Alone in the Bronco, Wes clicks into his Spotify playlists, landing on Sarah McLachlan. Lilting from the phone speaker, a haunting melody touches Wes from within as the music's conviction and vulnerability transport him to an unearthly space. An ad interrupts the music. Jen lightly taps her fingers on the driver's side window.

"Try to be gentle with yourself," Jen says forgivingly. "I didn't mean to get jealous over a necklace, or an innocent air kiss. It sounds like Gabi was a nice girl finding her way."

Their hands touch briefly, and Jen joins Wes in the parked Bronco. On his phone, Wes is getting to know California by scrolling into some local news. "KTLA reports that the shooting was gang related," Wes comments, clicking into the latest article on the drive-by shooting in Torrance.

"Let's move somewhere nice," Jen says to Wes on their way out of the Bronco. "I can't wait to unpack all those suitcases and start our life together."

Together in the hotel room, the three of them retreat to the twin beds. On their phones, Jen and Wes scour the rental apps for a home. Zen searches the listings in Laurel Canyon, where Ava lives, but Wes reminds him everything that far north is beyond their budget.

"Here's a nice little house in Venice Beach," Wes says, passing his phone to Zen. "The kitchen looks a little narrow, but it's a two-bedroom bungalow not far from the ocean."

Jen leans closer to check out the listing. "They're having an open house the day after tomorrow."

"Aren't there any listings with open houses today?" Wes asks.

She texts him links to five different rentals. "Let's also check these places out," Jen suggests.

They hop back into the Bronco to head up the coast, and take a walk with a landlord through a condo in Santa Monica. Too small, too city, too much trouble to park. Then comes a cabin at the end of a long street twisting up into the Topanga Canyon, which even the landlord says is one spark away from perishing in the Santa Ana winds. In the afternoon, they drag their heels to Burbank, West Hollywood, and Los Feliz. Too much filming, too much tourism, too much of everything.

The next morning, Wes and Jen are in Downtown Los Angeles checking out a space with lots of exposed brick, an old warehouse remodeled as a chic urban loft. The price is right, but the wide windows and elevated ceilings spell trouble.

"When something feels like a fire hazard, you've got to go with your instincts," Wes says bluntly to the landlord, a college kid renting it out to pay for school. "Thanks for your time."

The westward drive is traffic hell. Only one hour remains before the open house in Venice Beach is over. On the freeway, Wes inches his way to the fast lane, worrying that someone else has already snagged the house.

"Let's claim it," Jen says, pressing her palms together in a moment of manifestation. "If we say it's ours, so it shall be. I'm going to pray on it."

"We've got this," Wes concludes, cruising along the pale golden coastline in El Segundo. "Venice or bust!"

The house in Venice Beach looks a little more worn out than the stylish Spanish cottage they saw on Redfin. Instead of the lush, green lawn in the photos, the grass is brittle and dry. The door of the attached garage sits slanted in the frame, and one of the window panels is busted out. The home's owner, Abdul, lifts the garage door. As Wes rolls the big SUV into the tight space, Abdul assures him the broken electric door opener will be repaired soon after the house finds a renter.

"We've been all over L.A. these last couple days," Wes tells Abdul on a walk through all the rooms in the single-story dwelling. "This house might not be perfect, but it's perfect for us."

Abdul's eyes gleam with satisfaction as he forwards Wes the rental agreement from his iPad. "I'll e-mail you the documents," he offers. "If you can pay three months upfront, it's yours today."

"Done," Wes says, sealing it with a handshake.

They settle into the cozy little house, a modern mint-green bungalow tucked neatly on a quiet street not far behind the boardwalk bustle. After returning the Bronco SUV to the Hertz lot near LAX and leasing out a used Toyota Corolla, Wes pulls into the garage and doomscrolls on Facebook for updates on the shooting in Torrance. No arrests, no leads, and nothing new since the story had first broken on Long Beach's Patch. On a long thread of sadness and shock, Wes posts a comment, aiming it at her assailants: **Bangers always ruin everything. Justice for Gabi!**

"Nice ride," Zen calls to Wes from the front yard.

"It's not quite the Bronco, but it'll do," Wes says. "Have you heard from Ava?"

"We're meeting early tomorrow morning at the Venice breakwater. Gotta get out there before the winds pick up."

Wes checks his phone, diving into his notes for a web link he'd saved at the car dealership. "When you have a minute, Zen, I wanted to share something with you. Here's that contest I was telling you about."

Wes passes the phone to Zen, who looks at the screen like he doesn't believe his own eyes. "The 2024 Huntington Beach Surf Off?" Zen asks. "What's this all about?"

"You could win a lot of money for school. It's open to surfers of all levels, ages eighteen to twenty-two. Every weekend, the best surfer in each heat goes to the next round until one grand prize winner gets a quarter million dollars to attend any college or university in California."

"I don't know," Zen says doubtfully. "People here have been surfing their whole lives."

"Maybe they have," Wes responds. "But do they know how to use technology and reach an online audience? Not many surfers can break the Internet like you.”

“I’m glad you believe in me, Dad. But this isn’t Amsterdam, where me and my mates were like the only surfers in town. Californians were born to surf.”

“You called me Dad,” Wes responds, cherishing the powerful milestone. “And yes, I do believe in you. I think you’d have a really good shot at winning. That video you made with Ava the other day was pretty breathtaking.”

“Man, that shit already got a hundred thousand hits on Insta,” Zen comments, reveling in his newfound success online. “Ava’s showing me how to monetize my socials, so maybe I’ll just stick to that.”

“Imagine if you win this thing,” Wes goes on. “It’s a full ride. Don’t worry about the entry fee. It’s a few hundred dollars. I’ll cover it.”

“It’s cool, I’ll enter the contest,” Zen nonchalantly replies. “But what am I going to spend four years of my life studying?”

“That depends on you,” Wes answers. “Surfers should probably understand the business side of surfing, and so you might go for a marketing degree. Maybe take environmental studies or political science to give yourself a full picture of what today’s surfers are up against. The University of California has ten campuses. All of them are known for having different standout programs across the arts and sciences.”

“Oh, so you’ve already looked into this?” Zen asks, recoiling in suspicion.

“Sorry if I’m bombarding you with information,” Wes says. “And sorry…”

“Come on. Don’t start that *sorry* shit again,” Zen cuts in. “Like I said, text me the link and I’ll enter the contest.”

“It’s just an option. Today at the car dealer, I talked to a father and son who were amped about the surf off, and I thought it might give you an opportunity to surf competitively, or even earn a living at it.”

“Ava’s got my new video blowing up on her socials,” Zen boasts. “I’m going to start my own YouTube channel and post the videos there, too. More views, more money.”

“Look, Zen, there’s no pressure if you feel college isn’t for you," Wes tells him. "I read some of the fine print, and the HBSO winner can also take a cash prize option. Then you could decide whether to spend that money on education for your career, or on a career for your lifestyle."

"Okay, let me win first and decide later," Zen says evasively. "It's kind of ridiculous how Americans pay so much money to study at university, when all that's free in Europe."

"Here in California, I think community college is free."

"Why would I waste my time at a community college?" Zen responds. "With that kind of money, we could start our own reality TV show."

"Ugh," Wes groans as Zen walks away in a wetsuit. "We haven't been here a week, and already my son is sounding like a typical American."

At the kitchen table with a fresh coffee carafe, Jen is plugging away on her MacBook. With her new screenwriting software, the pages already look like a movie script, with pure emotion radiating off the perfectly arranged lines. Jen stops typing and looks up from the keyboard, and Wes apologizes for interrupting her flow.

"It's okay, babe," Jen says, closing up the laptop. "I could use a break."

"How about we get some ice cream on the boardwalk?" Wes offers.

Jen doesn't respond right away. "I have a different kind of break in mind. I want to meet someone in Hollywood who can get my script on the silver screen."

"That could be something," Wes concurs. "How do you feel about Venice so far? I think it's kind of like Amsterdam with a beach."

"The thing is, my script isn't a beach story," Jen says. "Venice is not Hollywood. Here, people are quirky and free. No one's trying to become a star. Because it's so touristy, Venice Beach is as removed from Hollywood as Disneyland."

Wes grins affably. "That's true. Venice is a beach town, not a movie hub. But one of these days on the boardwalk, you might connect with someone who knows someone."

"Venice is too mystical," Jen observes. "Everyone knows

Hollywood is where all the big deals are made. I'd rather knock on doors than to sit around and wait for a one-in-a-million chance encounter to happen."

"If only it were as simple as pounding the pavement. We'll hit up Sunset and Santa Monica soon."

"Anyway, I'm really happy that Zen is finally thinking about his future. Do you think he'll go for the scholarship contest?"

Wes cracks a half-smile. "Zen called me dad for the first time today. That's why I've been on a cloud. About the surf competition, I offered to pay his entry fee, but he wants to give it some thought."

"Well, I suppose it's never too late to study for free in the Netherlands," Jen replies. "How's the job hunting going for you?"

"I sent my resume to some high-end restaurants in Beverly Hills and Brentwood," Wes says. "The pay for a manager with my experience is pretty good, but it's demanding work. And since we don't really need the income, I was thinking to ask Zen if I can be his manager."

Jen shoots him an incredulous look. "And what exactly would you be doing, Mister Manager?"

"I'll help him balance his books and manage his schedule. He'll need someone to help boost his online presence as well. I can ask my cousin Evan in San Diego to give us the down low on search engine optimization."

Zen walks into the house in a black wetsuit, his feet caked in sand and his surfboard bone-dry. "Choppy waves today," he says. "No one was going out on *that* water."

"Hey bud," Wes greets Zen. "Can I ask you something?"

Zen shrugs and nods. "Go for it."

"Is there a chance you might be looking for a manager to help you get ahead in your surfing career?"

"Sure, I guess. Why do you ask?"

"And there's a second part to my question," Wes continues, taking a deep breath. "Am I the manager you're looking for? As your dad, I'll put in the work for you without asking for a cut. Just remember me when you're rich and famous."

They come to an agreement with a soft handshake that

quickly warms into a tight hug. At the kitchen table, where Jen opens her laptop to get back into her screenplay, Wes and Zen crunch some numbers on their phones. The math adds up to a sweet pot of streaming royalties when Zen works out the current projections of his weekly social media metrics.

Zen gets another clip from Ava, who texts him a slow-motion video of that early morning barrel he'd slayed on their first morning in Manhattan Beach. Together, Zen and Ava are setting goals: a viral video every week, and a hundred-thousand followers on Instagram within a month.

Zen's going viral, again. The visceral buzz of six-digit reactions to his surfing content sends him dashing into the kitchen with sand between his toes and a phone so hot he almost drops it. Onscreen, Zen's latest surf video is streaming, and he huddles with his parents to watch it together.

At the beach, the scene turns tense. A middle-aged surfer shouts at the ocean, spitting in Zen's direction when he steps out of the water. Jen and Wes review the footage closely, backtracking thirty seconds to see what all the fuss was about. Wes holds his breath and closely follows Zen on his board. As Zen soars with the crest, the other surfer buckles under pressure and his leash snaps, leaving his board to float like driftwood in the sweeping current.

"You cut me off on the green wall, motherfucker!" the older surfer yells. He fumes over his broken leash, kicking his damaged board into the sand.

"I was blindsided, man, take it easy," Zen tells him.

When the older surfer yanks off his swim cap, his balding mullet ages him another ten years. "Easy for you to say, kook. That wave was mine."

Zen steps closer to the angry man, crossing into the volatile orbit of his bitter rage. Wes and Jen stare at the screen, dreadful that their gentle son and the burly surfer might come to blows. "You came out of nowhere, man," Zen says innocently, reaching out for a handshake. "Sorry I didn't see you."

"Where'd you learn how to surf anyway, you grom?" the surfer grumbles to Zen.

"Hey big guy," Ava says, capturing the footage from behind the camera. "Did you lose your toupee in the water? Give him a break. It was an honest mistake."

"Fuck this, I'm out," he growls, stomping his way to the sand dunes.

Sitting at the kitchen table, Wes watches the clip again and again. He studies Zen's moves, the paddling and pivoting, all of it seeming so lighthearted and effortless. When the older surfer throws a fit and kicks sand, Wes has a good laugh and rewatches the scene until his phone battery drops below ten percent.

"I'm glad you're going viral," Wes says to Zen. "But are you sure this clip is good for your online image?"

"Ava thinks it is," Zen immediately replies. "The guy was pissed because I caught the peak and he flopped out. But I swear I didn't see him."

"Even though this clip is getting lots of views and likes, I'd probably advise you, as your manager, to consider taking it down. Not all publicity is good publicity."

"It's not like I have that much content to begin with," Zen responds. "And of all the clips we posted this week, that's the one with the strongest metrics."

"Of course it is," Wes responds knowingly. "Especially online, people gravitate to drama. You don't want that to overshadow your talent."

"Thanks for the advice, Dad. I'll think about it."

"Did you have a chance to think about Huntington Beach?"

"I'm gonna go for it," Zen replies. "Today, I finished applying to U.C.L.A. Ava says I have a killer candidate profile."

"Zen, that's epic!" Wes cheers him on. "Have you told Mom yet?"

"Mom checked the grammar in my application essay," Zen says as Jen comes into the room to give him a smile and thumbs-up.

"This calls for a celebration," Wes proposes, glowing at the news of his son gearing up for college. "Tonight, we'll have dinner in Hollywood."

Rocco's is on the corner of Santa Monica and San Vincente. A handlebar-mustached host in short-shorts greets Zen first. Wes and Jen follow him into the dimly-lit dance floor and indoor bar, but instead they decide to dine outside on an elevated patio overlooking the Hollywood Hills and West Hollywood's sheriff station. Jen orders a bottle of red wine, while for teetotaler Wes and underaged Zen, it's sparkling water. Soon, their plates arrive: penne pesto and grilled shrimp for Zen, and an arugula salad for Jen. From the table, Wes notices a pavement rainbow brightening the crosswalk and points to a colorfully affirming billboard on a nearby hill, "You Are Enough." The cosmopolitan vibe in West Hollywood inspires Wes to choose an animal-free entrée. He gets a vegetarian burger, and says it's what his mom would've ordered. Before their food comes out to the table, Jen knocks back a couple glasses of Cabernet.

"Everyone here looks so young," Jen says loudly enough to raise a few brows at a nearby table. "Do you think this is the place where I should be pitching my script?"

Wes gives her an assuring smile. "Go for it, babe."

Wineglass in hand, Jen staggers slowly across the terrace. Loud and tipsy, she approaches the table of twenty-somethings. They offer her a chair and exchange quick pleasantries. When Jen takes a seat, the other women at the table engage her first.

"Are you in the industry?" one of the women asks Jen admiringly. "What do you do?"

"I'm writing a script," Jen says. "An Amsterdam sex worker is murdered, and a good cop faces off with crooked cops while searching for the perp who did it."

"You lost me at 'good cop'," says a disheveled-looking man with a pierced septum. "All cops are bastards."

Jen tries to smile, but can hardly hide her disappointment. "Well, it's about time for Amsterdam to have a Hollywood movie. Sex workers deserve visibility in films, don't you think?"

"Are you giving sex workers visibility as human beings with agency and autonomy, or casting them as helpless victims thrust into a dangerous lifestyle against their will?" asks a purple-haired young woman sipping an Appletini. "Why not have the cop murdered by a corrupt pimp, with the hooker caught in the middle?"

"Hey, that's actually a pretty cool idea," Jen quickly concurs, slurring her words. "Thank you for talking to me, I guess. I'm going to go back with my family."

The hipsters quickly turn inward, mumbling among themselves while Jen takes clumsy steps away from their table.

"I think I want to change the story around," Jen tells Wes.

"Yeah?" Wes responds. "Try not to take whatever they said to heart. Always remember, you're the one writing it."

"I don't think they like my story. They don't seem to like me much," Jen says, topping off her wineglass again.

From the table of hipsters, the worst drunk staggers across the terrace. "Hey. Jen, is it?" he says, swirling the ice in his whiskey highball. "See that little dog over there?"

Unsteady in her chair, Jen turns around and scans the terrace. Perched on a picnic blanket a few tables over, the feisty brown chihuahua is lapping up a plate of scrambled eggs.

"Oh, how cute! They probably ordered from the doggy menu."

The straggly-bearded drunk scoffs, knocking back the whiskey and thumping his glass on the table. "Yeah, well, I bet that dog shits out better screenplays than yours. But, hey, don't give up on your dreams."

"That jerk," Jen tells Wes. "Are you going to let him disrespect me like that?"

"No, I'm not," Wes says, offering Jen the remaining half of his veggie burger. "I'll be back."

Wes returns the empty glass to the table. "Forgetting something?" Wes asks the whiskey-swilling hipster, who's now nursing another tumbler. "What you said to my partner was rude and uncalled for. Is it because she's got an accent? Does her voice not sound American enough for you Hollywood hillbillies?"

Whiskey Hipster tries to stands up, grasping the seat for support. The chair flips over and he falls on his ass. Jen gets the last laugh and lets him know it.

"Instant karma!" Zen says to his mom.

"Hey, it serves that asshole right," Jen stammers, sipping her wine as she turns to Wes. "Babe, why don't we take this party elsewhere?"

"Before you go," says a man snuggling his chihuahua in a tiny quilt. "I'm Ross. Just want to say I heard everything and love your story. My husband works in Hollywood and he also digs the murdered sex worker trope. You'll do fine, girl!"

"Really?" Jen mumbles, looking at Ross as though she didn't hear him properly. "You think so?"

"I really do," adds Ross's white-bearded husband. "I'm Kyle Langley. In the nineties, I discovered the screenplays of two Academy Award winners. These days, I deal mostly with mergers and acquisitions."

Jen leans closer to Kyle, proffering her hand. "It's nice to meet you. But do you think someone can make a movie out of my story? Are all the cool kids in Hollywood going to like it?"

"Don't listen to those pretentious assholes," Kyle tells her. "They're exactly what's wrong with Tinseltown."

"So, who's this adorable bundle in your arms?" Jen asks curiously.

"That's our best girl, Fefe," Kyle says. The chihuahua wriggles her tiny head out of the quilt to sniff Jen's hands. "Fefe knows good people when she sees them."

"We'll be heading home now," Ross tells Jen. "Our little chalupa is getting sleepy, and we're out past her bedtime."

"Do you live here in WeHo?" Wes asks Ross and Kyle.

"Oh, God no," Ross replies. "Hollywood's too young and woke for a couple of old farts like us."

"We moved from Burbank to Sierra Madre a couple years ago," Kyle replies. "East of the city, out in the San Gabriel Mountains."

"Just a month ago, we were still living in Amsterdam," Wes replies. "Now Venice is home."

"Ah, Amsterdam," Kyle says. "Home of Netflix. They're giving Hollywood a run for their money."

"Really?" Jen asks. "We should talk more about this."

"Sure, we'd love to have you over for dinner," Ross says,

reaching out to shake Zen's hand. "You must be the hot young surfer your mom and dad were going on about earlier."

"Um, yeah, I guess," Zen responds, distant and jittery. "On YouTube and Instagram, my handle is Zen Surfs LA."

"Got it," Ross says, distracted by the raucous laughter at the drunken table of hipsters in their twenties. "Be right back."

With Fefe in his arms, Ross loosens the quilt and carries her across the crowded terrace. Immersed in their chatter, the young hipsters sip their drinks, seemingly oblivious to their surroundings. None of them bother to look up at Ross gently rubbing his chihuahua's tummy with her backside pointing at the table. A faint, piercing sound escapes Fefe's tiny body. Wes and Jen retreat indoors to the bar area to escape the rotten stench that overwhelms the terrace, where everyone is gagging and coughing.

"Don't like the smell?" Ross says sassily, swaddling Fefe in her little quilt. "Then why don't you take your heads out of your asses? Enjoy your night, dipsters."

The drive home starts in the slow grind of westside traffic. WeHo sparkles in the rearview mirror: the bucolic backdrop behind a blazing, red-hot nightlife, where hillside rainbow flags blanket the hills behind Santa Monica Boulevard. To get back to the coast, Wes steers west of West Hollywood. As Santa Monica becomes La Cienega, the boulevard jams up. Slowly, the panoramic hillside vistas overlooking Hollywood fade into the background.

"I'd say we've just made a nice little inroad," Wes says. "Let's take them up on dinner."

"I've been trying to edit my screenplay for a year now, but still haven't talked to a professional," Jen says anxiously. "What if it's still not ready?"

"Kyle and Ross seem well-connected," Wes responds. "Just follow up with them tomorrow. If Kyle wants your script badly enough, maybe he'll pay for an editor."

"Hey, the dude asked for my socials," Zen reminds his parents. "What am I supposed to say to him? 'Hope you like my surf videos, can you put me in a movie?'"

From the driver's seat, Wes looks at Zen in the rearview

mirror. "You gave Ross your Instagram handle. Let him reach out to you."

Zen's expression turns sour. "But why are you telling Mom to make moves? Am I supposed to just sit back and wait?"

"Kyle and Ross seem interested in helping your mom turn her script into a film," Wes says. "That could be life-changing."

"So you're saying my shit doesn't matter as much?"

"I didn't mean it like that," Wes replies, quickly and clearly. "Zen, this is Hollywood. Just play it cool and don't let them see you sweat. I'm here for you both, and that won't ever change."

"I love you, Wes," Jen tells him, lacing her fingers with his.

Wes exits the boulevard to take the 405 to Venice Beach. Everything flashes before his eyes: the quick seduction of twenty years ago, the chance encounter of two months ago, and the international relocation of two weeks ago. Traffic once again jams up, and in that moment, Wes turns to face Jen.

"There's something I've been wanting to say to you," he reveals as cars on the freeway start inching forward again. "Hope it's not any less meaningful because you said it first. I love you, Jen. And I love you, Zen."

In the rearview mirror, Zen glimpses his father's eyes. "Does this mean we get to be a family?" Zen asks from the backseat.

"We already are," Wes answers, cruising toward the fiery, tranquil glow of a vibrant coastal sunset. "You're my family now."

6

It's a crisp and drafty morning in Venice Beach. A cold onshore flow makes it feel chillier, even indoors. For a defense against the postfrontal air, Wes and Jen are cozying together in the living room under a knitted quilt, cell phones in hand and warm coffee cups on coasters nearby. On her screen, Jen focuses closely on Chimamanda Ngozi Adichie, the author speaking on a TED Talk about *The Danger of a Single Story*. Beside her, Wes is swiping back and forth on banking apps to review his accounts. He admits his half million-dollar net worth has taken a hit since setting up a home base in L.A. But Wes is sure he's got enough of a bankroll to bleed money for a good year while Jen and Zen pursue their dreams, as long as they keep their nut small.

"How did you save so much money in Amsterdam?" Jen asks.

"Twenty years of free housing didn't hurt. For the loft, I only had to pay the electric bill. Living upstairs from Sub Dude, I hardly ever bought groceries," Wes continues. "No car, no insurance premiums. Guess I made out like a bandit."

"Did you have any investors?"

"In a word, Harry," Wes answers. "He would've given me the shirt off his back if I asked him for it."

"When was the last time you saw him?"

"Six years ago. Harry hung himself at his home in London. He had to play straight in order to get an inheritance from his Victorian-era grandfather. Harry was always living a double life. In time, everything takes its toll."

"God, that's terrible," Jen says. "I spent two years hiding my relationship with Abby from my mom. We were all living under one roof."

Zen comes charging into the living room. He tousles his thick dark hair and reaches for the rack above the TV stand to grab the longest surfboard in his quiver.

"I'm going out with Ava," Zen says, running his nails across the board. "Does anyone have a hairdryer and a credit card? I gotta scrape off the old wax before putting on a fresh layer."

"My dryer's under the bathroom sink," Jen offers. "Your dad's the one to ask about the credit card."

"Zen, remember we've got dinner in Sierra Madre with Ross and Kyle," Wes says, handing Zen an American Express card. "That's three freeways in rush hour traffic, so can you be home by four?"

"I'll sit this one out," Zen shoots back. "The mountains aren't my scene."

"Come on, Zen," Jen says to him. "I'm sure they're looking forward to seeing you."

"Well, maybe I'd rather be at the beach with my girlfriend than to hang out with old gay guys in the middle of nowhere."

"Not cool," Wes says to his son, who he still doesn't know well. "I was just remembering my friend Harry, a gay man who took his own life. He'd be alive today if the people in his life weren't so narrow-minded. Without Harry, I would've been stuck in Thailand without a dollar in my pocket."

Zen cocks his head and looks askance at Wes, clutching his longboard and turning away. "Come on, Dad. Not another sad tsunami story."

"It's a truth I'll always live with," Wes replies. "But Kyle and Ross could help your mom break into the biz. They can show you the ropes in Hollywood, if you're interested."

"Interested in sucking dick to get a role in a movie?" Zen asks facetiously. "No thanks."

Wes shakes his head in dismay and rests a hand on Zen's shoulder. "They deserve respect like everyone else. Do you dig what I'm saying?"

"Dude, why all the touching?"

Wes gets the message and backs off. From the driveway, a car horn sends Zen with his surfboard on a dash through the door. "My woman's giving me a ride to beach," Zen says in his guttural Dutch accent. "Later, gators!"

"Later gators?" Jen echoes as the front door slams shut. "What did he just call us?"

"I guess she's his woman now," Wes remarks to the rattle of Ava's vintage Volkswagen cruising shoreward.

"Don't mind Zen's tough little homophobic front," Jen says with a sigh. "He'll tell you more when he's ready."

Wes and Jen head east to Sierra Madre. After feeling some heat on the freeways, the drive unfolds under shaded green canopies of oak tree branches hanging over the street. In the foothills of the San Gabriel Mountains, Wes steers carefully through a tight path that narrows into a single lane. Around the bend, they arrive at the house on a lush, rugged hillside overlooking a canyon. Magenta bougainvillea vines decorate a trellis outside the arched doorway of the sprawling estate.

As Wes rings the doorbell, Jen hands him the bottle of Chardonnay. Now Wes's hands are full with gifts, freeing Jen to greet Ross with a big, loud hug when he opens the door. Wes hands Ross the mixed bouquet. A little red, a little orange, and a lot of sunflowers. From behind Ross, little Fefe comes yapping and jumping.

"Oh, you're too good to us," Ross says, lightly squeezing Wes on the arm. "Come in, lovelies."

"I forgot to bring something for Fefe," Wes says. "Back in town, we passed by a cute little pet store. Let me go and bring her back a treat."

"Don't you dare," Ross turns serious, quickly snapping back to his usual bubbly self. "We spoil our girl plenty."

"Beautiful place. Gorgeous flowers out front," Jen tells Ross as she looks around and takes in the spacious digs.

"Thanks, dear. Kyle designed our little shack from top to bottom. He wanted a place that felt like daytime TV, while I was going for a crib on a cliff. You know, something more cinematic? And this is where we landed. Make yourselves at home, loves. Drinks are in the fridge, *mi casa su casa.*"

The living room is wide open and minimalist, a white stucco décor with a mishmash of modern art and lots of space between furniture. A long canvas of gold glitter sparkles across the wall in an expansive living room, where Kyle sits with his MacBook at the end of a long blue velvet sectional.

Kyle stands up to shake Wes's hand, though his eyes are on Jen. "I was just reading your screenplay. It's really drawing me in."

"That means a lot to me," Jen tells him.

"I've been reading scripts all my life," Kyle says. "Not so much in the last decade or so, when streaming platforms have come along and changed the game completely. Your lines are fabulous, Jen."

"It's my first screenplay, and that gives me a lot of hope," Jen responds. "It's a real dream come true to be in this position."

"I don't want to over-promise anything, as I haven't pitched a script in a while. These days, I work mainly on the financial side of movie production. At U.C.L.A., I double majored in film and finance."

"Zen's girlfriend Ava is about to graduate from U.C.L.A.," Wes chimes in. "They've really been cranking up the metrics with Zen's surf videos. He's is a natural. His abilities are mind-blowing. Maybe you can help him land a role in a surf flick."

"I'm definitely not on *that* end of things anymore," Kyle says abruptly. "Casting is a sleazy business. And you don't want to know how corrupt Hollywood can be."

"All the sexual crimes coming to light have been horrific," Wes comments.

"It's not just that," Kyle goes on. "In the last ten years, Hollywood has become insufferably woke."

"I think what Americans call woke is common courtesy in Europe," Wes says. "I haven't lived in the states for twenty years, so I can't fathom why basic human concepts like dignity and respect have gone out the window."

"Well, let me put it like this. I hate all politicians," Kyle declares with calm, measured grace. "Power corrupts. And in Hollywood, they let power go to their over-inflated heads."

"They also have the power to turn someone's story into a movie," Jen says. "Don't they?"

"In theory, yes. But for whatever reason, if they think your script is not quite woke enough, they'll instead go with one that meets their impossible standards. It's all so performative, with everyone constantly trying to out-virtue signal each other. Every writer in L.A. has no choice but to bow before Hollywood's vision for a perfect world."

"A lot of movies on streaming platforms look more like life as it is experienced by the everyday masses, don't you think?" Wes asks from the kitchen. "You know, more grit and less glamour?"

"I guess what I'm trying to say is that it's not like the old days anymore," Kyle responds, turning to Jen. "Because if Hollywood says no, Netflix could say yes. Either way, we can work with editors and directors who might, as one option, turn your script into a series. The plot might also unfold with episodes instead of a feature film, if you're open to that."

"I'm open," Jen says, sliding into Wes's embrace as he hands her a can of High Noon.

Ross turns up in a chef's apron with a steel spatula in hand. "Hey, loved ones! The lasagna is cooled off and ready."

At the chrome-rimmed oval dinner table, the conversation shifts from professional to personal. Originally from a Chicago suburb, Kyle relocated to Los Angeles as an undergrad, starting university with a scholarship and the full support of his parents. By graduation, Kyle had already served an internship on the business end of Hollywood, but instead took a job advising investors at a financial firm in Burbank. With a bankroll to fall back on, Kyle became a casting agent during the 1980s, calling that decade the golden age of modern cinema.

"It wasn't the golden age for being a gay man," Kyle says,

emphatically holding up a finger. "In the eighties when people started getting sick and dying, it felt safer to keep certain parts of my life hidden."

"Kyle has the greatest parents in the world," Ross adds. "I love my in-laws!"

"I came out to my mom and dad at fourteen," Kyle reveals. "They were my first and biggest allies."

Wes smiles politely. "Are you parents still…"

"Yep," Kyle cuts in. "They're both in their early nineties, still eating big Midwestern breakfasts every morning."

"How about you, Ross?" Wes asks, digging into his lasagna. "You must be a native Angeleno."

"Ha! If only," Ross replies with a caustic laugh. "I come from a large Catholic family back east, about an hour outside Philly. By twenty-five, I'd had gotten tired of trying to figure out why half of them handled me with kid gloves while the other half very plainly did not enjoy my presence. Soon as I got here, I changed my name and cut ties with everyone, except my Aunt Tina. Before I moved to California, Aunt Tina told me she knew I was gay since I was six years old. After retiring from social work, she moved to Ireland."

"We should all have an Aunt Tina in our lives," Jen says, grinning shyly. "For a while, I was in a domestic partnership with an American woman. We pretended to be roommates, putting on for my mom that we were just friends making ends meet. My family is all spread out in Indonesia, Brazil, the Netherlands, Albania, and Morocco. Everyone's either a serious Christian or a devout Muslim. It's like being caught between a rock and a hard place."

"Yes, honey, I know that feeling all too well," Ross replies. "Did Zen forget all about us?"

"Oh, um, no. It's not like that. He just went surfing with his girlfriend today."

At the word girlfriend, Ross tenses up, but quickly composes himself with a devilish grin. "I can see where Zen gets those thick, luscious lips," Ross tells Jen, staring at her intensely. "So full and fabulous. God, a mouth like that could suck a breadcrumb off a rooftop."

"Ross, don't joke like that," Kyle says curtly, reproaching him with a knit brow.

The table falls silent in the aftershock of Ross's offhanded remark. Everyone focuses on their plates. After another mouthful or two of lasagna, Wes breaks the awkward silence.

"Where's Fefe?" he asks Ross. "It got quiet all the sudden."

"Oh, she's fine," Ross answers breezily. "When she ain't yappin', she's just nappin'."

"So," Jen says. "What do you do, Ross?"

"Well, about ten years ago, I was starting to hit my stride with some minor roles in TV and film," Ross recalls, scratching the stubble of his auburn beard. "Most of my income was always from commercials. These days, I teach theater classes at two community colleges in the Valley. My heyday in Hollywood, if I can say that I had one, is long gone."

"Come on, now," Wes says, trying to encourage him. "You've got a dazzling personality. I'm sure your best roles are still ahead of you."

"Oh, listen to you, Wes. You're such a kind man," Ross responds. "I'll go check on dessert. Homemade blueberry ice cream is thawing out on the patio. It tastes so good when it's just soft enough to sip, but still hard enough to..."

"I think I'm going need something stronger than Chardonnay," Kyle blurts out, turning a finger pistol to his temple and pretending to unload.

As Ross walks across the living room to another wing of the house, the conversation takes on a different order. Kyle talks about his good fortune in crypto trading, and how much he's been saving on property taxes since leaving L.A. Eventually, he circles back to Ross's suggestive comment and apologizes for him.

"Zen had a bad experience a few years ago," Jen shares, holding a hand over her mouth.

"What?" Wes asks. "What happened?"

"I've already said too much," Jen answers, politely clearing her throat. "Kyle, please pretend I didn't just say that."

"Of course," Kyle says, setting his wineglass on a ceramic coaster.

Wes sits tensely in his chair. "Jen, he is my son. I want to know if he…"

"All I can say is that it could have been much worse," Jen says guardedly. "But that's Zen's story to tell. Not mine."

"Okay," Wes agrees, looking across a white marble floor that from the dining room appears to go on forever. "I need to use the restroom."

"That way, past the art gallery," Kyle says. "Second door on the left."

On the white floor tiles, Wes follows an odd trail of big, brown footprints. He feels the soles of his Patagonia sandals. A thick dusting soils his fingers. Next to an art gallery, Wes finds an open door. In the small bathroom, Ross is standing in the dark. He's nervously tugging on strands of his hair and his cherubic, jowly face is beet red.

"There's a bear in the house!" Ross says, trembling in horror. "And I can't find Fefe!"

Wes approaches Ross with deliberately quiet steps. "Try to stay calm," Wes whispers, pointing to big brown tracks across the white floor. "Looks like the bear went that way."

"My poor Fefe," Ross cries into his hands. "Our little girl would be a snack for a bear. Fefe's little dog door is busted out!"

"Look," Wes says, moving closer to Ross. "Something on those tracks is wet and blue."

Ross points a shaking finger at the broken screen door to the limestone patio. "Oh my God," he wails uncontrollably, raising a finger at the big, brown bear nestling comfortably in the corner.

"Hey guys, what's going on?" Jen asks them from behind.

Ross shushes her. "Please. Tell. Kyle. To. Call. 9-1-1."

Fefe's shrill barking comes out of nowhere. She sprints into the room at a breakneck pace, lunging at the brown bear.

"Fefe! No!" Ross yells while the huge bear uncurls from a resting position and waddles to the broken dog door. "Come back now!"

Fefe is going off like a firecracker. Swaying slowly through the open door, the bear sniffs and snarls out to the patio. Fefe stands her ground in the middle of the doorway and Ross is on his knees, begging Fefe not to follow the bear outside. Wes checks his sandals again and finds more dirt, with a loose blob of blue-purple goo smeared into the soles. The commotion turns calm when Jen reaches out to Fefe, who edges closer and jumps into her embrace.

"Your little girl is safe," Jen says to Ross, handing him Fefe.

"Well, Jen, now it's official," Ross exhales, cuddling Fefe closely. "You're Fefe's doggy godmother."

They tread slowly outdoors, taking gingerly steps on the square stone patio. Beside the table, the stainless-steel loaf pan of blueberry ice cream is licked clean. Wes looks beyond the edge of the patio at the evergreen coyote brushes across the canyon, where the bear is now sprinting between fissures in the rocky terrain. A fowl, fruity-smelling stench strangles the air. Wes gasps, and Jen stops short of stepping into a loose mound of bear scat. She shrieks in revolt and bolts for the nearest bougainvillea bush, vomiting into a pruned thicket of purple flowers.

While Ross cuddles Fefe in the living room, Kyle walks out front to say goodbye to Wes and Jen. He sees them off with lasagna squares in Tupperware. Back home in Venice, Zen is rooting through the kitchen cabinets in search of food. Wes hands him the leftovers, and Zen is so hungry he digs into the cold lasagna with a spoon.

"Did you and Ava not have a chance to eat today?" Jen asks.

"Nah, we spent the day making an epic video. One of her interns filmed me and Ava catching waves together. I texted you guys a link. Did you check it out?"

"Haven't had a chance yet," Wes says. "Up in the mountains, a bear got into the house. Little Fefe chased the bear away. We almost got sick from the smell of bear shit."

"Dude! Dad, do you mind? I'm trying to eat!" Zen shoots back.

"Oh, and by the way, no one was hurt, Zen. Thanks for asking," Wes quips.

"Glad you're all okay, but damn!" Zen hollers. "How does a bear get into your house?"

"Ross left a gallon of homemade blueberry ice cream to

thaw outside," Wes recalls. "Not a smooth move. The bear ate it all, and was probably too bloated to come after any of us."

"Let me know if you got that video," Zen reminds his parents. "It's so good, but we're not posting it on our socials."

"Really?" Wes asks. "Why not?"

"Ava says I shouldn't give my followers such a personal look into my life. She says it's bad optics. When it looks like you're already in a relationship, people can lose interest in what you do. I guess I can see that."

"You two look so good together," Jen tells Zen. "Ava's got such an amazing body. I didn't look that good in my twenties."

Wes turns to Jen, smiling sincerely. "From the moment I saw you that day in Amsterdam, I knew you were the most beautiful woman I'd ever seen. Twenty years later, and you're stunning as ever."

"Yo, lovebirds!" Zen interrupts his parents as they kiss. "Are you watching that video I texted you or what?"

They gather around the Zen's phone. As the video streams, Ava paddles alongside Zen, her wet blonde hair whipping in the water as she carves her way across the long barrel. Overall, Ava catches more waves than Zen, who sometimes paddles to the side to watch her shred.

"Why not put this on your YouTube channel?" Jen asks.

"Like I said, my social media followers should know that I'm a surfer, not someone's boyfriend," Zen says when the scene changes and he's kissing Ava, their black wetsuits pressing together as one.

"You look so cute," Jen says. "This is like a movie where you're both stars."

"I mean, it's not like we're competing, but she's a next-level surfer," Zen confesses. "It'll be years before I can shred as naturally as Ava."

"Doesn't Ross make great lasagna?" Wes asks Zen. "He asked about you today. Maybe we'll have Ross and Kyle over for dinner, if that's okay with you."

"Sure, that's fine," Zen replies with a frown. "Look, Dad, I'm not down with homophobia or anything. Guess I should tell you about something that happened a few years ago."

Wes's heart is pounding out of his chest while Zen revisits a fateful day in Amsterdam. It happened at his schoolmate Marx's house, where Zen suddenly felt drowsy after eating a chicken sandwich Marx's uncle had made. In the guest room, Zen went to bed and dosed off. When Zen opened his eyes, the uncle was totally naked and touching him below the waist. Zen sprang from the bed, running out of the house barefoot.

"And the uncle?" Wes asks. "Did he get away with it?"

"As it turned out," Zen goes on. "That pervert had sexually assaulted other teenagers in Amsterdam. I told a schoolmate about what happened, and he got a gang together. Five or six of them beat him into a coma."

"I wish I could've been there for you," Wes tells Zen. "Maybe it wouldn't have happened if I'd been around."

"It's all good, Dad," Zen replies, at once unbothered by the harrowing memory. "This life is full of sliding doors, one after another. Either we walk through or we don't."

"I guess you can say that again," Wes says, forcing a laugh. "A freaking bear came through a sliding door today."

"Life comes at you fast," Zen says to his dad as everyone heads to bed.

That comment stays with Wes while he tries to fall asleep. Those five words remind Wes that the son he loves had lived through the first two decades of his life without a father. *Life. Comes. At. You. Fast.* Each word echoes in Wes's head until his temples are throbbing.

"Don't be so hard on yourself," Jen breathes a sleepy whisper into Wes's ear. "Life comes at you fast, and here we are. We've saved the best for last."

They kiss goodnight. Just as Wes starts drifting off, a buzz on the nightstand tethers him back to his phone. On Facebook, he gets a friend request from Ilan Lopez, a surname Wes remembers seeing online in news articles about Gabi. But the devout profile picture with a full beard and side curls doesn't look familiar. Wes turns on the nightstand lamp as his phone vibrates again. This time, it's a new message popping into his inbox.

Hi Wes,

Please accept my friend request. I'm Ilan, Gabi's uncle. This is a difficult message for me to write. My beloved niece Gabi was taken from this world in a random act of senseless violence. While she was on her way home that day, she called me to say how happy she was to meet you. Gabi said you gave her your Magen David pendant. I kept the necklace when Gabi's brother in Mexico came for her other belongings. I'd like to return it to you, and to thank you personally for being with Gabi during her final moments on this earthly plane.

Take care,
Ilan Lopez

The plane lands at Cancun International, where the sheer heat makes me feel twice my age.

It's beyond balmy here. The humidity is sticky and intoxicating, and I probably look a little drunk to the militarized security forces patrolling the arrivals gate. Muscular men with machine guns unzip and inspect each piece of luggage, checking one passenger at a time with a metal detector wand. After my travel bag makes it to the other side, I switch to Spanish and thank the officers, who say nothing and don't smile back.

Beyond that checkpoint, an eager mob of taxi drivers and tour guides are waving brochures at incoming travelers. I cut through the crowd at the arrival gate and follow the signs outside to a bus bound for Playa Del Carmen. That's the picture perfect, palm tree-lined beach town on the postcard Dad mailed me a few years back on my birthday. He scribbled a few loving words on the postcard, but apparently forgot to include an address or phone number.

I get it; Mom hates Dad not only for leaving us, but for leaving us in a big financial hole. Still, I can't understand why she's always been against this trip and even tried holding college tuition over my head to get me to reconsider. But it's my grandparents on Dad's side — my Jewish side; the side that hid, fled, and survived — who want nothing more than for me to locate and reconnect with their only son.

The air-conditioned hotel is a haven from the heat that's been wearing me down since the airport. My plan is to start locally, and to ask around if the name Stanley Levine rings any bells. With my Berlitz *Say It In Spanish* phrasebook and a pocket full of pesos, I decide to cool off at the hotel bar with a Corona.

A stunningly cute woman with short black hair tucked behind her ears approaches the service rail. At first glance, I mistake her for a bartender. I crack open my Spanish phrasebook, my eyes scouring the pages for a greeting. But my heart is beating too fast and I can't make out any of the words.

"We can talk without the phrasebook," she says in a relaxing voice.

"Oh, you speak English," I say.

"I do," she returns with a warm smile. "My dad is from Dublin, while my mom is a proud *tapatía*. I'm Nayeli. What brings you to Playa Del Carmen?"

"Hi Nayeli, I'm Wes. I came here to look for my dad. He's been living in Mexico for a few years now."

"Why don't you just give him a call?" Nayeli asks.

"I would if I had his number."

"You might want someone to show you around," Nayeli says. "It's safer than going out alone at night."

"Could you point me to Coco Beach or El Cielo?"

Nayeli smiles. "Wes, it's my first time in Playa Del Carmen, too. I've never been to the Gulf Coast before. I'm from Guadalajara. That's two thousand kilometers from here."

"Are you on vacation?" I ask.

She takes a long sip from her margarita glass and loosens the buttons on her white V-neck shirt. "I'm here for a business meeting with software engineers. They are developing a computer program to change how people learn languages."

"Sounds exciting."

"To be honest Wes," she says, stirring the crushed ice in her glass. "I'm not sure if I want to work for a corporation much longer. I want to travel and see more of the world."

"Having options is good. Would you like to have dinner with me tonight?"

"Tomorrow for sure," Nayeli replies. "I must prepare my presentation tonight. And you've got to find your dad."

I nod to agree, but the truth is Nayeli could be the most beautiful woman I've seen in my young life, and now my runaway gambler father is far from the forefront of my mind.

"I'll try to find him tomorrow around the beaches," I say, glimpsing a man across the bar in a John Lennon tee captioned *Man Plans And God Laughs.*

"We can meet here tomorrow, yes?" Nayeli asks.

"Definitely," I answer right away.

"See you then," Nayeli says, reaching out for a hug. "Wish

me luck."

"I'm sure you'll do great," I say. "Maybe I'm the one who needs luck."

"*Dulces sueños*," she says to me. "Hope your first night in Mexico is a nice one."

I wake up cold and sweaty. From bed, I look through the small window with a poolside view. It's still nighttime, and the only light is from the moon and the pool's glow-in-the-dark blue tiles. At five-thirty in the morning, I'm internally still on American East Coast time and an extra hour of sleep holds no appeal. After a quick shower, I throw on some beach clothes, a bucket hat, and an extra layer of sunscreen. At the brink of dawn, I'm out going out to search a foreign beach for the man who named me, raised me, and showed me how to love the ocean.

Outside the hotel, a driver standing beside his yellow taxi greets me. In my pitiful-sounding Spanish, I request a ride to Coco Beach. Responding confidently in English, the driver asks if I want to stop at the promenade or the pier. From the window, I see a white-sand beach resort that bristles with palm trees swaying in the breeze. On the way out, I slip him some pesos. He then hands me a yellow business card: **Jorge, Bilingual Commercially Licensed Driver.** Jorge's a tall, thin, thirty-something fashion plate in a black suit and skinny tie. I love how people in Mexico take their professions so seriously, making it all look so easy. Jorge gets out of the taxi to open my door, which makes me feel like a rock star.

I walk out to the shoreline, glimpsing a pool that stretches around a beachfront hotel. In the distance I see a sprawling cluster of thatched-roof bungalows and imagine my dad lives in one of them. The sunrise beautifully bleeds yellow and orange. My feet touch the white sand and, alone on the beach, I breathe in the sweaty scent of algae glistening on the shore. Smelling the salt water makes me thirsty. Beyond the beach, I find a walkup café on the boardwalk and buy a little bottle of orange juice. I try to sip it slowly. Three orange juices later, I've gone into my phrasebook more times than I can count, asking the same question, "*¿Conoces a Stanley Levine?*"

I explain, to anyone willing to listen, that Stanley Levine is my father, a local scuba diver who lives near the beach and might be working as some kind of watersport instructor. They respond with polite smiles and dismissive waves. Everything but the answer I seek. Flipping through pages in my phrasebook, I feel like a fool whose piss-poor grasp of the world's most beautiful language is getting me nowhere. With a payphone on every corner, I stroll up and down the promenade and try chatting with a few more people in the boardwalk bustle before calling Jorge. Back at the hotel, it's only eleven in the morning and already I feel a need to peel out of my sweaty clothes and shower for the second time today.

I return to the hotel bar, where I'm meeting Nayeli later in the day. She's already there with a salted margarita glass in her hand. Curious as I am about her business meeting, I'm even more drawn to her casual, dressed-down vibe. A suitcase sits beside her barstool, and it looks like she might dip out at any moment.

"I quit my job," she says. "They weren't taking my ideas seriously."

"Oh, wow. Sorry to hear that. Are you still staying in town?"

Nayeli looks up from her glass. "The company just canceled my room, and my flight back to Guadalajara on Sunday is non-transferable."

"You know, I'm here for the whole week and my room came with a second bed. You're welcome to crash there if you need to."

Nayeli's warm, dark eyes light up. "Really? Is that okay?"

"Um, sure. Of course."

"How old are you, Wes?" Nayeli asks, sizing me up with a once-over.

"I just turned twenty."

"I'm twenty-four, and I want to move out of my mom's house," Nayeli tells me. "Maybe I can start my own language school. A place where people can learn languages from qualified, passionate teachers. Not from corporate hacks."

"I think you've just described my dream job," I tell her as I wave to the bartender and order us a round of tequila shots.

After lunch, Nayeli grabs her luggage and we head to my room. Standing between the twin beds, she lifts her suitcase on the mattress beside the window and tells me five words that send my heartbeat into overdrive. "One bed will be enough."

We perch closely at the bedside and go straight to open-mouthed kissing. With rain tapping on the window, a loud thunderclap startles me, but not Nayeli. She laughs through the storm, which doesn't last for long.

We hardly leave the room for days on end, mornings turned into afternoons of passionate, carefree tumbling in the sheets. Nayeli and I go out each night for a daily meal and feast on all things spicy and sweet. While the week blows by and our remaining time together slips away, the sex only becomes more intense. We explore each other's bodies by communicating in a language all our own. Our hands are like stone tablets, and with fingers and tongues we trace our desires, touching and kissing our way through a crash course in ecstasy.

Sunday comes, and it's time for us to check out of the hotel and fly into opposite directions: Baltimore for me and for Nayeli, the other side of Mexico in Guadalajara. The weight of our inevitable goodbye is like an anvil sinking in my chest. We've known each other for a few days, but it feels like we're a long-time couple at the front desk, where we return the room key before heading out. We hold hands for the entire bus ride to the airport. Outside the window, with all of Mexico's rustic natural beauty flashing before my eyes, Nayeli is all I see. In our seats Nayeli and I kiss and touch like we're invisible to everyone else on the bus. Already, I'm in love and everything is becoming *we.* Whenever we're both ready, I hope to marry Nayeli twice, in two ceremonies, one Jewish and American and the other Catholic and Mexican. The cloudless sky eventually gives way to a lush green landscape and soon, the bus arrives at Cancun International Airport.

"I'll take summer classes so I can graduate early and come back to Mexico," I tell her when it's time to say goodbye.

"Mi amor," Nayeli says, seeing me off at the ticketing counter inside the airport. "I'll email you tomorrow once I'm back in Guadalajara."

At home in Baltimore, I'm now walking a little taller. My heart is full of pride and satisfaction when I tell my mother all about the Spring Break trip she never wanted me to take.

"I didn't find Dad, but instead met an amazing girl named Nayeli. She's a language teacher. We're talking about starting a school in Mexico after I graduate."

"Mexico?" Mom replies in disbelief. "Are you kidding me?"

"It's not what you think. Mexicans are world class professionals. Everything they do, they put their heart into it.

"So, who's this girl? I mean, I'm sure she's pretty."

"She's Irish and Mexican, a total stunner. But it's not just about that. I think I'm in love," I say point blank. "And so, I'm going to take classes in the summer and try to graduate a year early. Maybe even sooner than that if we can afford it."

"Are you sure this is what you want?" Mom asks with genuine concern. "You could make more money teaching English in Korea, Hong Kong, or Singapore. Why does it have to be Mexico?"

I look squarely into Mom's eyes, giving her my bravest face. "Because Mexico is where my heart is."

The semester is back in session. Between my classes, I stand in line at the Student Union: two front-desk computers, a five-minute courtesy time limit, and usually a couple people ahead of me in the queue. When it's my turn, I sense impatient eyes looming at me as I type my heart out. The guy behind me groans when I look up a word in my Spanish-to-English dictionary. In the long, flowery message, I assure Nayeli that one day we'll be the dream team at our new language school in her hometown. Sure, I didn't see it then, but now understand that I was really trying to assure myself.

After a month of seeing Nayeli in my inbox almost daily, I don't hear from her for a few days. The semester is heading into final exams week, and I've registered for five summer classes. I'm constantly clicking into the outbox to reread my last three e-mails to Nayeli, each time reliving all that desperation and doubt. Feeling sorry for myself that she hasn't written back, I walk off campus to the Greene Turtle and wash down a dozen buffalo wings with a pitcher of Bud.

When I get back to the Student Union, it's almost ten o'clock. I'm the only one at the front desk until a campus cop starts marching circles around the computer station, calling out a five-minute warning. Just as I'm about to sign out, a new message from Nayeli drops into my inbox.

Dear Wes,

I hope you're doing well. Sorry for not getting back to you sooner, as I've been pursuing a new job offer. A university in Prague has offered me a position as a lecturer in Linguistics!

Since quitting my job, I've been borrowing money from my parents. I need to start working again as soon as possible, and this is an opportunity for me to experience what it's like to live in another part of the world. The dream of starting my own language school may have to wait.

You know, Wes, I have to tell you something. I've felt a little guilty for distracting you from finding your dad. At this time in our lives, you and I have different things to pursue. Maybe we'll meet again, or not. Either way, I know you'll make an amazing teacher one day and thank you for letting me stay with you in Cancun. Those sweet memories will always be there.

Wishing you the best.

Nayeli

7

Zen thinks it's a bad idea. He almost changes Wes's mind about meeting Ilan Lopez. Wes is more trusting, but Zen is sure that lurking behind the Facebook profile is a neo-Nazi or gangbanger instead of the Mexican-American Orthodox Jew draped in a tallis with professional details posted on his bio: **In West Orange County, my pronouns are local/jeweler.**

"I just messaged him back," Wes says between bites of a lox and avocado bagel. "I asked for a photo of the pendant."

"What?" Zen's mouth hangs open. "Are you seriously meeting him off a picture? That dude's giving you too much personal info. I don't trust it."

Wes frowns, shaking his head. "Have a heart, Zen. The guy just lost his niece to a random gunshot."

"What if the dude in your DMs isn't the same dude IRL?"

"I agreed to meet him in a public place. Happy now, Zen?"

"I'm just looking out for your six, Dad," Zen says with a smirk. "I mean, how many Jewish Mexicans do you know?"

"My dad lived in Mexico for a decade. He found out from a Chabad rabbi in Playa Del Carmen that my grandparents had passed away in Baltimore."

"It just seems sketchy," Zen goes on. "I'd talk to this guy for a while before meeting up. See if he's legit first."

"I know you can never be too careful online these days," Wes replies, passing his phone to Zen. "But I've checked out Ilan's online profile. I'm sure he is who he claims to be."

"Dad, are you joking or what? Any two-bit crook who knows a little AI could put up that profile in five minutes."

"I'll meet him somewhere outside and in the open, like the Huntington Beach Pier," Wes suggests. "While you and Ava get your bearings at the surf off, I'll pick up the necklace."

Zen holds up a finger and points to the Facebook app on his smartphone. "Okay. As long as that's who he really is."

"Oh, look," Wes says, fixing his eyes on the blinking ellipsis in Messenger. "He's writing back now."

Ilan responds, first with a picture of the necklace. The Star of David is still smeared in blood, the silver link chain caked with flaky crimson remnants. Immediately, Wes feels like an asshole for demanding proof like that.

Don't worry about the blood. I own a jewelry shop, and have made sure the necklace has been sanitized and disinfected for your protection. My shop is in Seal Beach, and so meeting you in Huntington would not be out of the way for me. See you at the pier this afternoon.

Not knowing what else to type, Wes reacts to the message with a thumbs-up emoji. "It was covered in her blood," he says grimly. "Maybe if I didn't give Gabi that stupid necklace, she'd be alive today."

"Dad," Zen says, patting Wes on the shoulder. "Go easy on yourself. It was by sheer happenstance."

From the breakfast table, they swing by the living room to gather Zen's surfing gear: two boards, spare snap-on fins, a freshly-shampooed neoprene wetsuit, and a bottle of Panama Jack. Elevating her laptop on a pillow, Jen sits on the edge of the sofa in a sleek red party dress. With jittery fingers, she signs into a Zoom meeting with Kyle and some power brokers from a Hollywood firm.

"This is big," Jen silently mouths the words to Wes while attendees on squares pop into the grid and introduce themselves.

Walking from Main Street to Pacific Coastal Highway and finally the Huntington Beach Pier, Wes and Zen check out the surf. Already more than a dozen heads are in the breaker zone. While carrying Zen's board from the main drag to the beach, they encounter local bylaws on posted signs banning dogs and other animals, bicycles and skateboards, and even shark fishing. The beach, the pier, and the ocean all have different curfews.

"Welcome to Huntington Beach," Wes utters in dismay. "Surf City, U.S.A. sure has a lot of rules."

In slip-on leather sandals and a raffia straw sun hat with spiraling stripes, Ava crosses the intersection of PCH and Main. As soon as they meet, Ava and Zen are kissing deeply, and he's got his hands all over her.

"It was taking forever," Ava tells Zen, who blankets her with kisses. "Parking was such a drag."

"Now that you've found each other, I've got to meet someone at the Pier Plaza," Wes says. "Nice to see you, Ava. Knock 'em dead, Zen."

Wes follows a trail of tall palm trees to the plaza. Merchants under canvas roofs sell tee shirts on the beach, where Wes walks on a grassy knoll and climbs cement stairs to the amphitheater. From the pictures on his Facebook profile, Ilan is instantly recognizable in the black fedora hat, and the coiled dark *payot* hanging over his ears. He looks a little older and more rugged than what appears on his social media profile.

"Thank you for meeting me today," Wes says, touching the back of Ilan's hand. "Gabi was a real light in this world."

Ilan takes off his round rimmed glasses to rest his eyes in a white handkerchief. He seems hot and stifled in his black suit. "She was working two jobs and going to community college. On Tuesday nights, Gabi had been taking a class to convert to Judaism."

"I'm so sorry, Ilan. I wish I was saying this in happier times. *L'shanah Tova.* May you and everyone who loved Gabi know peace and comfort once again."

"Why did you give Gabi this necklace?" Ilan asks, handing it to Wes in a blue velvet keepsake box.

"It meant a lot to her," Wes answers. "The necklace had already served me and I thought it might still serve Gabi. Can we talk about it more over lunch?"

Ilan smiles at the offer. "I've been getting in my paces today. I forgot they have all this new parking by the pier. My car's at the Chabad, two miles down PCH."

"That's quite a walk. Can we get lunch somewhere local?"

"Thanks, I guess," Ilan returns, hesitant and guarded.

"My son Zen told me about a deli called Sessions. Come on, man. You shouldn't be alone on Rosh Hashanah. It'll be my treat. It's the least I can do for bringing the necklace."

Ilan smiles wanly. "Wes, I appreciate your warmth. But if you already have plans with your son, I should be on my way."

"Zen's out surfing today," Wes says. "I wouldn't mind having a local to show me around. We're still new in town."

They walk into Sessions, a laidback joint with window tables looking out at the bustle on PCH. Wes and Ilan settle into barstools overlooking a slog of cars speeding and slowing on the ocean-facing highway. They both start with drip coffee, and Wes suggests avocado toast because it's the only thing on the mostly meat-and-cheese menu that looks halfway kosher.

"Just so you know, I don't always observe *kashrut*," Ilan says, idly twirling a wooden stirrer in his coffee. "Gabi loved avocado toast."

"They call it the Avocado Party Toast," Wes cheerily describes the plates he brings to the table. "It comes with cheese and greens. Both of the cashiers say it's their go-to breakfast."

Wes tries to get Ilan to talk about himself, to pivot away from grief and maybe find joy in revisiting his life story. Born in Poway, San Diego County to Sephardic-Jewish parents from Mexico City, Ilan got his start working at his father's diamond center, further north in Carlsbad. Ilan's father set him up with a retail jewelry storefront in Seal Beach, a locale catering to a middling clientele with spending power somewhere between outlet mall bargains and Rodeo Drive boutiques. Ilan says that his parents have both since passed, with most of his surviving relatives still living throughout Mexico.

"When I was young, I fell hard for girl from Guadalajara," Wes confesses.

"How did you meet her?" Ilan asks.

"At the hotel bar. I'd flown into Cancun to look for my father, who'd basically abandoned me and my mother in Baltimore. It's a long story, but his business dealings caused a lot of debt. Someone wanted him dead."

"So, your father left the debt for you and your mother to handle?" Ilan probes further. "It's okay if you'd rather not talk about it."

"No, it's okay," Wes quickly responds, worrying Ilan might instead circle back to his grief. "My mom became quite successful in the financial sector. She always said that if it weren't for my dad's debts, we would've been millionaires by the late nineties. The truth is, we were just trying to get dug out like most middle-class families. In college, I was paying for off-campus housing so Mom could rent out my bedroom to a New Yorker in Baltimore for medical school."

Ilan reclines in his seat and takes another bite of avocado toast. "Did you ever find your father?"

"Our paths finally intersected in Thailand, where I taught English and Dad was a scuba diver. He went out on the morning of the 2004 tsunami, and that was it. After ten years apart, we only got to spend spent three days together."

"I'm sorry to hear that. Maybe I should be thankful that at least Gabi got to stay with me for three years."

"Brief as it was, I try to look back with gratitude. I will say that they were three of the best days of my life," Wes continues. "Sure, I wish we would've gotten more time together, but at least we had a chance to finally see each other again. My dad and I scaled the bottom of the ocean and saw every color of fish. And the very next day, I saw people getting swept away by unbelievable waves. Even now, I still find it hard to relax on a beach."

From his barstool, Ilan looks to Wes with quiet admiration. "You've lived a very interesting life. I'm sure you're a great father because you've had so many different experiences."

Wes nods humbly, cracking a small smile. "How about

you?" he asks Ilan. "Married?"

"No," Ilan replies reservedly, looking out the window. "Working in the diamond business for most of my life, I've seen love at its best and worst. That roller coaster is not for me."

"May this year bring new joy into your life, Ilan," Wes tells him. "I really mean that. And I hope you might come visit my family at our new home in Venice."

"Your friendship is a blessing," Ilan says in Hebrew to Wes, a former scribe who'd once handwritten a Sefer Torah into a kosher parchment.

For a moment, Wes looks on in bewilderment, moving his lips while translating in silence. "Your friendship means a lot to me too, Ilan," Wes returns, reaching into his pocket to tap the box holding his Star of David necklace.

After the light meal, Wes and Ilan take a walk on Main Street, eventually finding their way back to the garage. On foot, they enter through the exit gate, where parking spaces ascend on an incline. Scanning the row of cars for his gray Toyota, Wes hears the clatter of skateboards scraping against the pavement. A young skater with blond dreads is hovering around Wes's car.

"Hey man, I need a video," the kid demands from Wes, holding out a phone with a cracked screen. "Just press record."

Wes waves off the kid and his phone. "Okay, this is weird."

"Please," the wild-eyed kid persists as the approaching skateboards roll louder and fiercer. "They're coming to get me."

"Hey!" a voice bellows from the parking level above, and at least four more ramp rockstars are whirling behind a burly skater. "Get that piece of shit!"

"Dude, come on," the kid pleads with Wes. "You've gotta give me a ride."

"What kind of trouble are you in?" Wes asks curiously, though the dreadlocked kid's bony frame, buggy eyes, and the spittle-flecked corners of his lips seem to answer the question. Without responding, the kid slips into the backseat of Wes's car, leaving his skateboard to roll down the parking aisle.

"Hey man," Wes casually greets the broad-shouldered

leader of the pack. "What's the issue?"

"That's between me and this thief," says the muscular skater, bumping Ilan from behind.

"Forgetting something?" Wes asks the gang of skaters, holding out the board.

"I'll take that," one of the skaters steps out of the pack and tries snatching the skateboard by the bearings.

Wes pulls the board against his chest. The bald, bearded skater moves in on him, going for the grab. Holding it at an upward angle, Wes releases his grip and the board slams the aggressor on the nose. His nostrils squirt blood. He barely flinches as his white tank top soaks it up and one of his homeboys throws him a tee shirt to quell the bleeding.

Ilan opens the passenger door. "Wes," Ilan whispers from the front seat, staring at the shirtless skater's waist. "He has a gun."

"Does this belong to any of you?" Wes shouts at the gang of skaters, brandishing the bloodstained skateboard by its trucks.

The skater without a shirt reaches into his baggy stonewashed jeans and pulls out a black handgun. The burly skater steps in front of him. "Yo, put that fuckin' thing away, homie!"

Alarmed, Wes drops the skateboard, letting it roll down the aisle of parked cars. He ducks into his Toyota Corolla and floors it in reverse. The squealing tires sear tracks into the pavement and the car rolls over the skateboard, snapping in it two. In the backseat, the skater kid is suddenly lucid and looking out the window at what remains of his board. Wes sees them in the rearview mirror, the menacing skaters throwing down their boards, pumping their fists.

"Sorry about your skateboard," Wes says, plowing into a narrow lane and smashing through the mechanical arm at the garage exit. "Do you have a name?"

"I'm Corey," he says.

"Corey?" Wes repeats, revving the engine. "Make sure your seatbelt's on."

The engine roars through the gate. Wes peels out on PCH, hightailing it off the coast to a cul-de-sac. From the tranquil subdivision, Wes turns into a shopping plaza, burning rubber all the way into a parking space. Ilan quickly detaches himself from the passenger seat and thanks Wes for the ride, for a chance to suspend his grief and feel a little excitement at the start of the High Holy Days. In the relative calm outside Chabad, Wes walks with Ilan to his car and restarts Maps to enter Corey's address.

On the phone, Siri tells Wes when and where to turn on the streets of Huntington's flat terrain. The virtual assistant's navigation takes them further from the coast, deeper inland into neighborhoods of stucco houses under palm trees. After a few minutes the houses start getting bigger, with meticulously manicured lawns and lush, colorful gardens, and Wes is not so sure that he's dropping Corey off in his own neighborhood.

"What's up with your homeboy's big ass hat?" Corey asks Wes. "Was that spaghetti in his pocket?"

"It's not spaghetti," Wes responds. "Those threads are called *tzitzit*. My homeboy is religious, while I'm not."

"Thanks for saving my ass from those guys," Corey says to Wes from the backseat. "The crib's right over there."

Corey points Wes to street parking across from a sprawling house behind a gated front entry. More than a house, it's an estate with a massive garage and private terrace, tinted windows and accordion glass doors. In the back, Wes glimpses an infinity edge pool, a gazebo, an aluminum louvred pergola, and a sleek glass cabana he almost mistakes for a different home.

"So, this is where you live?" Wes asks skeptically.

"Nah, dude. I'm from the hood in Inglewood," Corey says on his way out the car. "A MILF I bang lives here. You know the homeboy who pulled the gun? That's his mom. Thanks for the ride. For real, dawg."

"You bet," Wes replies as Corey steps to the gate. "Take care of yourself, man."

Corey dials in a code to buzz the gate open. He walks on the luxury property with crooked steps, approaching the modern mansion like a prowling thief. Wes drives down the street while typing his home address into Maps. In that moment, a text from Zen comes through: **hey dad, I'm crashing at Ava's tonight. Caught some killer tubes today and I'm going to the next round.**

Wes reacts with a thumbs up. As much as he'd like to give Zen the full love and support that only a heart emoji can convey, Wes doesn't want to blow smoke without knowing the whole story. A moment later at a red light, Wes holds the phone below the steering wheel to sneak a quick reply.

Congrats Zen! Wes types out. **You know that I am proud of you.**

Blue and red lights flash in the rearview. Wes pulls over on PCH, stopping on a narrow shoulder uncomfortably close to the fast-flowing traffic. The police officer at the window looks young with her dirty blonde hair and sunny, freckled complexion. Her Spanish accent sounds like Ilan's, passionate yet calming. She asks Wes for his driver's license, and takes it back to her cruiser to scan his driving history.

"I see your driving record's very clean, Mister Levine," she says, returning the documents through the driver's side window. "But I can't let you off with a warning because you almost ran a red light while a pedestrian was in the crosswalk."

"I don't normally do that."

"Today I'm giving you a ticket. That amount will increase with each violation. So, do your part to keep the roads safe. While driving, your phone should stay on a mount at all times. In California, touching a mobile phone when driving is illegal, and that includes while stopped at a red light."

"Understood, Officer," Wes pauses to read the name Lopez on her name badge, dangling the citation out the window. "My friend's last name is also Lopez."

"It's a common name," Officer Lopez replies flatly. "I can't take your ticket back."

"I won't let it happen again."

The young officer turns around to check on her cruiser, and two more police cars are whizzing into the fast lane. "Stay safe," she tells him in a hurry.

Wes doesn't touch his phone until he's home in Venice with the car parked and the ignition off. A text message with a timestamp from an hour ago flashes onscreen. It's from Jen, who is having dinner in Beverly Hills with Kyle, Ross, and some Hollywood power brokers from the earlier Zoom meeting. Wes lets the message sit, taking in the cosmic, pink-purple sky at sunset. Inside he finds a pack of Stargazers on the kitchen table. Beside the slim pre-rolled joints, a Post-it note from Jen invites Wes to help himself.

At some point during the last twenty years of running a restaurant in Amsterdam, Wes simply had forgotten to keep smoking pot. But with the rare lucent sky sparkling outside his door on this starry night, Wes holds one of the skinny joints under his nose and gives in. A sharp, sudden whiff of piney grass awakens his senses. On the front porch, Wes sparks up, savoring the warm gentle breeze. In his mellow state, he starts typing out a text to Jen, but takes the joint inside when he sees a couple with small children walking past the house.

Did Zen tell you he's going to the next round? Today I got a \$162 traffic ticket for texting and driving. Lesson learned. Say hi to Kyle and Ross, and hope they might join us for dinner in Venice Beach, a bear-free zone. Best of luck tonight, babe. You've got this!

The house feels strangely empty to Wes when he heads back into the living room and turns on the television. On the news, the headlines are equally stunning and soothing, with synagogues taking increased security measures for the High Holy Days and former Congresswoman Liz Cheney endorsing Kamala Harris for president. Wes takes another puff and coughs, and then comes another shocker: Liz reveals that her arch-conservative father, former Vice President Dick Cheney, is also voting for Kamala. Soon, Zen is blowing up his dad's phone with more texts and links.

Hey Dad, watch this video Ava made on Insta360. It's a weird lens that makes the water look fake. She swears by this lens, which covers every angle at once. I don't think it should go on my YouTube channel because it looks so unnatural. That's the last thing we need. Do you think this video is worth the views?

What would the HBSO judges say? As my manager, what do you think?

Wes watches the clip, but he's too stoned, too close to seeing double to offer Zen a meaningful symbol of approval. On the clip, Zen looks like a cartoon character, a big head and stick figure body surfing on an inch of water. Wanting to show support, Wes raves about Zen's footwork and adds a few words of praise for Ava. **Great camera work, Ava! Everything you do is so amazing. You know Zen, I think that's the most you've ever texted me at one time LOL. You look bold and brave on your board. Enjoy your night, you two!**

A knock at the door snaps Wes out of his daze. Jen's home, with Kyle standing somberly beside her.

"Hey there! You're back early," Wes says, a little loopy with the smell of weed still permeating in the living room.

"Fuck Hollywood," Jen utters point blank. "I'm so done."

"We had a tough time pitching her screenplay to some big shots," Kyle admits. "But like I've said, Hollywood has become a cesspool of know-it-all elitists."

"What in the world do they want?" Wes implores Kyle. "Jen speaks five languages. She has traveled around the world. If her life was made into a movie, it would be a blockbuster hit."

"Tell that to the ultra-woke pricks from today's Zoom meeting who did a complete one-eighty at dinner in Beverly Hills."

"What did they say?" Wes asks Kyle. "And how exactly is multi-cultural Jen not woke enough?"

Kyle takes a deep breath and sighs before responding. "They don't think a director in 2024 will touch a script with a good cop. It's been like that since George Floyd was murdered. I get that. And I hate to say this, but Hollywood these days is too uptight to green light a screenplay set in Amsterdam. One of the bigwigs at dinner said the Red Light District is too cheap and exploitative for a major motion picture."

"Babe, don't sweat it. Everyone's got an opinion." Wes says to Jen. "Hey Kyle, did you hear that the Cheneys are endorsing VP Harris?"

"I'm done with the elites," Kyle replies, cold and dismissive. "Politics sucks. Our country is fucked. And if China gets their way, we'll all be picking pine nuts at Trader Joe's for ten cents an hour."

"I suppose there's always Amsterdam," Jen puts in.

"Something's got to happen for you, dear," Kyle says. "I'll make some more calls and get back to you tomorrow afternoon. Is that cool? Are we cool?"

"Thanks, you're the best," Jen tells Kyle, walking him outside where Ross waits in the car.

"Let's go!" Ross calls out, honking the horn. "Fefe's home alone. She's probably worried sick!"

"Do you want to go to the boardwalk with me, Wes?" Jen asks as Kyle drives off in a hurry.

In the street outside the house, a disjointed musical throng forms along the avenue, overtaking the street on a march to Ocean Front Walk. Some of them carry djembes and shakers, these Venice Beach denizens on a tuneful westward stampede. A few acoustic guitars add to the scattered melodies blending together in joyful dissonance. Quietly, Wes and Jen slip into the growing cavalcade of noisemakers taking their collaboration to the oceanfront. When they reach the boardwalk, Wes feels a vibration in his pocket, an incoming text from Faisal in the Netherlands. He reads the message out loud. **My brother, Wes. Please FaceTime me soon as you can. It's about my father.**

Venice Beach, May 1999

The outstretched expanse between Ocean Front Walk and the coastline makes the beach feel empty as a desert. With each step I take, the dry sand drags heavier on my sandals. Mom and I push forward to the shore. Though we're halfway there, the ocean still appears out of reach.

"Damn tar," Mom gripes, trying to pick something sticky off her loafers. "So much for a day at the beach."

The substance on her heel feels like hot, dry bubble gum. "That's probably one of two things, Mom. Either that's from an oil spill or a little volcano fragment."

"A volcano what?" she asks. "Did it occur to you we're the only ones on the beach?"

Close to the pier, a brawny shirtless man in sweatpants slowly makes his way across the sand.

"We're not," I remind Mom. "People actually live here."

Waves crash hard around the concrete Venice Fishing Pier; a bridge to nowhere, really, jutting into the Pacific Ocean like a final western plank. Below the wooden deck, the beach dweller pulls back his long dreadlocks and splashes ocean water on his face. A dog with pointy ears follows him across the flat beach. They settle outside a small tent where a chicken clucks and pecks around a plastic cooler, lending the exposed domain a touch of permanence.

Back on the boardwalk, Mom and I unlatch our bike rentals from a shaded rack under a neat row of palm trees. Instead of riding, we push the handlebars along the walkway, where I stop to slip a dollar bill into a tin box held by the trembling hands of The World's Greatest Wino. That's how the cardboard sign at his feet identifies him. The World's Greatest Wino sits on a frayed straw mat. There's a sparkle in his big blue eyes and an empty paper cup in his shaky, bandaged hand. With a little surge in his energy, I think he could light up the silver screen as a leading man. It saddens me that he looks so beaten, so broken, his leathery skin so dangerously sun-damaged. And so, I reach into my pocket for another dollar, having no illusions that he'll put the money into acting classes instead of booze.

"Hey, thanks! You're a swell guy," mumbles The World's Greatest Wino. "Can I have another?"

I look to my mom, trying to read her eyes from behind those thick black sunglasses. She's not in a particularly charitable mood. We're in Southern California for a three-day weekend. On the other end of Venice, Mom is helping her friend Jeannie flip a house, an ivy-covered hideaway somewhere north of the boardwalk bustle. We're staying two hours east of L.A. at a Best Western in Palm Springs, a decision Mom made to cut down on expenses. These days, money comes up a lot. I reach into my pocket, offering a third dollar. Once it's in his grip, The World's Greatest Wino jerks his hand away and we walk on.

"You're a bleeding heart like your father was," Mom says.

"Like my father *was?*" I question her choice of words. "It's not like he's dead."

"They're everywhere," Mom goes on. "Professional panhandlers."

"You know, I always thought that being on your own as a single mother might've made you a little more compassionate."

"Don't start with that," Mom snaps back. "The writing is on the wall. California is going to the dogs. Jeannie says she can't wait to leave. That's why she's selling her house and moving to Nevada, where her money will go a lot further."

"Mom, I came with you on this trip thinking we might enjoy a little getaway," I say. "Can we try to do that?"

"You've got to decide what you want out of life, Wes. Back at college, Jeannie majored in theater. She needed me to explain the documents to sell her house. Jeannie's financially illiterate. But at least she has enough common sense to know when it's time to give up on a dying dream."

"Jeannie's the daughter of a wealthy college president back east," I quip. "I doubt she's giving up anything."

"Once she moved here, Jeannie swore she'd never leave California. She was as L.A. as they come. But lately she's singing a different tune. And I know you don't want to hear this, but it's because immigrants are taking over the state. It's very hard to get ahead here if you're not a minority."

"Mom, you do realize I'm Jewish, don't you? That means I

am a minority. And come to think of it," I respond, hearing my own heartbeat throb. "I'd rather live next door to an immigrant than a bigot."

Mom takes off her sunglasses to give me a deep, disappointed stare. Out of nowhere rolls a young woman on freestyle skates with big curly hair, cutting between us as she calls out what sounds like a curse in Spanish. Before I catch my breath, a beach bum in a yellow Lakers tank top steps into our space with a rack of handmade jewelry held to his chest. He points to the long sharp tooth hanging from his puka bead necklace.

"Shark teeth! Get some shark teeth! All these pieces are made with real shark teeth," he pitches his wares, revealing a wide gap between his own front teeth. "This one's a megalodon. These earrings are from sand sharks."

"I don't want your fucking shark teeth!" Mom shouts.

"Alright, we're chill," Mister Shark Teeth says to himself after we walk away. "It's all good, I'm chill. Stay chill, lady."

"Mom, you need to relax," I tell her discretely.

"Everyone here is on the take," she whispers. "The beach is empty. That should tell you something's off. I want to go back to the peace and calm of Palm Springs before sunset."

"Let's try to have a moment of fun before we do," I say when a pink neon Psychic Reader window sign comes into view.

"Hello. Come in for a reading," a woman wearing a bright silk head wrap waves us inside. She asks us our names (Cathy and Wes), what we do (university student and financial planner), and where we're from (where else? Baltimore). She points to a shiny array of crystals and a deck of Tarot cards spread across her table like a hand fan.

"Have you ever had a reading before, Cathy and Wes?"

"I guess my dad was into that sort of thing," I confess, browsing the options on the menu display. "We're traveling on a budget, so would you read our palms for ten dollars each?"

"Of course, dear," says the woman, who might be around my mother's age. "I'm Linda, and I'll let you know what I see in your future. Cool?"

"Definitely cool," I reply, handing Linda a twenty. "Mom, would you like to have your reading first?"

"Hello, my dear sister," Linda turns to Mom, who smiles politely at the intimate greeting. Linda traces a finger across Mom's palm, focusing on one long line. "Your lines are clearly showing prosperity. You are very smart with money. But I sense something is missing in your life."

"I've been on my own for five years now," Mom tells Linda. "But I'm not looking for a relationship. One marriage was enough."

"No, it's something else," Linda says bringing her face closer to Mom's palm. "You don't have any pets, do you?"

Mom shakes her head. "How can you tell?"

"In your future, I am seeing a dog," Linda predicts, smiling sweetly. "A dog will bring you clarity. Sometimes dogs give us answers when no one else can. Companionship is only the beginning."

"Thank you for the reading," Mom says, subdued at last. "Maybe you are like the sister I never had."

Linda laughs daintily. "Oh Cathy, you'll do very well in your life. A dog is coming to you soon. Then, you'll find what you've been looking for."

Linda turns to me. I reach out a hand, my heart beating faster than usual when she runs her finger up and down the palm lines. Her eyes gleam with excitement. I've always felt strange seeking psychic advice after Dad's over-the-phone fortune teller sent him running away to Mexico.

"Wes, I see that you'll make your family very proud. You're going to travel the world and find great success working with letters. And when you return, you'll really hit it home. Do you know what I mean?"

"Working with letters?" I ask. "Like a writer?"

Linda nods once and smiles. "It is written in the stars."

"Can I ask you about a relationship I was in?" I change the subject. "A year ago in Mexico, I met a woman named Nayeli who went to teach English in Europe. Do you see her coming back into the picture?"

Linda's cheerful expression fades into a sympathetic frown,

her eyes lowered and brimming. "Wes, my dear. The young woman is in your past. It's time for you to move on."

"Are you sure?" I press on. "Will I ever see her again?"

"Do you want her to tell you something different?" Mom impatiently asks me. "She hasn't written you in a year. You have to let her go."

"Don't worry about your love life, dear," Linda warmly replies, clasping my hand. "I see family in your future. I'm also seeing that you'll find your father. It'll be a joyful reunion. And in the same year, you will meet one of the great loves of your life.

Mom nudges my arm. "That sounds like a bright future, Wes," Mom says, but it doesn't cheer me up.

"May God smile blessings upon the both of you. If you'd like me to get my Tarot cards, I can tell you more."

"Maybe another time," I respond with my head already sticking out the door. "Thanks for the reading."

Outside, Mom and I retrieve our bikes, walking them across the promenade to share a beachfront trail with rollerbladers, skateboarders, and runners.

"I wish Linda saw something with Nayeli," I say to Mom as we mount our bikes.

"She predicted so many nice things," Mom tells me. "Why not focus on the travel and success Linda saw for you, instead of worrying about one relationship that didn't work out?"

"I've been alone for a while, and with Nayeli I felt so alive."

"Come on, honey. You spent a week with her in a hotel room. Besides, she's moved to Czechoslovakia, for God's sake. Do you think you even cross her mind?"

"I don't know," I answer, staring into the low barrel waves crashing on the shore. "But you don't have to make me feel bad about it."

"You've got to stop being so negative, Wes. Don't stay stuck in the past. It'll only hold you back."

"I wonder if I'll ever see my dad again, wherever he is," I say. "Last year, my poor grandparents really wanted me to find him in Mexico. What a disappointment."

"Wes, I don't mean to cause you any heartache. But I don't

trust your dad's parents."

"What are you talking about? They're my dearly beloved grandparents. They escaped the Holocaust. They're two of the most honorable and trustworthy people I've ever known."

"I've always suspected they told your dad to run away to Mexico," Mom's words spill out like an overdue confession. "Since I'm not Jewish, they didn't care if we stayed together or not. Besides, your dad wouldn't do something so drastic just because of what a phone psychic told him."

"Did it ever occur to you that maybe they know a thing or two about running at the first sign of danger?" I ask Mom, turning my back when she doesn't respond. "Think about it."

A loud, snarling dog snaps me out of my thoughts. The skaters rolling past us barely flinch, but a skittish elderly man takes feeble backward steps on his walking stick. The dog lunges closer and bares sharp teeth, barking in a grotesquely low register. The shirtless man from the pier slides his knees into the sand, pinning his forearm against the dog's throat.

"Get down, get down!" he yells, grunting into his dog's snout. "Stay down!"

The dog gasps for air, desperate to squirm free. My bike drops to the ground and I find myself drawn to the hoarse, agonizing sound of the dog's compressed airways.

"Go easy on your pooch, dude," I say. "He can't breathe!"

The dog owner grits his teeth, lifting his arm to instead bury a knee into the dog's neck. The growls and barks of a moment ago are now hollow wheezing sounds.

"Okay, tough guy. I think you've made your point. Let him go!" I shout.

Still gripping his dog by the collar, he staggers closer and steps to me. "'Sup, bro?" he says with his fists up and chest out. "You want a piece of me?"

Mom flips on her sunglasses and steps between me and the man with a worn-down dog in his arms. From her purse, she whips out a can of mace, pointing it at the wild-eyed He-Man brandishing his pet like a weapon.

"Back off freak," Mom orders him, her thumb on the spray dispenser. "Leave my son alone and go back to your little tent, or I'll burn your goddamn eyes out."

He drops the dog and steps back. With thumbs held to his lips, he whistles through his teeth and throws a tennis ball at the ocean. The dog chases after the ball, hobbling through the sand with the owner running ahead, leading the way back to the pier.

"That was animal abuse," I say to Mom, noticing the dog's tail now drooping between his legs.

"What were his other options?" Mom asks me. "He told his dog to stop barking at people, and that didn't work."

"Don't you get it, Mom? It's not just about the dog. You didn't have to threaten him with mace. I'm a red level Masada fighter. That was embarrassing."

"I was just protecting you, Wes."

"That's not protection," I say, picking up my bike to pedal off. "You're suffocating me!"

I try to lose myself in the electric neon lights of Venice in the late afternoon: the glistening signage of trinket bodegas, tee shirt shops, practically every tourist trap known to man. Another cluster of palm trees comes to a stop at the rusted Stone Age exercise equipment of Muscle Beach. A bodybuilder in a tight tank top passes a pungent joint to a haggard, ascetic-looking bohemian on a bench, where an acoustic strummer sings for passersby flocking to tattoo studios, massage parlors, and ice cream shops. Street corner hawkers under flimsy umbrellas push their products in the oceanfront bustle. It's a lot of people. I need some time to myself, and maybe Mom does, too.

Eventually, I'll turn around and look for Mom so we can return our bikes to the rental stand on Main Street, a couple miles north where Venice Beach becomes Santa Monica. But for now, I just want to feel free as the wind and take in the eclectic mix of wild souls under the purple-orange tinge of a creamsicle sunset. I pedal until the boardwalk narrows into a single lane and merges with yet another bike path. When I turn around and make my way back to Ocean Front Walk, I trundle through a mix of walkers and skaters.

Down the boardwalk, I see Mister Shark Teeth again. A

flurry of twenty-dollar bills is drifting into his hands while he offloads sharp-edged pendants to a few surfboard-toting guys, a blonde boho chick or two, even a balding dwarf backpedaling a unicycle. Mister Shark Teeth hustles hard, and he deserves it. I hope that he makes it, and that everyone on the boardwalk makes it. Hollywood is for finding fortune and fame, but in Venice Beach, you make it when you find yourself.

I'll find Mom soon enough. You can't miss her, when she's the only person in this funky L.A. beach town wearing a pantsuit and business blazer. Eventually I see Mom's bicycle leaning against the windowfront, where soft neon light radiates from the Psychic Reading sign. Inside, the kindhearted clairvoyant Linda divides her Tarot deck into three stacks. Unusually subdued, Mom sits at the table in spellbound silence. Mom opens her purse and slips Linda a few more twenties. Linda holds her gaze on the crystal ball and starts to speak. What she says seems important, but I can't quite read her lips through the window. I trust the universe, and believe none of this is by accident. For better or worse, my adventurous dad found his way to a safer life in Mexico on the advice of a psychic. And behind the gilded curtains of a visionary Venice Beach mystic, my cautious mom might be finding herself at last.

8

"Dad had a heart attack," Faisal reveals to Wes on their international FaceTime call.

"What?" Wes goes silent. "What happened, bro?"

"A week ago, he walked into the hospital with chest pain."

"How's Omar been holding up? Is he going to be okay?"

"For the last few days, Dad's been resting at home. I'm not letting him touch that grill. I don't care if I have to work double shifts seven days a week."

On the mellow periphery of the boardwalk at night, Wes finds a quiet bench facing the ocean. Luminescent blue waves break gently on the shore and at this hour, Venice Beach is a warm and moist seventy degrees with no sun to melt off dense coastal fog obscuring the water. Along the oceanfront walkway, the scene comes alive with skateboards, scooters, and even a few breakdancers. Five different styles of music are blaring at once. Everyone is grooving to the beat of their own speakers. The noise and chaos make it hard for Wes to focus on the call with Faisal.

"Can you hire some new cooks?" Wes suggests.

"We're not in a position to do that, brother. That guy you punched through the window could still take us to court. I asked three lawyers, and they all said the same thing. We're still responsible for what happened."

"Damn," Wes responds, a little deflated. "Do you have any good news?"

"That depends how you feel about selling the business. The Sub Shoppe wants to buy us out. Amsterdam is the latest location they're targeting in their quest for global dominance."

"Really?" Wes says, with Jen looking on in surprise. "How much are they offering?"

"We haven't gotten into negotiations yet," Faisal answers, counting on his fingers. "Dad's got monitoring, medications, and meetings with a nutritionist. I'm more concerned about his health than anything else. Anyway, the best we can hope for in a buyout is forty-percent of what we made last year."

Wes runs the figures in his head. "That might be a quarter mil. Split three ways, we won't be left with much."

"Can we ask for more?"

"We have to," Wes insists. "Before signing anything, I'm going to talk to a lawyer. Jen, can you text me Kyle's number?"

"Who's Kyle?" Faisal asks.

"Kyle's in the movie industry, mostly on the business end. I'm sure he can recommend a good lawyer."

Wes clicks out of the call in a hurry, and is quick to type out a text to Kyle. **Hey! Jen gave me your number. My sub shop in Amsterdam is entering into negotiations for a buyout from a corporate giant. You've probably guessed it: The Sub Shoppe. Since you're in acquisitions, I thought you might know an attorney who can help us get a fair offer. Thanks, and please get back to me when you can!**

Once Wes clicks send, a read receipt with a time stamp appears under the text almost immediately. Every time a wave breaks, Wes checks his phone, expecting a reply from Kyle. Faisal is getting ready to open Sub Dude in Amsterdam, where it's now six in the morning.

At nine p.m. Pacific Time, the boardwalk is too loud and hazy for Wes to think clearly. Stretching far into both directions, the rhythmic gathering that started on their quiet little avenue is still churning out a joyfully discordant melody. With music in the streets reaching a fever pitch, Wes and Jen dip out of the festivities. They walk home holding hands. Wes reaches into his pocket a few more times to check his texts. A half an hour later at the house, and still nothing from Kyle.

"Usually, he writes back fast whenever I text him," Jen says.

"That restaurant is my life's work," Wes adds. "We should take the buyout while we have the chance. My first thought is to sell it off before Sub Dude can get sued by the freak that attacked me and Omar. All I know is that without a good lawyer, we'll get hosed."

"Let's go inside, babe," Jen gently suggests, taking her time on a backward walk to the bedroom. "Things didn't go my way today, either."

"Don't worry about that little setback in Beverly Hills," Wes says to Jen, wrapping her in his arms. "Maybe Kyle can still pull some strings for you."

"I can think of something else I'd like to pull," she whispers playfully into his ear.

They climb on their giant California King mattress, a planet unto itself. Wes and Jen collide under the sheets, their clothes flying into the air. Wes stops, and digs into his pants pockets for the vibrating cell phone. It's not Kyle, but the message is from Kamala Harris, who is asking for a campaign contribution in any amount. Jen stashes the phone under a pillow. To distract him from the business dealings in Amsterdam, she kisses him on the navel and around his waist, and lower still, bringing Wes back to the moment in Venice Beach.

They stay in bed late into the morning, stirring awake when Zen bursts through the front door. Scanning the floor for their underwear, Wes and Jen can hear their surfer son running the spray water over his wetsuit, hanging it on the shower rod before he heads back out with a fresh, dry one. Wes dives into his inbox and call log, hoping to see a missed connection with Kyle, or Ross. Jen dials Kyle's number for the third time since the night before, while Wes once again tries getting Ross on his cell.

"Guess I was a real bitch at dinner last night," Jen says, glancing for the hundredth time at her unanswered texts to

Kyle and Ross. "Those Hollywood big shots went out of their way to trash me, my script, and everything I've worked so hard for. Okay, so I had a few glasses of wine and Kyle was a little embarrassed. But he doesn't seem like the ghosting type."

Wes comforts Jen, circling his hand on her back. "Let's see what's on TV."

Flipping stations from a predictably mild forecast on the Weather Channel to nervous election speculation on *The View*, Wes lands on a breaking news story coming out of Sierra Madre. A KTLA reporter is at the scene, standing on the shoulder of a wide boulevard with a silver mountain backdrop.

"A Sierra Madre couple with Hollywood ties died last night in a horrific cliffside accident," the reporter begins. The segment changes to footage of a late-night crew with a rescue crane dangling near a flowering purple wisteria vine. The clean-up crew untangles some shrubbery clinging to what remains of the car after a three hundred-foot death spiral off a winding road.

Kyle's car is reduced to ruins with the front end smashed into the windshield. Jen gasps, covering her mouth. Images of Kyle Langley and Ross Kelly flash on the television screen, pictures Wes recalls from their Facebook profiles.

"I can't even," Wes utters in disbelief.

News anchors at the desk discuss the tragedy in upbeat voices, recapping an eyewitness account of the driver swerving off the narrow road to avoid striking a bear.

"They were just here," Jen gasps, sinking with Wes into the sofa cushions.

A fast, forceful knock prompts Wes to turn off the television off and answer the door. Two police officers stand on the porch, where they brusquely introduce themselves as a detective and lieutenant from departments in Sierra Madre and Los Angeles.

"Good morning. I'm Lieutenant Lee, LAPD, here today on an agency assist," says the officer in a dark navy police uniform. "This is Detective MacCubbin from Sierra Madre, where Internal Affairs is investigating a fatal car crash in the San Gabriel Mountains. Do you have a moment to speak with us?"

"Of course," Wes replies, his words coming out forced and firm. "I'm Wes Levine, welcome to our home. We just saw the news."

"We'll just need a moment of your time," Lee says.

Wes leads the officers to the kitchen table and offers coffee, which they both turn down. The pack of pre-rolled joints slips off the table, and Jen quickly scoops it up, stuffing the Stargazers under her bra strap.

"Don't worry about that, ma'am," MacCubbin says with a toothy grin.

"What we just saw on KTLA is horrifying," Wes says to the officers. "Can you tell us what happened to our friends?"

The detective casts a sullen scowl. "The victims' cell phone data indicates their last stop prior to the crash had been at this address."

Wes nods as they take seats at the table, where Jen reaches for a napkin to pat her watery eyes. "That's right. They drove Jen home after having dinner in Beverly Hills."

Detective MacCubbin responds with a satisfied smirk. "Did the driver or passenger have anything to drink?"

"Here? No," Wes responds tersely. "Ross waited in the car when Kyle saw Jen off at the front door."

"Okay," MacCubbin accords, his eyes scanning Jen's fingers for a ring. "Are you married?"

"We're co-parents to our nineteen-year-old son," Jen answers, forthrightly defiant. "What exactly is being investigated? I mean, it's all over the news."

The detective clears his throat, straightening the silver badge on the breast pocket of his shirt. From across the table, the two-way radio hanging on Lee's duty belt goes off. *Copy this, copy that,* a code foreign to the public's ears.

"The cellular data on their phones was being tracked by the insurance company," MacCubbin adds. "The driver, a Mister Kyle Langley, was holding his phone in the moment the accident took place. Mister Langley was driving over the speed limit and slammed his brakes hard before losing control of the vehicle."

"The roads near their house are really narrow. Could they

have been derailed by another car?" Wes asks.

"Mister Langley's use of a handheld phone while driving is likely what cost him and his husband their lives."

"The news report said that they swerved to avoid hitting a bear," Wes says. "When we were at their house, a bear came through the back door. Their little dog chased it away."

"Bears sightings happen all the time in the San Gabriel Mountains, but that's neither here nor there," MacCubbin diverts. "The driver had a very high-cost life insurance policy. And so, if Mister Langley was intoxicated or driving irresponsibly, his insurers deserve to know."

"Kyle seemed fine to me," Wes responds flatly.

Lee plucks the two-way radio from his belt. "It's a Code 1," he mumbles into the speaker.

"Wait, what's a Code 1?" Wes asks nervously.

"In police terms, it means everything is copacetic. All is swell in the land of swells," Lee concludes, turning to Detective MacCubbin. "Look, I need to get back on the beat in East L.A., where everything is not Code 1. Are we just about finished here?"

"One more thing," MacCubbin says to Wes. "Can you forward us any text messages between you and Mister Langley? That would be a great help to our ongoing investigation."

"Like I said, we were friends but not quite texting each other every day," Wes reiterates to the detective.

MacCubbin twitches his auburn mustache and takes a deep breath. "I'm just asking you to go into your texts and let us know if there's anything that can help us find the truth about what happened last night."

Wes shakes his head. "That goes against the Fourth Amendment of the Constitution. What you're asking violates my right to privacy."

The detective's frown twists into a half-cocked smile. "Are you trying to hide something, Mister Levine?"

Wes stands up, his chair scraping loudly on the kitchen floor. "If you want my phone, you'll need a warrant. Until then, we're done here."

When the cops leave, Wes double-bolts the door. "Holy

shit," he utters to Jen as the two police cruisers drive off. "Do you think Kyle crashed while reading my text message?"

A week later, Wes gets an unexpected call from Craig Berman, the L.A.-area attorney Kyle had texted at Wes's request on the night of the accident. From the moment Craig picks up, the call is somber and commemorative. But soon they're talking business, and Craig is certain he can get the Sub Shoppe to shell out big bucks for prime commercial real estate in Amsterdam. On the phone, Berman insists that Sub Dude, a fixture outside the Central Station for over twenty years, deserves far more than the standard buyout rate, on the grounds that not many food service operations last so long in such a competitive, high-end location.

"I'll let my business partner Faisal know," Wes says. "Can you give us a timeline?"

"Will have to get back to you," Craig responds. "I'm about to drive."

"Be safe," Wes says, setting his phone on the kitchen table.

A moment later, Zen is ambling through the front door. He's in his own world, bumping his surfboard into walls and avoiding eye contact on his way to the living room rack.

"Hey," Wes breaks the silence. "Everything okay?"

"I'm going to the next round," Zen replies, flat and unconcerned.

"That's great! Is something else on your mind?"

Zen puffs his cheeks. "It's Ava," he confides to his dad about the cracks starting to appear in their passionate, productive relationship.

"Ava?" Wes asks, surprised and concerned.

"Let's just say there are creative differences," Zen clarifies. "I want to focus on catching waves, not collecting Instagram followers. But Ava's all about cameras and attention. She enjoys feeding content to social media's endless picture show."

"Have you and Ava considered a compromise?"

"You can't compromise with technology," Zen responds. "The filters, the frames. It all makes me feel like a fraud. We've been using Insta360. I hate surfing with a stupid selfie device.

It doesn't even look real," Zen complains. "But this is what Ava says will keep our online audience engaged."

"Why not do both?" Wes suggests. "I mean, I also like the longer videos too. But they aren't seeing as much traffic as the shorter clips, and they're more work for Ava."

"Don't you get it?" Zen implores Wes to hear him out. "I want to surf. I don't want to be just another jerk off on YouTube."

"You've got more than just followers, Zen. Many of them are subscribers. Just take a moment and consider the magnitude of that."

"Come on, Dad. A lot of that is bought and paid for."

"Look at what Ava's helped you build, Zen. Your metrics are making you money. You're on the verge of having a million followers, and the world's number one surfer has got, what, three or four mil? I've never been social media savvy, and Sub Dude's never had a website. No Facebook, no dot-com, nothing. And that's not a flex because these days, we all need to harness technology and social media to achieve our goals."

Zen casts a quizzical glare. "What do you mean, goals?"

"As your manager, Zen, I'd like to ask you to describe your main goal as a surfer?"

"To keep surfing. That's my goal," Zen declares boldly. "I want to be in a position where I can spend more time surfing on the water, not the World Wide Web. That's Ava's thing."

"Have you offered a cut of the loot to Ava?" Wes asks, and Zen goes silent. "I think that's an easy question."

"I mean, she must be getting something out of it. Every video we've made is also up on her channel. I'm sure that's monetized, too."

"She's put in a lot of work, and you've been seeing some nice returns," Wes reminds Zen. "Wouldn't it seem fair that if someone works and makes you money, they should also get paid?"

"Ava's definitely not hurting for money," Zen says. "Her parents own two houses in L.A., one in Hawaii, and a condo in Vegas. Besides, why would I pay my girlfriend? We started this thing together, but not with any kind of business plan in mind."

"Maybe it's time to get one. Just think about it," Wes continues. "Get focused. This is where I take off my dad hat to put on my manager hat. To stay in the surfing game, you need a clear vision of what it is that you're after."

"I've never had my hands on this kind of money before. But at the end of the day, it's really not much. Twenty or thirty grand would go a lot further in Indonesia or Thailand. In L.A., it's chicken scratch. Do you really think I should be paying Ava when her parents are loaded and I haven't got a pot to piss in?"

"What do her parents do?"

"Her dad's a venture capitalist. Mom's a sex therapist."

Wes chuckles. "Oh yeah. With job titles like that, they're definitely loaded."

"Ava's not even done with school yet, and she's already a millionaire," Zen adds. "And as an only child, she'll get everything when her parents pass away. Cha-ching!"

"Just make sure Ava feels like you truly care about her," Wes reminds Zen. "Don't let a good thing slip away."

Jen comes out of the bedroom in a bright fleece robe. "Good morning, loved ones," Jen greets them in a mellow drawl. "What did I miss?"

"Just a little parenting," Wes says with a wink.

"Welcome to the last nineteen years of my life," Jen quips, reaching for a clay coffee mug.

At first, Wes doesn't say anything back. But his downward glance speaks to a regret over what could have been. "Jen, I wish you would've walked into Sub Dude the first year we were in business. That way, I would've never missed a moment of Zen's life. I can't change the fact that we didn't have a chance to reconnect until year twenty."

Jen pats Wes on the shoulder. "What I'm saying is it's not too late," she rephrases, flipping open her laptop on the way to the living room.

A message with **urgent** in the subject line hits Zen's inbox. It's from Coach Jon Spencer, who says he needs to meet with Zen as soon as possible. Zen gets the coach on the phone to ask what the meeting is all about. Jon only tells him that his concerns are administrative and confidential in nature.

"No one's in trouble or anything," the coach says. "I need to meet with the international surfers in the HBSO about some prize eligibility issues we've come upon. Also, bring a copy of your passport or birth certificate."

After slogging through congestion on the 405, Wes and Zen finally pull up to the Huntington Beach Pier. They're both in pissy moods from sitting in traffic for two hours. At the start of the wooden path, Coach Jon Spencer is standing alone with his back to the pier.

"So, where's your office?" Wes asks impatiently.

Jon points to two benches facing coastal highway traffic. "This is it."

"We really could've done this on FaceTime," Wes shoots back. "What are these administrative concerns, anyway?"

Jon turns to Zen. "I reviewed your application, and noticed you're an EU citizen. Until recently, we've been an international contest through and through. We've had winners from Australia and New Zealand five years in a row. But our legal team has just informed us that non-U.S. citizens are no longer eligible for the scholarship award. The cash option is now your only option."

"Okay," Zen replies indifferently.

On his phone, Jon scrolls into his inbox and forwards a contract for Zen to sign electronically. "Your online presence is second to none, Zen. I know you'll keep blowing away all the judges. And if you win, the HBSO Committee is asking you to sign a contract agreeing to take the cash if you win."

"Then who gets the scholarship?" Wes asks Jon. "You're saying that the winner must be an American citizen?"

Jon cracks a wry grin. "If Zen wins, then no one sees that scholarship. Between you and me, the committee would prefer to disburse a cash prize. From the HBSO's standpoint, the scholarship is twice the work and double the payout."

Zen twists out a polite smile. "If the scholarship prize is so much trouble, then why have it at all?"

"I'll level with you," Jon concedes. "The whole college scholarship thing is for optics. We're supposed to encourage young surfers to stay in school. And in the last ten years, only one grand prize winner has chosen the scholarship. With your talent, Zen, you could make a living off endorsements alone."

"What if he gets into U.C.L.A?" Wes asks the coach.

"Then he'll have the option of using his prize money to pay for tuition and expenses," Jon answers. "But personally, I wouldn't. Sometimes you've got to take the money and run."

"I'll do it," Zen readily agrees. "Send me the documents, and I'll e-sign them right now."

"Make sure you wear this at the next round," Jon says, handing Zen a Maui and Sons rash guard. "Judges like seeing up-and-coming surfers wearing hot brands."

"When will I actually start getting paid by these brands?" Zen asks, stretching out the rash guard emblazoned with big names.

"They'll be paying you soon enough," Jon replies with a sparkle in his eye that makes anything seem possible. "I'm pulling for you, Zen."

From bustling Huntington Beach, Wes and Zen cruise up PCH to a calmer, quieter Seal Beach. They park on Main Street and make their way to the pier. Wes and Zen walk past a bulldozer moving mounds of sand to form a berm as a buffer against the expected winter storms and high tides in the months ahead. Standing under the wood pilings that hold up the pier, Zen wants to get familiar with the surf break. He dips his toes into the chilly water to get an idea of what to expect in the next round, different as the wind and waves will be on that day.

Since relocating to California, Wes has become more at ease with the ocean. His past trauma is becoming like a massive cruise ship shrinking into the horizon, too far out to matter much from the shore. Memories of the tsunami still persist, but no longer dominate. By now, Wes can accept and even honor what happened without feeling stuck in a battle with himself over a moment that came and went more than twenty years ago. What had long been an albatross on his neck is now but a dot in the distance drifting closer to the vanishing point. Wes and Zen practically have the entire beach to themselves, save for a sketchpad artist cloaked in a Ghostface mask and black cape.

"How you making out, Dad?" Zen asks.

From behind his aviator sunglasses, Wes stares into the placid Pacific waters, where a trio of shaggy blond adolescents paddle out on their longboards.

"It gets easier with time," Wes finally says. "By now, I should've come out to see you surf. Not on Instagram or YouTube, but in person. I'm your father and your manager, Zen. I should take on a more active role."

"It's alright," Zen says, shrugging it off.

"No, it isn't. Before my dad left for Mexico, he was always too busy flipping pizzas back in Baltimore. I always told myself that if I had a child, I'd never put them through that."

"Well, Dad, if it's any consolation," Zen begins. "I'm not a child anymore."

Those words hit Wes between the eyes. He turns to face the ocean, wishing he could block out the gravity of Zen's comment. "Your mom showed me the photos on Facebook. It wasn't that long ago when you were a little boy growing up without his dad. And as it turns out, just like my own father, I was slinging subs instead of being there for you."

"Maybe after selling the Amsterdam joint, you could take Sub Dude to L.A.," Zen suggests. "You'd probably do better with a vegetarian sub shop. The Greens here are nuts. Last week in Brentwood, someone threw a brick through a steakhouse window."

"The future of food is animal-free," Wes responds candidly. "I've haven't been eating meat lately, and don't miss it. But launching another restaurant would really eat into my savings. A food truck might be the way to go."

Tracing on a sketchpad, the silent, black-clad Ghostface artist creeps closer, but Wes and Zen don't seem to mind.

"It feels like L.A. is becoming home," Zen says. "But I don't want to hold you back. Like I said, I'm no longer a kid."

"I'll be here to love and support you any way I can."

With the gentle murmur of waves lapping on the quiet beach, Zen takes a deep breath. "After the surf off, I might move to Hawaii with Ava," he admits like a long-held secret.

"Hawaii?" Wes asks.

Zen nods. "She's shown me some videos. Man, those winter swells are out of this world. Big, monster waves in Hawaii make California's seem like child's play."

"Hawaii's expensive, and it's so far away from everything."

"Yeah, but Ava's parents have their second house in Maui."

"And Ava?" Wes asks. "Is she okay with you two moving in together so soon?"

"It was her idea," Zen says. "I mean, you and Mom moved in after a month of dating, so I figured, why not?"

"And what about college?"

"Did I tell you I didn't get into U.C.L.A.?" Zen says, clicking onscreen for the message in his inbox. "This morning, I got a rejection letter."

"Oh, man. Zen, I'm sorry. I guess that's why you were quick to sign away the scholarship prize."

"Anyway, I was facing some pretty steep odds. A university like that takes less than one in ten applicants."

"Just focus on the here and now," Wes advises. "Look, I'd miss you if you moved to Hawaii. You're my son, and it feels like we just met. But you've got to live your life."

They dust the sand off their shorts and head back to the Seal Beach Boardwalk, taking a long walk across the shops on Main. In the car, Wes is laying out towels on the front seat and his phone rings. It's another FaceTime call from Faisal.

"I thought I should let you know, brother, that we served our last cheesesteak today."

"What you mean?" Wes asks. "Everything okay?"

"Craig Berman is on top of it, brother. Already we are in negotiations for a buyout. Staying in the restaurant game for such slim profit margins just doesn't make sense."

"I hear that. Enough of this business shit. How's Omar?"

Faisal sighs. "Dad's doing better every day. He's been through a lot. I think he's starting to understand why it's time for him to retire."

"Give Omar my best," Wes says. "Can you do me a favor and save all the signs out front?"

"Um, yeah. Sure," Faisal answers tentatively. "Are you thinking to rebrand out in Cali?"

"Never say never," he replies, speculative but weary. "My share of the buyout might get me and the fam a year in California, no more than two. Sooner or later, I'll have to go back to work. Take good care of your dad, *akhi.*"

"I will, brother. Catch a wave for me if you can."

Back in Venice, Wes parks near the boardwalk. He scans the side streets for a familiar taco truck. Standing in the middle of the promenade, Wes and Zen are nearly run down by two white face-painted unicyclists passing bowling pins back and forth. They think fast and split apart. The riders in loud, circus-y suits come to a stop at a merch table in front of an ice cream walkup. They have a tip box at their feet, and Wes drops them a couple dollars. "Nothing but love, guys. That's totally Venice!"

Further down the boardwalk, Wes and Zen encounter an electric guitarist, a dead ringer for John Frusciante with long windswept hair and a dark stubbly beard. On a beat-up Telecaster, he picks through the opening chords in 'Under The Bridge,' the muffled notes crackling on a tiny Fender amp. This time, Zen drops a couple folded dollars into his tip bucket. From a nearby side street, Wes and Zen still hear the busker singing the Red Hot Chili Peppers song, mixing Spanish with English.

In the next alley, Wes finds the taco truck where he and Zen had grabbed lunch earlier in the week. The cashier behind the service window speaks little English, so he calls someone on his cell phone and holds it out with the speaker turned up.

"Hi, I'm interested in getting my own food truck," Wes says into the phone speaker.

"How many years you been in the business?" asks the food truck owner, who sounds gruff and hurried.

"Twenty years. But I don't make tacos. I own a sub shop that's being bought out, and have been thinking about downsizing."

"Do you my honest advice?"

"Yeah, please."

"California's not the place to do that. I own three taco trucks in Venice, Boyle Heights, and Downtown L.A., and they're all barely getting by."

"Are you saying a brick-and-mortar restaurant might have more potential?"

"You're a white guy, right? Gringo?"

"I'm a member of the human race, and I live on Planet Earth," Wes responds in a clarion tone. "Does that answer your question?"

"What I'm trying to say is that it's becoming a predominately Latino industry," the taco truck owner rephrases it. *"Ángel, por favor dale el teléfono.* No speakerphone."

Through the concession window, Wes takes the cashier's cell phone.

"Okay," the owner says. "You should probably know that I don't make most of my money selling tacos. I find work for Mexican migrants who want to try their luck on this side of the border."

"So, you help people get jobs?" Wes asks. "You're like a headhunter."

"Depending on how things go in this next election, I could become a hunted head. Do you catch my drift? Give the phone back to Ángel."

"Gracias," Wes thanks Ángel, returning his phone to the service counter. *"Cuídate."*

"What do you think, Dad?" Zen asks on their walk back to Ocean Front.

"Food service in L.A. seems complicated and problematic," Wes answers. "But I'm sure there are still some people here who believe in earning an honest living."

"You had it pretty good in Amsterdam," Zen puts in. "Why not just let your guys keep running Sub Dude?"

"Omar just had a heart attack and he's overdue for retirement," Wes answers. "And Faisal's working too hard to keep the place afloat. A buyout could be the best thing that ever happened to us."

"I don't know, man," Zen replies. "You're giving up your original, independent business to a faceless corporation. Are you sure that's what you want?"

"We've had a good run. In the last twenty years, Sub Dude has outlived so many restaurants in Amsterdam. But to what end? After all that work, a payout from a big company is like a pot of gold at the end of a rainbow."

A van without windows is blocking Wes's car. He flashes his headlights, signaling for the van driver to move. In the rearview mirror, Wes catches a glimpse of two men in black suits throwing their hands on a worker with a hard hat and a lunch pail. A third masked man takes the worker's belongings. Rolling down his window, Wes looks upon four more men with guns situating the worker in the back of another unmarked van.

"Mind your fuckin' business!" a masked man growls at Wes.

With hand gestures, Wes tries communicating with another militarized-looking man behind a bandana face cover and eventually maneuvers the Toyota out of the tight parking space. A half-mile drive home is ten minutes of gridlock and yellow police tape. Once they're finally in the driveway, Wes sees Jen standing on the porch, where she's cuddling a furry little creature in a quilt.

"Hey hon?" Wes asks. "Are you pet sitting for someone?"

"Do you remember our special little girl from Sierra Madre?" Jen whispers, looking lovingly downward. "A week before the accident, Ross changed his will to leave Fefe to her doggy godmother. Zen, come meet the newest member of our family."

Fefe leaps off of Jen to try climbing Zen's leg. They warm up fast and before Zen can blink, he's cradling Fefe closely.

"So tiny," Zen says gently. "You've got to eat something."

"On the phone, Fefe's vet told me she hasn't been eating much," Jen says, mixing water into a bowl of kibble.

"Hey Fefe," Wes says gently. "Welcome to the family."

Amsterdam, March 2009

Daisy is gone.

Mom has just said goodbye to her golden-haired Cocker Spaniel Retriever of ten years. It tears me up when I think about her as a little pup, in those early days of Daisy doing backflips off the sofa and chewing on everything in sight. Since that day we brought her home from a Pennsylvania rescue farm, Daisy's big brown eyes melted our hearts. Daisy changed Mom's life. After connecting with an animal for the first time in her early fifties, Mom switched to a vegetarian diet. She quit taking blood pressure medication, quit drinking, and quit watching TV sitcoms after work. With Daisy to care for, Mom swore off happy hours with co-workers she secretly disliked and started exploring the local trails and lakes and footpaths outside her door, reveling in every green space suburban Baltimore could offer.

Daisy mellowed Mom out; a lifelong Republican, Mom stunned me with news that she'd pulled the lever for Vice President Al Gore. Daisy was still a young pup back then, still nipping at rugs, sleeping on a straw nest bed and sometimes waking up the house with her late-night howling. Mom and I would talk for hours on the phone about the looming threats of climate change: industrial pollution and rising rates of childhood asthma, plastic in the world's oceans and the average American's resistance to recycling, a shortage of bike lanes in the face of overwhelming car traffic and highway expansions. In my senior year at university, Mom proofread my essays in Environmental Science, a class I'd ace with ease.

During the tense, unprecedented aftermath of the contested 2000 presidential election, Mom made a bold choice to ditch her Republican side of the family for the holidays. Instead, we went to my dad's parents' house for a big Jewish Thanksgiving. By that point, Dad was already six years disappeared into Mexico. What my paternal grandparents may have lacked in terms of familial connections in Baltimore they'd more than made up for with their vast social network of hip, cosmopolitan friends from Philadelphia and New York. As America's future hung in the balance, we feasted with creatives, hipsters, and mystics. Though Gore was running out of legal options, a sense of hope still remained that all votes would be counted and the twenty-first century might begin with a hippie renaissance, or something like it.

At the financial firm where Mom worked, the company and their shareholders broke strongly Republican. In the employee lounge, they mocked Gore as "Mister Green" and "Mister Internet." But thanks to the new environmentally-savvy friends she'd met walking Daisy on the trails, Mom was now a card-carrying member of Sierra Club. And with tech stocks blowing up in the late nineties, Mom had the foresight to know that the future was the Internet. And so, she figured, why not vote for the guy who's getting all this flack for supposedly having invented it?

I haven't seen Mom or Daisy since I first moved abroad six years ago. Still, I remember Daisy's long floppy ears hanging like side bangs. On this typically overcast day in Amsterdam, Mom meets me in the middle of De Wallen, the center of it all. It's around one in the afternoon when Amsterdam's neon lights start to come alive. None of it seems to phase Mom, who pays calm, respectful attention to the working girls in lingerie seducing passersby from behind rosy lamplit windows.

"It's good to see you, Mom," I say as we embrace.

"I missed you," she says tearily. Tears that I know are for Daisy, who's now three weeks over the Rainbow Bridge.

"Are you doing okay with everything?" I ask her.

"Well," Mom hesitates, resting a hand on my wrist. "Better than before."

"Did you get settled into the hotel?"

"I did, thanks," Mom answers. As she pulls back her hair, I notice a dried trail under her eyes and worry she's been crying nonstop.

"Earlier in the lobby, I saw someone with a service dog that reminded me of Daisy. I had to get out of there fast, or I'd be crying like a fool."

"Mom, I'm so sorry about Daisy. She was perfect."

"You know something? It's been ten years since the psychic in Venice Beach said that a dog would bring clarity into my life," Mom recalls, staring into the Amsterdam mist. "Without Daisy, I feel so lost."

I try to comfort her with another hug. "Welcome to the Old Continent, Mom. I guess this is home now. How's everything in Baltimore?"

"Not much changes in Baltimore," Mom says definitively.

"Even though I live in one of the world's most vibrant hubs, sometimes I feel like I'm missing out on life in America."

"Well, after taking Daisy to the vet on that last dreadful day, I just wanted to get away from it all. So, I took the option to retire early and travel around Europe."

"I've really been beside myself for poor Daisy," I say. "But I'm so glad to see you. It's been too long. How's everything else back home? All good with the family?"

From where we stand on the foot bridge, Mom looks down at the canal water, spotting her own reflection. "Some people on my side of the family have been suggesting I'm a bad mother for not seeing my adult son in six years."

I puff my cheeks, the air filling space where words are lost. "It's okay, Mom," I finally say. "We kept in touch over Skype."

"When I was working in Corporate America, I couldn't just ask for a week off to go to Amsterdam. They'd drug test me in a heartbeat."

"I hardly ever touch weed anymore," I say in the doorway of Voyagers, a narrow hotel with a narrow Dutch stairway also doubling as an unapologetically dank and hazy coffeeshop. Mom leads the way inside. We follow a lingering, piney scent of second-hand pot smoke to the service counter. She no longer tokes, either, but instead takes edibles. And so, I order us two magic brownies and a kettle of tea.

We settle at a window table. Mom looks as young as she did ten years ago on our trip to California. Her stylishly disheveled strawberry blonde bob shines uncommon light in gray, cloudy Amsterdam. Now that she's stepped away from the working world at sixty-two, Mom is renting out our old house in Baltimore and now plans to travel the world indefinitely.

"So, what's up with all the judgement from our relatives?" I ask between brownie bites. "Are they just bummed out you're living your best life?"

"I'm not concerned about them," Mom replies. "I've had plenty of time to think about where I might've gone wrong. If ever I seemed too focused on work or money, please understand the pressure I was facing."

"You did the best you could with those circumstances," I say as the magic brownie kicks in, gradually turning everything wavy. "I guess in his own way, Dad did too."

"It wasn't easy finding out that the man I married died in a tsunami," Mom admits. "But I'm sure you know that your dad and I couldn't stand each other in the early days. We waited four years after you were born before having a wedding."

"I know, Mom," I say, smiling. "I've seen the photo album. Remember, I was the ring bearer."

"We put off marrying because we weren't sure we'd last. I turned to my family for advice, and they stabbed me in back. There was always a lot of judgment coming from my side."

"Was it because of the Jewish husband thing, or the child before marriage thing?" I ask, backpedaling immediately. "You don't have to answer that if you'd rather not."

"I'll tell you the complete truth, Wes. It was both. For a family like mine, I was going into uncharted waters. Maybe things have changed a little since then."

"Hopefully," I put in. "Do you feel like you're better off without them?"

"Yeah, I do," Mom begins, picking at the edges of her brownie. "I spent years trying to be who I thought I was expected me to be. Everything sort of dawned on me after we came home with my sweet Daisy. She showed me the meaning of love."

I smile, a little tearfully, looking across the small table at my grieving mom while the magic brownie turns my senses into overdrive. "And that's exactly what you're always shown to me. I guess Dad would've been proud to see me with my own kitchen in Amsterdam."

Mom looks at me closely. "I'm proud of you too, Wes.

Amsterdam is lucky to have you."

"How long are you in town for? Maybe we could go somewhere for dinner."

Mom cracks a sympathetic half-smile. "Tonight, I've got to be on a train to Paris," she says. "But we've got time. I'll be staying in Europe for three more months until my landing visa runs out. Then I'm taking a trip with a friend to Peru. From there, it's off to Japan."

"What's going on in Paris?" I ask.

"I'm meeting an old friend," Mom says, nervous and blunt. "Okay, maybe old partner is more accurate."

"Really? That's great, Mom. Happy for you. Is he French?"

"She," Mom corrects me. "She's American. Before meeting your dad, I kept my relationship with Paula a secret. We even went on a girls' trip to Europe in our twenties. Paula liked it so much, she took a job in France and never looked back."

In the moment when everything starts making sense, it pains me to think about how much of my mom's life has been hidden away for so long. After Dad deserted us for Mexico, she never dated or even entertained the idea of getting into another relationship, at least not with a man. Though she was one of few female brokers at her firm, all of Mom's extracurriculars happened exclusively in women's spaces: from her annual Women In The Wilderness backpacking trips with Sierra Club to her weekly women's yoga classes to her all-woman book clubs.

"This is great news, Mom. How did you and Paula reconnect?"

"I looked her up on Facebook and we started sending each other messages. Soon we became close again."

"It goes without saying that I love and support you more than ever. I'm so proud of all that you are." I say.

"Thanks for being so supportive of me, Wes. You've always been an amazing son."

"It's never too late, Mom. Life is too short for anything other than truth and dignity."

She finishes half of her magic brownie and gives me the rest. I eat it all, thinking it might somehow take the edge off Mom's departure. But when she returns to the hotel lobby with her suitcase and we walk together to the Central Station, I'm choking back tears every step of the way. With so much to say, I keep quiet because it feels like if I move my lips, I might start bawling. At the ticket counter, I hand Mom her suitcase and we hug once more.

"Guess it's already time to say goodbye to your new and improved mom," she says with a wink when it's time for her to board the train.

It's who you've always been and *this isn't goodbye* are the words I'll always wish I'd said.

9

The Seal Beach round of the surf off opens on a clear, placid morning. Four wave chasers face an ocean on the cusp of a flood tide. With big brand names like Maui and Sons, Billabong, and O'Neill embroidered on Zen's rash guard, he waves to the cheering crowd with the cool ease of a seasoned public figure. The bright, warm tones and iconic insignia set him apart from the standard wetsuits wading into this crucial first heat.

From a seaward slope, Wes stands alone and watches Zen paddle out. Aside from Coach Jon Spencer, who's busy chatting with a lifeguard near the tower, Wes doesn't know a soul on the beach. During the early morning drive from Venice, they had not yet even touched the 405 when Zen mentioned Ava. But Ava is absent from this beachfront audience of middle-aged SoCal moms and dads who barely look a few years older than their young adult children toting surfboards into the ocean.

Zen bides his time in the uncertain breaker zone, making no sudden moves so early in the tidal cycle. Closer to the shore, Calvin claims a deceptive crest and pushes himself headlong into a barrel, gambling on a gust that doesn't come. He wipes out on a small but powerful wave, coming out of the ocean with a snapped leash. Wes keeps his focus on Zen by following the upward thruster fins on his board. Betting against the prevailing trade winds, Zen pushes himself to paddle beyond the breakers. From the beach it appears Zen could be playing the long game and saving his energy for a stronger groundswell. With shaky hands, Wes fumbles for his phone to get the camera ready.

With the wave cresting over his head, Zen steels himself up and holds his feet together. As Zen maneuvers at the base with a bottom turn, Wes snaps a flurry of photos on his phone. Along the coastline, the standing crowd politely applauds Zen on his smooth glide into the flats.

Still paddling in the lineup, Hillary pulls off her wetsuit hood to shake out her long ruby red hair. Working with the wind, she turns on the face of the wave and executes a flawless backside carve. With her wet hair thrashing, Hillary springs into the air and makes a big spray on the wave's lip, which gets a rousing ovation. Out of nowhere, a rogue wave suddenly converges with another swell, collapsing close enough to the shore to splash spectators up front.

"Hey, where's Keith?" Calvin asks Wes. "Did he even catch a tube?"

Further down the slope, Wes overhears the all-male panel grumbling about the shock value of Hillary shaking her hair loose in the middle of a heat. The four middle-aged judges argue for or against Hillary's surfing cred for a good five minutes. But before they can declare a winner, the crowd coalesces around Hillary, who's kneeling beside Keith in the wet sand. At the shoreline, she pushes rhythmic beats into his chest until it heaves and water flows from his mouth.

From the pier, an ambulance on standby rushes to the shore. The medics lay Keith flat on an orange stretcher, setting an oxygen mask on his face. Hillary calls to the other surfers, who gather behind the ambulance. With arms raised stiffly, Keith assures the concerned onlookers, holding his thumbs up. Once the emergency vehicles are off the beach, the judges call it a draw: both Zen and Hillary will advance to the next round.

"You're a hero," Zen tells Hillary.

"When I told my mom I wanted to be a surfer, she made

sure I learned CPR first," Hillary says. "Do you know CPR?"

Zen shakes his head. "Where can I take a class?"

"Are you on the west side?"

"Venice."

"Try Santa Monica College," Hillary suggests as a tall blond hunk in chino shorts and a Stanford sweatshirt hands her a black Givenchy tote. "Wes, this is my brother Kevin. It was a real honor to share some waves with you. You're quite popular with the surfers where we live in Malibu."

"Thanks, Hillary. But you're the MVP today. Thank God you were there when Keith got ragdolled."

"I saw it all go down from behind," Hillary explains. "The wind was working against him, and I knew he was in trouble when his wave turned out to be a wedge."

"Is he going to be okay?"

"They'll probably clear out his lungs and check for signs of inflammation while he's at the hospital," Hillary predicts. "That break pinned him into the ocean floor with almost as much force as a car."

"Poor Keith," Zen says. "He's a good guy."

"Anyway, good luck with CPR," Hillary reminds Zen. "See you in La Jolla."

The following weekend, Wes and Zen pack up the Toyota Corolla for a long drive to San Diego. In this round of the HBSO, the surf break is north of La Jolla Cove. As soon as Zen touches the sand, the crowd disperses and the surfers are packing it in. Close to the shore, a few gray-speckled seals are cuddling in the coastal waters. Soon, a small colony comes hauling out and the faint smell of sea waste quickly turns noxious. Zen holds his breath, evacuating the sewer-smelling reef break where dozens of whiskery, slithering seals are making themselves at home and getting down to business, unbothered by the panicked humans scampering for the dunes. From underneath the pier, Zen and Hillary hold out their phones to capture distant snapshots of seals in mating season galumphing on the sand.

"I checked out your YouTube channel again," Hillary tells

Zen on a slow walk back to the parking lot. "Is your crew getting any footage of the HBSO?"

"I don't have much of a crew," Zen replies. "My girlfriend Ava helped me launch my channel."

"What's Ava's last name?" Hillary asks curiously.

"Davidson. Do you know each other?"

"Yeah," Hillary says, blushing a little. "Ava and I surfed together. Back in the ninth grade we'd spent a few weeks at a surf camp in Mission Beach. I'm guessing she never told you?"

"She hasn't mentioned a surf camp. So, what's the story?"

"It's not my story to tell," Hillary firmly concludes.

"Okay," Zen slowly replies. "So, I guess I'll see you at the next round?"

"I won't be in town for the rescheduled date," Hillary says. "Did you get the group text?"

"I haven't checked my messages yet. When's the next round?"

"Next Saturday in Mission Beach. I'll be at an orientation at Harvard, the law school."

"Oh, cool," Zen says. "Are you into the environment?"

"I'm planning to go into immigration law," Hillary answers. "And since I can't make the next round, I'm dropping out of the HBSO."

"That's a bummer. I learned a lot from you. I even signed up for a CPR class in Santa Monica that starts next week."

Hillary casts a polite, fleeting smile. She flips on a pair of black Ray Bans, silently staring at an ocean aglow with golden rays.

"I don't have good memories of Mission Beach."

"I'm sorry to hear you had a bad experience. Was it at the camp or on the beach?"

"Both."

"Can I ask what this has to do with Ava?"

"Okay," Hillary agrees tentatively. "A migrant family had been staying in a tent not far from our surf spot. During the sessions, we'd see them coming and going. Then one of the girls at camp came back to her room when a man was going through her drawer looking for a snack. The intruder got arrested and immigration officers swarmed the beach to look for his family. They all got deported, Zen. All over a fucking bag of trail mix."

"All of them, deported?" Zen asks. "How?"

"Because the person who filed the police report also said there were undocumented immigrants in a tent near the camp. After that, we never saw the family or their tent again."

"Was it…?" Zen begins to ask. "Did Ava call the cops?"

Hillary pauses, sighs, and takes off her shades to look Zen dead in the eyes. "Like I said, it's not my story to tell."

They walk together to the beachfront parking lot, where Hillary straps her board to the rack of her old school wood-paneled station wagon.

"Stay stoked," Hillary says. "Hope you win this thing."

Zen smiles, catches himself staring. "Wish you could stick around, but I'm sure you'd out-shred us all."

Hillary waves off the compliment. "Come on, Zen. You're a rock star."

A beeping car horn cuts into their conversation. It's Wes, double-parking his Toyota Corolla between two cars in the crowded, beach-facing lot on La Jolla Shores Drive. Zen sends Hillary a Facebook friend request, which she confirms before driving off.

"Sorry to be in a rush," Wes says to Zen. "Just trying to not get any more tickets."

"What are you talking about?" Zen asks with an insouciant shrug. "It's free parking."

"Making friends?" Wes asks as Zen fastens his surfboard on the roof rack. "How's Ava doing?"

Zen doesn't answer right away, not until they're back on the road. "I invited Ava to Thanksgiving. She said this year she'll be alone. Her parents are celebrating their anniversary in Vegas."

"That's cool," Wes says, starting out on the 5 North for a grueling commute back to L.A. "We'll be home in about three hours."

"What a waste of a day," Zen gripes when freeway traffic slows to a grind. "The next round is all the way in Mission

Beach."

"Hope the seals don't get horny and crash the party again," Wes jokes, cruising ahead with the ocean behind them and houses on lush foothills to their front.

"I guess in California, you've got to be ready to roll with what nature has in store," Zen responds with a reverence not typical of him.

"Wise words," Wes agrees. "Is Hillary going to be in the next lineup?"

"She's dropping out of the surf off and going to Harvard," Zen answers. "Hillary told me something went down with Ava at surf camp in ninth grade."

"Really?" Wes asks. "What happened?"

"A migrant laborer went into a girl's room looking for some food. Hillary dropped some hints about who got the intruder and his family deported."

"Now Zen, will you listen to me?" Wes asks impatiently as he cuts across the freeway to cruise into the fast lane. "Don't let what Hillary said come between you and Ava. Why ruin your relationship based on hearsay?"

"But what if it's true?" Zen returns. "Why would Hillary make something up like that?"

"Think about how young they were, Zen. People change."

"I think Ava got the family deported," Zen utters, his inflection uncertain.

"You think? Or are you sure?" Wes presses on. "Ava couldn't have been older than fourteen. For her, that was practically a lifetime ago."

"Anyway, Hillary wants to be an immigration lawyer. She's got a real for-the-people vibe. I dig that about her."

"That's an admirable career path, and Hillary seems cool. But Ava is your girlfriend. Think about everything she's done for you. Ava helped you break into the surf scene, and her videos turned you into an Internet sensation."

"Dad, don't you get it?" Zen asks. "Hillary's actually doing something meaningful with her life. She inspires me to be a better person. Meanwhile, Ava is like a typical California beach girl. Me and Ava have been together since the day we got here, and I still don't know what she stands for."

"But Hillary is going to law school all the way in New England, and you're talking about moving to Hawaii with Ava. Are you sure you're both ready for that?"

"I've talked about it with Mom," Zen replies. "She says we should at least get through the holidays before moving in together. Ava's vegetarian, like you."

"Now that's inspiring," Wes says. "Should we make it an animal-free Thanksgiving this year?"

"No way!" Zen laughs. "I'm not giving up on my meat for anyone!"

"Don't give up on your girlfriend, either. You've got a good one," Wes says with the dense traffic thinning out under a green directional sign pointing north to Los Angeles.

At home in Venice, the bills are piling up on the kitchen table. Wes opens an envelope from the law offices of Craig Berman to discover a five-thousand-dollar invoice for the retainer fee. He tears into water and electric bills, three credit card statements, and five different insurance premiums due. With each click on Autopay, Wes parts with hundreds or thousands of dollars to cover this expensive month.

"Well, there goes around ten percent of my life savings," Wes sighs, crunching the numbers on his phone.

"Once the screenplay gets sold or optioned, I'll start taking care of more expenses," Jen says, rubbing the back of Wes's shoulders. "Did you ask Craig Berman if he can help with that?"

"He'll get back to us," Wes says cautiously. "On the phone, Craig didn't want to overpromise anything. He's a lot like Kyle in that way."

"I feel like all my hopes went off the cliff with Kyle and Ross that night they died," Jen confesses. "I need someone to believe in me, or I might go back to doing medical transcription."

"Let's stay positive, babe. I'm still getting a small salary from Sub Dude, but here in California, that's hardly beer money."

The bell rings. Zen opens the door and three women are standing on the front porch in silken, sculpted dresses. They're around his mother's age, all toned and slender with pretty, personable faces and sun-soaked hair. Zen stands in the doorway with a towel draping from his waist. Still dripping wet from his shower, Zen greets the women with a sales pitch.

"Subscribe to my YouTube channel, and I'll sign your yoga mats."

They laugh lightly. "Cute," one of the women says. "You must be the surfer your mom keeps going on about."

"Come on in," Jen says, introducing the friends from her yoga class. "Ashley, Amy, and Alicia. This is my son Zen and his dad, my partner Wes. Tonight, our yogini Clara is celebrating her birthday. We're taking Clara to her favorite restaurant, a vegan Ethiopian buffet up in Santa Monica."

"You lost me at vegan," Zen quips, firming the towel around his waist and returning to his room.

From the doorstep, Wes overhears the women chatting on their way to the car. "He's hot," one of them says. "Hey, Jen. So, are you and Wes open?"

"Have a great time," Wes calls out to Jen and her yoga friends, who hop into Alicia's convertible for a short drive from rustic Venice to Santa Monica Boulevard's urban bustle.

While Zen is out picking up pizza, Ava turns up at the door. Wes invites her to come inside and wait for Zen to bring dinner home. He can't stop raving about the thrill of watching his son catch waves.

"The next round is in Mission Bay," Wes tells Ava. "I know it's quite a drive, but you're welcome to ride with us. I'm sure Zen would love to see you there."

"Mister Levine, can I be real with you?" Ava asks.

"You can call me Wes. What's on your mind?"

"I see real potential in Zen," Ava goes on, twirling strands of her long blonde hair.

"He's been talking about Hawaii. Are you moving?"

Ava nods. "And sooner or later, Zen's going to outgrow the California surf. It gets predictable here. To stay competitive, he needs to keep up with the big wave chasers in Maui, Bali, and Portugal. His online followers will lose interest, unless Zen proves he can handle a more challenging environment."

"I think he can handle it," Wes says with a shaky confidence to mask unspoken fears of his only son getting swallowed by a rogue wave taller than China's Great Wall. "His coach says he's got a good chance of winning it all."

"What about after that?" Ava asks. "Zen's not just competing with other surfers. With AI churning out all these fake videos of insane waves, every surfer on the planet has to outperform them just to stay relevant."

"It's pretty nerve wracking to watch my only son going up against big waves," Wes confides to Ava. "I was in Thailand during the 2004 tsunami, where I lost my dad."

"So sorry that happened to you, Wes. Were you…"

Ava freezes up when Zen barrels through the front door, trailing the savory aroma of two pizzas: a pepperoni and a vegetarian. With ceramic plates in hand, Wes and Ava take jalapeño-topped slices. Zen eats his pizza straight from the box. From her cushy wicker basket bed in the living room, Fefe springs to the kitchen table. She's jumping and pawing at Ava for a slice. Ava abandons her plate to make room on her lap.

"Pizza is a big no-no, Fefe," Wes cautions, offering her a sweet potato-flavored chew stick instead.

"My little Bella was a Pomapoo," Ava says, cuddling Fefe. "Pomeranian and poodle mix. Before her trachea collapsed and we saw Bella over the Rainbow Bridge, she had seventeen good years with no major health issues. We never fed her from the table."

"Yo," Zen says with his mouth full, focusing on the pepperoni pizza as if it were his last meal. "I think I could eat this whole thing myself."

"You might have to, since Ava and I are both vegetarians," Wes quips, looking to Ava for approval.

"Well, pescetarian," Ava clarifies. "My mom is from Baltimore and dad's a Seattle guy, so crabcakes and salmon are still my go-tos."

"How about we grill some salmon for Thanksgiving?" Wes suggests. "I'm from Baltimore and all, but crabcakes aren't really in my wheelhouse."

"Works for me," Ava agrees. "No turkey?"

"We'll have one," Wes answers. "Just in case anyone might

want some. Since moving to California, I've been feeling more of a connection to animals."

Ava softens her gaze. "Aww, sweet."

"So, do you have any brothers or sisters, Ava?"

"I'm a first and only. What about you?"

Wes nods and smiles. "Same. That makes all three of us a first and only."

Stuck in his thoughts, Wes pulls apart his pizza crust and takes small bites. "I hope you'll make it to Hawaii together, but I'd be lying if I said I'm not terrified by the Maui waves I've been seeing lately on my Facebook reels. Who knows if they're real or fake? It makes being a surfer's dad even scarier."

"Come on, Dad," Zen says, digging into the pizza box yet again. "The tsunami was twenty years ago. Sooner or later, you need to move on."

Wes quietly gets up from the table, taking his plate to the kitchen sink and staring through the window at palm trees swaying in the sunset.

"You know, Zen, I wish it were that easy," he says, tossing half a slice of pizza into the trash. "I could use some fresh air."

"Wes," Ava calls to him across the living room. "Why don't we get our paces in together? Zen, let's go with your dad."

"I appreciate that," Wes says, grabbing his camel brown sherpa-lined jacket. "But I might make a couple business calls, and don't want to bore you with all that. If you like, help yourselves to the joints in the fruit basket. We just signed up for Netflix. The password's taped to the remote."

"My dad's cool as shit, isn't he?" Zen says to Ava, who casually admits she's been getting high with her mom since the tenth grade.

"Just remember to keep her water dish fresh. And no human food unless it's approved by Fefe's doggy godmother," Wes says from the doorway.

Wes heads outside and in the corner of his eye, he sees Zen picking pepperoni rounds from the pizza box. From the front porch, Wes can hear Ava trying to talk some compassion into Zen.

"A tsunami is as traumatic as it gets," she says.

Strolling down the avenue, Wes goes deeper into the neighborhood and soon, the Venice Canal Historic District opens in front of him. He checks his texts and quickly dials into a FaceTime call with Faisal, who's now getting ready for bed in Amsterdam.

"I know it's late there. But I just saw your text and thought it might be important," Wes says to Faisal on the phone screen. "What's the word?"

"We closed the deal, brother! The Sub Shoppe is buying both Sub Dude and the building space outright," Faisal announces. "I just got out of a Zoom meeting with Craig Berman and a Sub Shoppe lawyer. Two-point-five mil."

"That's more than I thought we'd get," Wes responds. "I'll breathe a little easier once we take those checks to the bank."

"You'll have to come back to Amsterdam to get your share," Faisal tells him. "In case you want to give it another shot, I've saved all the signage for you."

"You're the man," Wes tells Faisal. "Right now, my entire being is humming with gratitude."

"Sorry to kill your buzz," Faisal replies. "But the Sub Shoppe has already got their hideous logo planted on our awning."

"Life moves on," Wes replies. "Now I'm getting an e-mail. Let me read it and call you back."

Wes's zips through the message, going straight to the bottom line: Craig Berman and Associates have negotiated a two and a half million Euro management buyout.

The train station-facing franchise would have to serve two-hundred thousand full-length subs before seeing a return on their investment, Wes figures in his head. Even with plans to operate on a twenty-four-hour schedule, it seems senseless for a big company to start out so deep in the hole. Instead of responding by e-mail, Wes sends Craig Berman a text message.

It'll take Sub Shoppe's Amsterdam location two years just to turn out a profit. Is this what they want?

A moment after Wes sends the text, already Berman is typing something. **What they want is the location. And I wasn't going to let them shortchange you for it.**

Wes texts him back in a hurry. **Okay, and on an unrelated note, I also wanted to ask you about Jen's screenplay. Is there a chance you might know someone at Netflix in Amsterdam?**

Berman reacts with a heart emoji, but doesn't text Wes back until sometime the next afternoon, while Jen is at yoga and Zen's spending the day at Disneyland with Ava. **Two things about pitching a screenplay,** Wes reads Berman's text from inside his parked car. **1.) I can pitch a script, but it won't be cheap. 2.) We should draft a business plan and find a director and maybe an actor or two who are interested in the project. Again, I can help you with assembling a team in Hollywood, but all of this is logged as billable hours. Making it an Amsterdam-based production will cost considerably less. Let me know what Jen thinks.**

At home, Wes finds Fefe asleep in her basket. Her faint breathing sounds more like a cat's purr, a squeaky snore that flutters in and out of her tiny nose. On the kitchen floor, Zen is on his knees pressing into the chest of a plastic CPR manikin.

"I've got all these numbers to memorize," Zen says. "The rhythms and chest compressions are easy, but these ratios are turning my head in knots. It's the price I must pay."

"You can't put a price on saving a life," Wes tells him. "I'm really proud of you, Zen. I think about that a lot, and wanted to tell you."

Zen looks Wes over. "Are you sure you're thinking about that? I think something else is on your mind."

On his phone, Wes shows Zen the photo Faisal sent him of new Sub Shoppe signage, the instantly recognizable cursive corporate logo in place of Sub Dude's signature silhouette of a surfer clutching a long board and a hoagie roll.

"Damn," Zen looks his dad over. "I know how much Sub Dude meant to you."

"We're getting a nice lump sum in the buyout. I'm so close to hitting my first million, I can almost taste it."

At the mention of money, Zen turns to his phone and checks his ledgers. Projected payouts from new subscribers and social media royalties are starting to add up. Soon, he's back on the Quizlet app, thumbing through flashcards again. "I really need to study, Dad. I don't want to pay course fees again if I fail."

"Like I said, I'm proud of you no matter what," Wes puts it bluntly.

Zen sustains his gaze, trying to see through his dad. "Come on. What's *really* weighing on your mind?"

"Okay, here goes. I always wanted to be a surfer," Wes reluctantly admits. "Sure, my dad took me scuba diving. But he became so obsessed with it that he never made time for anything else. I tried surfing lessons one summer with my cousin Evan in San Diego. Out on my own, I caught a wave or two in Laguna. That same day, I saw a guy getting banged up pretty badly on the rocky reef. He had to be airlifted to the hospital. Then after the tsunami, surfing became unthinkable."

"What seems unthinkable today could become reality tomorrow. I'll teach you to shred, Dad," Zen offers. "There's not much to it."

"Who am I kidding?" Wes asks. "Every time I'm at the beach, it's another panic attack waiting to happen. Maybe I should stick with what I know and go back to cooking."

"You could do that," Zen replies. "Or, after you get the money from Sub Shoppe, you'll have time to focus on surfing, if that's what you want to do."

Wes stares at the image on his phone of the new corporate neon sign illuminating the space that had been his workplace and his home longer than any other place he'd ever worked or lived. An unsettling feeling rises in his throat and he can barely get the words out. "I don't know."

"What do you want to do with the rest of your life?" Zen asks his dad point blank.

"The question is, what have I done with my life? A year of teaching English in Thailand, then scribing a Torah in Amsterdam. Sure, I've owned a business since I was twenty-six. But, dude, I was flipping cheesesteaks in the middle of my forties. At this point, who would hire me? My work history looks like it belongs to three different people."

"And that's what makes you who you are," Zen counters,

returning his hands to the manikin chest. "Okay, now it's really time for me to get back to this. The exam's tomorrow and Mission Beach, the day after."

"I'm proud to be your father," Wes says. "You're living a life that I always dreamed of, but was never quite brave enough to go after."

"Hey Dad?" Zen asks. "I think you'd make a good politician. Why not run for mayor of Venice Beach?"

"I appreciate the vote of confidence," Wes thanks his son after a moment of careful consideration. "The only vote I am seeking."

On the morning after Zen passes his CPR exam at Santa Monica College, he's ignoring health advice in San Diego. At Mission Beach, the murky waters are high and dark. Coach Jon Spencer informs the lineup that the runoff is potentially a health hazard, but also that the HBSO committee can't afford to cancel yet another round. While waiting for the judges to assess the stormwater and make the official call, Zen weighs the risks. In the wake of a late October storm that just hit Southern California, the judges are talking about the runoff-to-rainfall ratio, quibbling among themselves about the exact numbers but agreeing that another cancellation might doom the surf off altogether.

"On the bright side, you'll have high waves today," Coach Spencer says, checking the forecast on his phone. "It didn't rain much. But with runoff water, there's always a risk."

"I'm not going out there," says San Diego-based Sam, the local contender balking at his hometown ocean. "Good luck to you all."

"The judges decided not to cancel today's round, so it's your call," the coach says. "Surfing entails risk. We all know that. And only you can decide if it's worth taking a chance on getting sick."

"The only thing that's going to get sick are those waves," Zen replies.

Alex from Huntington Beach scoffs at Zen's bravado. "I'm not touching that dirty water," Alex says. "I've got to stay in and win this thing."

"I don't care if I have to paddle out there in hazmat gear," Zen says, dashing to the water with his board. "Those waves are mine."

"Is that dude crazy or what?" Sam says to Alex, who is having a word with Coach Jon Spencer.

"I'm not giving up, Coach," Alex says. "I'll pay the registration again if that's what it takes."

Zen paddles into the breaker zone, ahead of his only competitor, a young self-described prodigy from Calabasas. The two surfers in the lineup split apart, with Zen angling for a backdoor entry and the prodigy facing the oncoming wave frontally.

The prodigy touches the peak of a steep swell and starts off strong, but he loses balance and flops off his board. As it breaks, the wave appears to swallow the prodigy and his longboard. Not a good look. The next swell rises even higher and Zen charges from behind to get himself deep into the barrel. While everyone else in the standing crowd hardly moves a muscle, Wes is jumping up and down for Zen.

Between the two contenders in this heat, it isn't much of a contest. Judges in the tower announce the winner before the surfers touch the beach. Though he took a tumble, the prodigy recovers first. Zen takes his time in the swash, treading heavy steps through shallow water.

"Of course he won," Alex grumbles to Sam.

"He's out of his mind," Sam puts in. "We aren't nuts enough to go into nasty runoff water."

"If he wins, this whole thing's rigged," Alex says tauntingly. "Zen's not even from California."

"Tough shit, quitters," Wes snaps at the nonparticipants sulking from the sidelines. "That's my son you're talking about."

"Oh, hey. My bad," Sam quickly apologizes to Wes. "I didn't know."

Zen hobbles out of the water, slow and subdued like an injured man tethered to a surfboard. Heartfelt applause greets Zen when he and his father come together at the coastline for a deep hug.

"I'm so damn proud," Wes whispers to Zen, who stumbles into his dad's arms.

"Thanks for being here today," Zen replies, his voice weak and mellow.

10

Zen's on his knees in the bathroom, praying to porcelain. After vomiting, he spots a trace of blood in the toilet water and starts freaking out. With Zen shivering in bed, Jen comes quickly to wrap him in a quilt. Wes drives them to Urgent Care. Once they're in a patient room, the doctor goes straight to the needle, rehydrating Zen with a clear liquid trickling into his vein. Zen waits behind the privacy curtain for the doctor to return with a diagnosis. Trying to relax on the clinical bed, Zen can't stop staring at the IV bag hanging overhead on a drip stand.

"I'm not going surfing again, am I?" Zen groans from under the blanket.

"Everything will be okay, Zen," the doctor says, turning the curtain open. "You'll recover with a few days of bedrest and a soft food diet."

The doctor removes the needle from Zen's arm and signs a weeklong prescription. Gastroenteritis sounds scary, but after a few sweaty days between the sheets with bowls of applesauce and mashed potatoes, Zen is doing push-ups and cobra poses on the Safavieh purple shag rug in his bedroom.

Wearing a medical facemask, Wes stands in the doorway of Zen's bedroom. "Should we tell Coach Spencer about it?"

Zen churns out a few more push-ups and springs to his feet. "I wouldn't. I can't afford to look weak."

"It's not about looking strong or weak, Zen. If you don't report your illness, you'll look irresponsible. If someone else in the lineup got sick, wouldn't you want to know about it?"

"Dad, chill! The doc said it's only contagious two days from my last puke. Now it's been three."

"Just remember to follow the doctor's orders and take your doses until they're all gone."

"That shit's giving me a headache and dry mouth," Zen complains, rubbing his temples. "Can I smoke weed with it?"

"You'll be fine. But have you thought about taking edibles instead? Smoking affects every organ in the body, and your organs have been through a lot."

"Alright," Zen begrudgingly agrees. "I'll look up some delivery options from the dispensaries on Weedmaps. What a country, huh?"

"You know, Zen. Before cannabis was decriminalized here, Americans used to flock to the Netherlands. Once upon a time, Amsterdam was one of very few places in the world where you could enjoy a safe, legal toke."

"I love America," Zen says gleefully. "But I fear what might happen when the new government takes over."

"Hey guys," Jen says from the hallway. "After the surf off, how would you feel about moving back to Amsterdam?"

"California life is second to none," Wes answers straight away. "I mean, if push comes to shove, Europe's always an option. I might not have anything keeping me here, but you've got a screenplay to pitch. Zen has a surfing career and a girlfriend to think about."

"Americans citizens are fleeing the country," Jen reminds him. "You know those Hollywood actors who always say they'll leave America whenever the elections don't go their way? Well, this time they're really packing their bags. If the stars don't feel safe here, how can we possibly be any better off?"

"Come on, Mom. If we move back to Amsterdam, where will I surf?" Zen asks. "Am I just supposed go back to catching kiddie waves in Bloemendaal?"

"You could surf in Indonesia, Zen, or maybe Brazil. You've got plenty of cousins all around the world who'd love to see you," Jen suggests. "Just think about it."

"But how would you go about pitching the script in Europe?" Wes asks.

"I just spoke to Craig Berman," Jen answers. "He says my screenplay has a better chance in the Dutch film industry. You know, with Dutch actors and directors?"

Wes wraps his arms around Jen's waist. "That's a real progress report, babe! Did Berman say why he thinks the Netherlands is a better bet than Hollywood?"

"Dutch films are making a comeback," Jen responds. "But here, everyone's stretched thin. Even the big money is tight. Maybe I expected too much from Hollywood, when all of this is so new to me."

"Mom, I don't think Hollywood's ever going to be ready for your screenplay," Zen says, setting his surfboard in the corner.

"What do you mean?" Jen asks.

"Sex work is too touchy a topic for a mainstream movie," Zen explains. "These days, people in the entertainment business probably want to sweep their sexual lives under the rug."

"Of course they would," Jen interjects. "One mistake could cost someone their entire career."

"Think about it, Mom. You're writing about Amsterdam. That's a world away from L.A.'s beaches and boulevards. On some level, maybe Amsterdam is becoming Hollywood's competition."

"I'm getting fed up with how hard it is to catch a break," Jen says. "But I'm not sure if I want to go home to Amsterdam just yet."

"When I win this surf off, nobody's moving anywhere!" Zen boasts, pumping himself up with more pushups. "Newport Beach, here I come!"

At the West Jetty View Beach, a granite wall absorbs the shock from incoming swells that splash forcefully against the rocky edge. The Wedge is Newport Beach's most famous and infamous break, with menacing, transparent emerald green waves that crest and crash dangerously close to the beach. Zen returns to the surf for the first time since falling ill. Plotting his comeback, Zen scans the waves breaking abruptly on the Balboa Peninsula, which encloses Newport's islands and gives the local surf its edge. Coach Jon Spencer is on his phone forwarding waivers for everyone in the surf off to e-sign in agreement that they're entering the powerful waves at their own risk.

First comes the Elimination Round, when a few surfers balk at the choppy waves. On their phones, two of them read over the fine print and refuse the waivers, effectively dropping out of the contest. But Alex is in the lineup after supposedly having quit the HBSO in the Mission Bay round. He prevails in this round with a near-perfect score while the other two surfers who start strong lose their footing in an insane closeout. All the surfers carrying longboards look more or less the same in their black wetsuits, but Zen recognizes Alex from his patchy, platinum bleached hair.

"Oh, hey Alex," Zen says, polite but unsettled. "I didn't know you were still in this thing."

Alex puffs his chest, gripping his board to avoid a handshake. "You've got a YouTube channel, don't you?"

Zen shrugs, a silent and humble admission that anyone with a phone and Wi-fi access can cultivate an online presence. "I've got some followers on Insta too."

"Uh, I got some followers on Insta too," Alex mocks Zen's guttural accent. "Let me tell you something, Zen. You might think you're hot with those big names on your rash guard. But I'm in this thing to win it, and Huntington's my home base. Do you know anything about America's Surf City?"

"Yeah, I've caught waves there," Zen says casually, detaching as he processes Alex's aggressive bitter taunts. "What exactly are you getting at, anyway?"

Alex cracks a sly, cynical smirk. "You should know that people in Huntington Beach want to live with as little government interference as possible. Don't forget that Surf City, U.S.A. is an American beach town, and America is for Americans."

As Alex steps back, Zen moves closer to him. "I'd like to challenge that notion," Zen responds diplomatically. "Why is there always a constant stick in your ass?"

"Huh?" Alex grunts spitefully. "I'd clock you right now if it wouldn't get me disqualified."

"Go ahead, man," Zen shoots back, clenching a fist. "What's stopping you?"

"Hey fellas. Everything alright?" Coach Spencer steps between them. "Zen, you're in the next heat. Get to your lineup, pronto."

"I'll see you in the finals," Zen says as the coach ushers Alex away with a congratulating pat on the back.

Zen jogs to the water toting his golden surfboard, bypassing his girlfriend, his parents, and his cheering supporters on the beach. Clutching their cell phones, Wes and Jen step closer to the water with two cameras at the ready. For Jen, it's her first time seeing Zen surf competitively. She's as nervous as Wes, who looks on with dread at another surprise swell that collapses directly on an unsuspecting shore.

After his spat with Alex, a friendlier energy awaits Zen in the water, where he stands in a line of foam with Moussa, a wave warrior from Senegal, and Luis, originally from Tijuana and currently a member of a Latinx surf club in East L.A.

"The wind is going that way," Moussa says, pointing to the rocky barrier. "For the best waves, the wind must come to us from the beach."

"The next set will be better," Zen predicts. "I want to go for something with a little more shoulder than that last one. We've got to get past the impact zone without getting clobbered."

"Read the swells," Moussa tells Zen. "Everywhere here is the impact zone."

"Instead of reacting to all these random swells in front of us, we need to find the pockets," Zen decides. "Nothing ever breaks in the same place every time."

"Don't sweat the choppy waves," Luis says. "Bad waves make good waves even more fun."

The three competing surfers paddle on the smooth concave surface of a glassy swell. Pointing to the first wave in the approaching set, Moussa stakes his claim and goes deep. For a moment, Moussa disappears behind a wall of water. The wave is too straight and high for Zen to find a pocket from the base. As it peaks, Zen takes a cue from Moussa and paddles for the next swell.

Making his move, Zen pivots for a straight drop down the wave's face. Towing through the turbulence, Zen pulls ahead and leaves a trail in the water. That trail signals to Luis where *not* to pop up. The wave breaks out of nowhere, but the way Zen jumps *with* his board speaks to his telepathy with the ocean.

From the back end, Luis cuts across, soaring from right to left. Moussa makes it to the beach without stumbling, but Luis slips off his board and tumbles into the swash. The crowd goes wild, cheering and checking their phones for the scores to post from the lofty heights of the judges' tower. Luis gets a solid eight-point-five and Moussa snags a nine. But Zen's ballsy pop-and-landing is what steals the show and sends him to the final round.

"We love you!" Jen hollers while Zen comes out of the shallow water. "I got so many amazing photos of you. So proud of you, Zen!"

"What an amazing jump!" Wes congratulates Zen, offering to carry his surfboard.

"Stop embarrassing me," Zen says under his breath, switching to Dutch. *"Bedankt, mijn geweldige ouders."*

"Which reminds me," Wes returns. "I think you're now the world's top surfer from the Netherlands. As your manager, can I suggest we make an effort to pump up your Dutch cred?"

"Wes, babe?" Jen asks, walking further ahead. "How much more time do we have in our parking spot?"

Wes checks the clock on his phone. "Not long. The meter said something about a two-hour limit."

When Zen and Ava find each other in the beachfront crowd, she leans closely to lower a red and white Hawaiian lei around his neck. She looks deeply into his eyes and turns her head softly in his direction, but Zen backs away without delivering on the kiss she'd been waiting for. He sounds off about not wanting to make a grand display of straight love in a sexually diverse public domain.

Ava turns away from him. "You sound like a lawyer," she says in a fed-up voice.

"We'll have time together later when we're alone," Zen tells her, sliding out of the embrace. "Think about it. If someone posts a clip of us making out and it ends up on Tik Tok or Instagram, thousands of my gay followers might unsubscribe."

"Whatever," Ava responds, distant but melodic. "Congratulations, Zen. I just want you to know I'm proud of how far you've come since the day we met."

With a sheepish grin, Zen scratches his head and tousles his thick dark hair. "Guess I couldn't have done this without you."

"I love you, Zen."

Zen grins and nods without replying in kind. They're still getting comfortable talking about love, and while Zen had been the first to tell Ava "ILY" after sex, the letters ring hollow without the words. Sometimes, Zen and Ava casually say "I love you" at the end of their phone calls. But in person, this is the first time for either of them to say three of the most powerful, binding words in the English language.

"ILY," Zen finally puts in. "You know I love you, baby."

"My parents said they'd be okay with you joining us in Maui for the holidays," Ava says to Zen, whose attention is on the judges up in the tower who'd already announced his win.

"Yeah, I'd like that." Zen's cool response dampens Ava's glowing aura. "I think Coach Spencer wants a word."

Ava looks to the ocean at a big, imposing wave that breaks big and startles the crowd standing close by. "Yeah," she says emptily. "Do your thing."

The cameras are clicking and flashing around Zen, Moussa, and Luis. They huddle closely with their backs turned on an ocean that changes course without notice. Behind them, two swells converge, becoming another wedge that strikes the shore like ten waves. The photo takers back off, shielding their smartphones from a forceful splash.

Stepping out of the group pose, Zen follows Jon Spencer to the west jetty.

"Hey Coach," Zen calls to him from behind. "Can I ask you something?"

Slowly, Jon turns around to face Zen. "What's going on?"

"Alex dropped out. Why is he back in the contest?"

Jon takes a deep breath before responding. "Zen, I don't make the rules for the contest, and I don't always agree with those rules as they are. But here's the deal. An entrant in good standing who quits the HBSO is technically allowed to rejoin by paying the registration fee again."

Zen's mouth hangs open. "What? That doesn't seem fair."

"What do you mean?"

"I just got over the worst stomach virus of my life, which could've been avoided if I knew it was okay to drop out and register again. I surfed in that dirty runoff water, thinking it was the only way I could stay in the HBSO."

"That's why we ask everyone to sign waivers," Jon responds evasively and backs away, patting Zen on the shoulder. "Great moves today, Zen. Way to slay it in Mission Bay, by the way."

Zen walks back to the coast and finds Ava standing alone on the beach. The shore takes another beating from yet another surprise wave that knocks two more surfers out of the contest.

"Did you feel that?" Wes asks Ava.

She doesn't answer, and instead nods in the direction of Wes and Jen, who are rushing to the sand dunes in a race against a ticking parking meter. Zen turns to the ocean to watch the next brutal wipeout, the wave closing in on a surfer who foolishly attempts to defy gravity over a curling foam ball that breaks big and consumes both board and rider. On the way to a small, tight parking area, Zen and Ava stroll by a beachfront row of boxy post-modern glass houses built into glistening golden sand.

"What's up?" Wes asks, reading the disappointment in Zen's downcast expression. "You won big today. Are you feeling alright?"

"No one ever told me you can drop out and register again," Zen complains to his dad. "I got played by the coach in Mission Beach."

"You live and learn," Alex bellows at Zen from behind.

"Hey Alex," Zen says, turning around. "We survived some

gnarly barrels out there today.”

Alex smirks conceitedly. “I’ve worked harder on my tan.”

“Gimme a minute,” Zen tells his mom and dad, who walk ahead to the dunes.

“So, that was a pretty swell little United Nations front you had going on there with the Mexican and the African,” Alex puts in. “One thing you should know about Huntington Beach is that political correctness won’t win you the surf off.”

“It’s called teamwork,” Zen responds firmly. “Maybe you should try it sometime.”

“I know you think you’ve got this whole thing locked up. But I intend to do whatever it takes to win.”

“You’re so full of yourself,” Ava tells Alex. “Come on Zen, let’s go.”

Kicking up sand, Alex steps closer and snarls at Ava. He charges into her shoulder and she panics, coughing and rubbing her eyes. Before Zen has a moment to react, Wes comes crashing into Alex like a freak wedge.

“You don’t ever hit a woman,” Wes grunts with a feral anger, his lips brushing against Alex’s ear. “Do you hear me?”

“Fuck you, old timer,” Alex growls back.

Wes ducks and delivers a sweeping kick to Alex’s lower legs, taking him down. On the dry end of a wet beach, he grips a clump of Alex’s hair and pulls his face in and out of the coarse sand. Zen stares in horror at Alex coughing out dusty grains. Alex gasps for air, and Zen holds out a stainless-steel water bottle, looking on with concern.

“Hey dude, you need some water?” Zen asks Alex, who wrests his way out of Wes’s grip and runs off spitting sand into his hands. “Dad, you didn’t have to do that. Thanks for being so diplomatic, yeah?”

Ava turns to Zen in disgust. “He came at me and kicked sand into my eyes! At least your dad did something about it. You didn’t even ask if I needed any water, you self-centered shit.”

“Hey!” Zen shouts. “He couldn’t breathe. Come on, Dad, what the hell was that? Were you trying to kill him or something?”

On the walk back to the car, Zen watches from behind as Ava whispers something into Wes's ear.

"Thank you. You're the best," Ava tells her boyfriend's dad.

Warm sunny days stretch into late November. Wes is in the kitchen at dawn, when he starts cooking before the sun can overtake the kitchen's comfortably cool and dewy atmosphere. By afternoon, the house is unpleasantly hot from hours of every burner going at once. The mild Mediterranean climate is a reason and an excuse to dine al fresco. Wes is a little nostalgic for something like the tie-and-sweater Thanksgivings he'd known back east. His brow gets hot as he sets folding desks on both ends of the oval dining table, merging them under a long red runner.

Wes and Zen take turns at the stove, where the turkey in the oven goes from yellow to golden. A few slabs of salmon sizzle on a skillet next to a root vegetable medley crackling in oil. Brush in hand, Wes turns off the oven to baste the turkey and step outside for some fresh air. The kitchen is getting hotter by the minute.

Turkey, salmon and tofu are the main courses. Wes and Jen arrange the festive banquet in three sections: traditional, pescetarian, and animal-free. In the living room, Fefe barks every time the doorbell rings. First Ava arrives and without a word, she disappears with Zen behind the closed door of his bedroom. A moment later, Ilan Lopez turns up with a wine bottle. He's not wearing glasses or his usual wide-brimmed hat, and his curly hair is fashionably loose. Wes receives the wine, setting it aside to hug Gabi's grieving uncle.

"Welcome to our home," Wes says, pointing to the chai pendant on his chest. "Thanks for helping me find my way back. I'm even thinking about putting a mezuzah in the door."

"Sorry, Wes, but I'm not feeling philosophical right now," Ilan replies. "On the freeway, I got cut off by some jerks who reminded me of the *cholos* that fired their guns upon Gabi. If you don't mind, I'd really like a drink."

"Did somebody say it's wine o'clock?" Alicia's bubbly voice bounces into the living room.

Amy and Clara follow Alicia inside, where they wrap Jen in a group hug. Soon Zen and Ava emerge from the bedroom in silky luau outfits, orchid necklaces and velvet shirts with flowery patterns and rhinestone accents. Ilan mingles with Jen's yoga friends, but he looks uneasy when Fefe paws at the hem of his pants. Holding a squeaky chew toy, Wes scoops up Fefe and carries her singlehandedly to a little rattan sofa bed on the patio.

"Jewish *and* Mexican?" Alicia asks Ilan, twirling her silken sunny brown hair as he pours her a glass. "That's hot."

"So, Dad, what time do we cut the turkey?" Zen asks. "I'm starving for real!"

"It's cooling off," Wes responds, a baking mitt in one hand and a thick dish towel in the other. "Did I tell you we've got a few Venice locals on their way?"

"Locals?" Zen asks curiously as a heavy-handed knock comes upon the door. "Like who?"

Wes welcomes Brad, an acoustic street musician from Wisconsin making his living on the Venice boardwalk. Not long ago, Wes and Jen connected with Brad one morning over coffee on Ocean Front Walk. That day, they left a few extra bills in his open guitar case. While Brad strummed through some nineties tunes, Wes and Jen also noticed the cardboard sign at his feet, unsure whether to laugh or cry.

Formerly homeless porn star seeks help paying off student loans.

No, but seriously, my mom in Milwaukee needs a new kidney, and I need travel money to see her. Thank you, God bless.

Soon after Brad comes LaRon, a local barista with a coffee truck specializing in candy bar-flavored lattes, and his girlfriend, who stands nearly a foot taller in high heels and a sequin mermaid evening dress.

"Happy Thanksgiving, LaRon," Wes greets the dapper couple at the door. "And what is your name?"

"Aaliyah," she introduces herself melodically in a deep register, her handshake unusually firm.

"Love your name," Wes warmly replies, waving them

inside. "So glad you came."

"Oh. My. God," Jen says in stunned admiration. "That is the most beautiful dress. Girl, are you in the movies?"

Aaliyah laughs out loud, a little bump emerging on the front of her throat. "I'll be on TV next week for a car commercial."

LaRon leans in to clasp Wes's hand in a close shake. "Hey, Wes," he whispers discreetly. "My momma hasn't met Aaliyah yet."

"Why not?" Wes asks. "She's lovely."

"Momma ain't ready. She real old school from Compton, man. Still against gay marriage. We didn't get invited anywhere else, so thank you for thinking of us, homeboy."

Wes firms a hand on LaRon's shoulder and they embrace. "Anytime, brother. The house came with a built-in espresso maker. Come check it out."

From the patio, Jen taps a fork on her wineglass. Everyone except Ilan and Jen's friends from yoga class are gathering in the backyard garden.

"This is our first Thanksgiving as a family," Jen begins as the chatter goes silent. "Thank you to my yoga girls, for helping me stay sane while writing a screenplay. Yesterday, I got some news about the script, which is on the way to Amsterdam. Soon, entertainment lawyers will be reviewing a contract with a little company in my hometown. That's Netflix."

"So proud of you, babe!" Wes calls out from behind the turkey, prompting a round of pithy applause.

"This is also my first time celebrating Thanksgiving," Jen continues, holding up her glass. "In the Netherlands, *Dankdag* is a religious holiday on the first Wednesday of November. Not many Dutch people celebrate it. And later, I'll definitely be kissing the chef who made this little feast possible. Love you, Wes. Happy Thanksgiving, everyone."

In his California bear apron, Wes takes a slim carving knife to the golden glazed gobbler. Most of the dinner guests skip the turkey and instead help themselves to salmon or stir-fried tofu. LaRon moves straight to the dessert table. When he digs into the pumpkin pie and Wes offers him a dinner plate, LaRon quietly confesses that before picking up Aaliyah, he'd had a quick, early meal with momma in Compton.

"Thank you," says Ava as Wes hands her a plate of salmon. "That's my favorite dish. You always think of me."

"Hopefully Zen thinks of you too," Wes returns, holding together a concerned smile. "Doesn't he?"

Ava doesn't answer. In the stony, hardscaped backyard where succulents bloom in dry shade, Zen is nowhere to be found. "Where did he go?"

Wes doesn't have to look very far. From the patio, he follows the earthy scent of skunk weed trailing from inside, where Zen and Brad are hitting the joint.

"Zen?" Wes says, trying to conceal his distaste for the ashes dropping into the kitchen sink. "Are you going to pay attention to Ava today?"

Zen coughs out a big cloud of smoke and rips into a cackling laugh. "You seem to be doing enough of that, Dad."

"I don't think that's funny," Wes responds.

Zen drops the roach in the sink and walks away, leaving Wes to run the tap over the ashes. Across the kitchen, Brad shrugs and returns to his gravy-drenched plate of stacked white meat, a mountain of sweet yams, and sliced cranberries. Slim and scrappy Brad is a real Midwesterner, a meat-and-potatoes kind of guy who could eat like a horse without gaining an ounce.

"Thanks for having me over, Mister Levine," Brad says, taking his plate outside.

"Hey, Prince Charming," Wes discreetly approaches Zen. "You should treat Ava better."

"Yeah, whatever."

Wes stands over the sink stacked with dirty dishes, where a dank stench lingers on. In a moment of solitude, Wes wonders if there's too much turkey or not enough animal-free options for the guests spilling in and out of the house. Through the kitchen window, Wes looks out to the patio, where Jen is serving Brad a second plate. A week ago on the boardwalk, Brad won Wes over with a stirring rendition of an emotional Collective Soul song.

"Happy Thanksgiving," Brad says to Jen. "Soon, I've got to

be back on the boardwalk with my guitar."

At the kitchen sink, Wes glimpses tension on both sides of the window. In the living room, he sees Ilan relaxing on the sofa between Alicia and Clara. The buttons on his shirt are halfway undone. Clara plays with Ilan's spiraling curls as Clara caresses his bare chest. Meanwhile on the other side of the glass, Ava and Zen are out on the patio getting into it. She points a finger at his face and a piece of salmon falls off her plate. They're both spitting words that quickly turn ugly.

"Did you want to give Alex mouth-to-mouth?" Ava acidly asks. "If Wes wasn't there to stand up for me, I would've had no one!"

"Ava, you need to chill," Zen responds. "Okay, so my dad didn't have to shove Alex's face in the sand like that. If I touched him, I'd get disqualified from the HBSO. Tell me what you would've done differently, Ava?"

Ava looks on in disbelief. "I'm done here," she says flatly.

"Come on baby," Zen pleads with her. "I am certified in CPR, because it is not in my nature to hurt. I'm a healer."

Ava looks away. "Aloha, Zen."

"What are you saying?" Zen asks her.

"After I graduate in December, I'm going to Hawaii without you," Ava replies. "Aloha means goodbye."

"Hey Ava," Wes gently says as he heads outside to the stone patio. "Can I get you anything?"

Ava's forced smile fades fast. "I'm have to go, Wes."

"Is everything okay?" Wes asks.

"I'm going to do what you told me I should do, and start surfing competitively again," Ava resolves. "You know, Wes, you would've also been an amazing dad to a daughter. I hope if Zen ever has one, he'll understand how things sometimes happen to girls that they're too ashamed to talk about."

Wes opens the patio door. "We can talk inside if you like."

"It's so obvious Zen didn't grow up with a dad," Ava says on a walk through the house with Wes. "Maybe things would've been different if you'd been with him all along."

Wes feels that remark like a knife to the chest. "I guess everyone's circumstances are different."

"Before I go, I should probably tell you why things have been weird between us. Zen's supposed to be my boyfriend, but he did nothing when Alex attacked me. And earlier, out of the blue Zen brings up surf camp in Mission Beach. I try really hard not to think about that summer when I was fourteen."

"Hey Ava," Wes says. "I don't want to pencil in the lines any more than you're comfortable sharing, but…"

"I was sexually assaulted," Ava shares straightforwardly. "The man who came into my room and groped me was a migrant worker. When I called the police, I only told them he was looking for something to eat. They arrested him, and his whole family got deported. As the whitest girl in SoCal, that was not a good look."

"Ava, I'm stunned," Wes says, equally surprised at the four-way make out session intensifying on the sofa behind them. "You're brave for sharing your story."

"Thanks for being so cool and kind to me," Ava says from the front door. "Happy Thanksgiving, Wes."

"Yes," Ilan utters from where he lay sprawling on the sofa with three pretty women descending on his bearded face with carefree kisses. "A very happy Thanksgiving."

"Just so you know, we do have other rooms in this house," Wes offers, slyly winking at Ilan and nearly half of Jen's yoga class twirling their fingers in his chest hair.

"This is more than I usually eat in a week," Brad says, cradling two foil-wrapped paper plates. "I need to grab my guitar and get back to work. Maybe next Thanksgiving I'll be able to afford a flight home to Milwaukee. My mom's health hasn't been good."

"I'm so sorry to hear that, Brad," Wes replies, patting him on the shoulder. "Just a minute. Let's get you a carrying bag."

Wes returns from the kitchen with a Ralphs tote and asks Brad to wait for another minute. On his phone, Wes scrolls through some last-minute flight deals on Expedia.

"I could have you on a plane to Milwaukee in two hours," Wes says.

"You could what?" Brad asks. "I mean, what do you mean?

"It'll be around ten o'clock when you land, but at least you'll get to see your mom."

"What are saying, Wes?"

"What I'm saying is that I'll buy you a round-trip ticket, from the City of Angels to Cream City and back again. Just tell me what day you'd like for the return flight."

Brad nearly drops the tote when he reaches out for a hug. "You're a legend. Thank you so much, man."

When they arrive at the airport, Brad steps out of the car with a bulky travel bag in one hand, his hardshell guitar case in the other. The departures zone at LAX is a clusterfuck as always, that sulfuric stench of diesel forever drifting to the curbside. Standing outside the parked car, Brad lingers for a moment, trying to speak over the din of airport traffic.

"Why did you do this for me?" Brad asks. "I mean, I don't know how I can ever thank you."

"You already have," Wes tells him. "That day on the boardwalk, the way you played 'The World I Know' really hit me in the chest."

Brad blushes and looks away. "C'mon. Don't bullshit me."

Wes grins, quietly cooking up a different response. "Okay. Here goes. Four years ago, my mom got COVID. Her health took a turn for the worse and I didn't get to see her one last time."

"I'm really sorry," Brad responds, offering a handshake. "This means so much to me."

"Go ahead, buddy," Wes says, slipping on his Ray Ban pilot sunglasses. "Just be there with your mom."

"This is going to be the best Thanksgiving," Brad says, taking sideways steps into the airport terminal, lumbered with the weight of his guitar case and duffel bag.

Brad's departure brings Wes to tears. He pulls himself together and cuts through some congestion in Inglewood. The westward drive home is wide-open freeways all the way to the coast. Wes returns to an emptier house, where the briefly festive holiday celebration is now eerily tranquil.

"Where did everyone go?" Wes asks.

"My girls and your buddy Ilan would've turned Thanksgiving into a full-blown orgy if I didn't tell them to go get a room," Jen calls out from the kitchen, where she's loading plates of leftovers into the fridge.

"Hey, hey," Wes utters from the doorway, where LaRon and Aaliyah are heading out. "Hope you both enjoyed yourselves. Sorry I had to step out for a minute there."

"All good, my brother," LaRon replies, leaning in for a hug. "Aaliyah's gotta get home to take her medicine."

Aaliyah smiles faintly, clasping hands with Wes, who squeezes her palm for a show of support. "Lovely to see you today, Aaliyah. Take care, now."

"Let's do espresso," LaRon says, giving Wes another close handshake on the way out.

"Drop by whenever, man!" Wes says as the last guests leave. "Feels like we've kicked everyone out early," he tells Jen, scanning the abandoned remains of the Thanksgiving shindig. "Even Ilan?"

"Especially Ilan," Jen replies. "It got weird when Amy tried to get us to join them."

"Us?" Wes asks.

"Yep. Like, me and you, and my yoga teacher. They say anything goes in California. But I don't share."

"Guess that's just life in the fast lane. After everything Ilan has been through, that man deserves all the joy he can get."

"You should have a talk with Zen," Jen says. "He's not taking his breakup very well."

Wes lightly taps on Zen's bedroom door. Laying on his rumpled bedsheets, Zen scrolls on his phone without looking up.

"Hey buddy, what's new?" Wes asks.

Zen mindlessly picks at the purple petals on his orchid necklace. "I should've never trusted her with my passwords. The fucking bitch took all my videos down."

"Come on now," Wes responds. "I didn't raise you to disrespect women like that."

Zen springs off the bed and throws his phone into the mattress. "You didn't raise me at all. You weren't even there!"

"I wish I was," Wes returns his son's anger with calmness.

"This is going to change everything," Zen says shakily.

"You know, the Internet isn't the only place where life happens. When I was your age, hardly anyone had a cell phone."

"Without those videos, I have no online presence."

"But you're so close to winning the surf off, Zen. That's the real money. You'll win the HBSO with or without those videos."

Zen cracks a smile and bumps his dad on the arm. "I'm thankful and all, but I don't know what to make of Thanksgiving. Feels like a pretty chaotic day."

"You know something?" Wes asks, bringing a few plates out to the patio. "Thanksgiving has always been one of my favorite holidays. Back in Baltimore, it's usually kind of cold in late November. And now, I'm loving this whole dinner outside thing. Just tank tops, board shorts, and my beautiful family."

"Dad, you're more Cali than Cali," Zen says.

"The truth is, all of this could disappear tomorrow," Wes replies soberly, raising his glass of dealcoholized Pinot Noir. "But I'm grateful for every moment we get to spend in California. Here's to our family and friends."

"To family and friends," Jen puts in, raising her wine glass.

"Cheers to freedom," Zen toasts, taking a bite out of a turkey leg. "Let's enjoy it while it lasts."

11

In utter darkness before the first daylight, Zen reaches into the nightstand drawer for his phone, a hemp wick lighter and a pre-rolled cone. He wakes and bakes, and burns a half-hour bed rotting with a finger on the block button. So far, around twenty of Ava's mutuals have dropped off Zen's friend list. Her relationship status is now unlisted, and she's taken down every photo of them but a smiley portrait drawn by a caricaturist at Disneyland. In a moment of clarity, Zen goes into Messenger to try and beg Ava to repost all the surf videos no longer appearing on any platforms. But before he can type a single letter, a notification informs him it's no longer possible to send messages to Ava Davidson on Facebook.

A wavy trail of pot smoke follows him to the bathroom. With the burning joint dangling from his lips, Zen takes down his wetsuit from the ceiling hook and packs it into a see-through dry bag. Instead of sitting around and waiting for the break of day, Zen springs for an early morning Uber to the Huntington Beach Pier. The Suburu has a hatchback but no roof rack. And so, Zen sits in the back next to his buckled-in surfboard, letting the tail stick out the open window. It's five o'clock in the morning and already cars on the 405 are snarling to a crawl.

Soon, the traffic jam loosens up and numbers on the fare meter start falling away at a mile a minute. At dawn on the day of the final round, a sliver of golden sunlight cracks a sky as dark as outer space. The bulky, broad-shouldered driver's name is Chinua. He's from Mongolia, doesn't surf but likes to watch, and doesn't charge Zen extra for the surfboard that barely fits in the backseat.

Alone on the beach at sunrise, Zen does his lunges and squats, arm circles and leg lifts. Between reps, Zen checks his phone to monitor his social media metrics, eyeing the royalty ledgers on four platforms for the money on its way. Even before Ava went nuclear and deplatformed him, Zen's numbers had been slipping. The next payment from YouTube is going to be a thousand dollars less than October's statement. On his empty Instagram profile, Zen's bleeding followers by the hour.

"All that content. Gone," Zen mumbles to himself, looking across the sand at someone approaching him from the pier.

"Hey Zen, you're early!"

"Hey, good morning!" Zen calls back to Hillary, who's walking across the sand in a maroon Harvard hoodie. "How was your trip?"

"Orientation was easy," Hillary replies. "But once I start law school next Fall, that's when the real grind begins."

"It's super cool of you to come out and support this event," Zen says. "I've been getting my stretch on."

"Same here," Hillary says, stretching her arms into a V-shape. "I'm back in the **HBSO**."

"Really? That's cool. While you were gone, things kind of went off the rails with **Alex**."

Hillary doesn't respond, and instead digs into her wetsuit bag. "I forgot sunscreen. Zen, could you spot me some?"

"Yeah, of course," Zen eagerly hands her a silver tube of Panama Jack. "I brought plenty of sunscreen. I'm from Amsterdam and didn't wear sunscreen much before we moved to California."

Hillary smiles warmly. "My mom's family is Dutch, and *mijn oma* was born in Utrecht."

"That's where some of my grandparents were from," Zen replies.

So, what happened to your socials?" Hillary asks. "The

videos aren't on YouTube anymore."

"Well, it's a long story," Zen stammers as the first spectators meander to the shore. "Good luck, today, Hillary. I've got to find the changing rooms and jump into my wetsuit."

"Okay," Hillary replies, rubbing a white layer of sunscreen on the back of her neck. "What about your…"

"Keep the sunscreen," Zen says in a hurry. "I got plenty."

When Zen returns to the beach, Hillary and Alex are standing beside their boards. The three finalists contemplate the uneventful waves. In a rare about-face, Alex gives Zen a high five and they wish each other luck in the final round.

"I guess it's just the three of us," Zen says. "Stay safe, and let's all come out of there in one piece."

"Hey, Zen!" Wes and Jen call to their son from across the flat beach.

Zen turns around. "Oh, hey Dad," Zen replies. "I'd ask you to wish me good luck, but these swells aren't giving us much to work with."

"Things can change in the blink of an eye," Wes tells him. "Anyway, your mom got a tripod, so maybe with a couple good video clips, you can build up your online presence again."

"I'm not really thinking about that," Zen says. "What you said last night is true. There's more to life than the Internet."

From the other side of the lifeguard tower, Coach Jon Spencer taps his necklace whistle, stopping short of blowing into it when introducing the finalists. Jon also has a bullhorn in his hand, but he decides against giving a long ceremonial introduction to the 2024 Huntington Beach Surf Off, because hardly anyone is showing up to watch.

The finalists move beyond the breaker waves, queueing in the sparse lineup. They paddle into different directions, biding their time for a decent tube. Alex and Hillary take their shots first, gliding to the shore with predictable, almost synchronized moves. Zen's wave is equally unspectacular. The entire vibe of the HBSO is strangely egalitarian.

An hour into the final round, the few remaining spectators on the beach disperse and leave. Coach Spencer admits that all the good waves came yesterday. But as soon as a gust of offshore wind comes along, Zen sees his chance. The wind holds up the liquid wall long enough for Zen to jump with his board as the peak starts to curl. Hillary and Alex are already on the beach, shaking hands and gesturing shaka signs to anyone still hanging around.

Jen yanks the camera off the tripod to show it to Zen. "So proud of you! I got the whole thing on video."

"Mom, please don't," Zen begs her. "The waves today were nothing to brag about. We might as well have done the finals at Water World."

"That was one hell of a finish," Wes says. "You'll win this."

"Win what exactly?" Zen asks bluntly. "It would at least mean something if we'd gotten some serious swells today."

Coach Jon Spencer looks tired and disappointed when he joins the three finalists outside a tower, where judges have been reviewing footage of the final round.

"I didn't see this coming," Jon announces to the surfers and the few remaining spectators standing nearby. "But today is ending in a draw. We're going to need you for one more event. Before leaving today, please confirm your travel availability by email, copying me and the committee. Make sure your passports are up to date, because the last round of the HBSO won't be in the United States."

"Where is it, then?" Alex asks. "I don't have a passport."

"For a fee, a passport can be rushed to you in a few days," Jon replies. "You'll have a week to get your plans in order."

"Who came up with this contingency plan?" Hillary asks. "By definition, the HBSO was supposed to be entirely in California."

"We've come too far to forfeit," Jon replies. "I'm looking at three world class surfers right now. One of you is going to win a lot of money."

"The only question is, win it where?" Zen asks.

"To answer Hillary's question about our Plan B," Jon circles back. "When you signed up for the surf off, you agreed to the possibility of international travel if a winner was not named after the final round. All of this is in the fine print."

"The HBSO is supposed to end today. It's really second rate

to spring this on us, Coach," Hillary says. "It's my last holiday season before law school. I was going to spend it with my family in Malibu."

"Look, I hate to beg. But I hope you'll stay in the contest for one more round," the coach says. "If you decide to bail, then we have to call on the runners-up. Most of them would give their eyeteeth for an opportunity like this, but they're not as ready you are."

"It's messed up," Alex tells the coach. "So, you're saying if I don't get a passport, I lose the surf off and the registration money I paid all those times?"

"The rules are the rules," Jon responds without emotion. "As soon as a decision is made about where we'll have the final round, you'll be the first to know. Keep an eye on your inboxes. Just stay stoked for a couple more weeks."

Jen and her yoga girlfriends are spending the weekend at a cabin in Ojai for a bachelorette party, and so Wes and Zen decide to get away, too. They temporarily abandon the familiar bohemian mystique of Venice, fastening two surfboards on the roof rack. Taking the freeways north for a change, they chase the swells to Santa Cruz. On the winding coastal highway, the rocky, rugged expanse feels open and endless. Fefe's in a basket harness with a secure strap. Zen stays in the backseat, keeping a water bowl and a chewy snack at the ready. Approaching the plunging cliffs in Big Sur, Wes loses signal for a while and his navigation system stops working. Parked on a curvy roadside, they take in sweeping coastal bluffs from atop a staggering cliff. Zen hovers protectively over Fefe when she does her business next to a hillside sagebrush. She doesn't seem to realize the heights of her surroundings, but Zen and Wes definitely do.

With the ocean at their backs, they huddle on the narrow shoulder of another wide-open scenic road to snap a few selfies with Fefe, and spend the evening cruising leisurely through a vivid golden sunset washing over a redwood forest. Awaiting them on the coast is a cozy, pet-friendly cottage in Santa Cruz. In the living room, the giant plush cuddler dog bed is too big for tiny Fefe, but it will have to do. Wes carries sleeping, snoring Fefe into the middle of the cuddler. Around midnight, they wake up to a shrill, empty-sounding cry. Wes and Zen come closer to comfort Fefe, when it becomes clear they must move her bed into one of their rooms. Fefe's frantic breathing settles once Wes is cradling her on his chest, and Zen helps her slip into a baby pajama jumpsuit. They both stay by Fefe's side while she falls back asleep, tucking her in with a pocket-sized patchwork quilt that came with the rental.

"I think Fefe woke up not knowing where she was," Zen whispers to his dad, whose face is covered in his hands. "Dad, what's wrong?"

"I'm okay," Wes responds, pulling himself together. "For a minute, I thought something was wrong. But she's okay."

He looks into his father's teary eyes without saying anything at first. "It's okay to cry," Zen says in a flat northern European monotone.

"I know," Wes sighs. "When I heard Fefe cry, it reminded me of everything I missed in your life, Zen. I mean, how did your mom even choose your name?"

"All she ever told me was that she got a vibe from you," Zen replies, trying to keep his voice down for Fefe nestling under the little quilt. "You made her feel calm and happy, so she named me Zen."

"We could've been a family," Wes says. "All those years, I was in the middle of Amsterdam and you and your mom were all the way on the other side of town. I guess it's a real cosmic miracle we even found each other."

"And Fefe," Zen blurts out. "Imagine if no one had come for her when those two gay guys drove off a cliff."

"Those two gay guys had names," Wes replies, clenching the chai pendant around his neck. "Their names were Ross and Kyle. May their memories continue to bring blessings into our lives."

"I didn't mean to disrespect their memories like that," Zen apologizes, sincere but irked. "Time to sleep, Dad. Epic swells are in the forecast tomorrow."

A mid-morning walk takes Wes, Zen and Fefe through a

quiet street of shuttered shops around Pleasure Point: Pleasure Pizza, Pleasure Liquors, Pleasure Window Cleaners. The slow, pensive stroll along a blufftop park leads them to beach access stairs at the edge of the world, where sand and stone are the only partitions between coastal range bungalows and the ocean. On the way down the steep wooden steps, Zen clings to his board, and to Fefe's leash. About ten surfers are paddling in the ocean. They seem to know the breaks intimately well, and most of them are quick to commit to easy swells. Zen recommends waiting for the current lineup to finish.

"Surfers are territorial," Zen says. "It's a weekday, so they'll probably come out soon and go to work. Look at that?"

Wes looks out to sea. "What am I looking at?"

"Those waves are easy rollers," Zen replies. "Perfect for you, but the more seasoned locals were probably hoping for some real swells."

"It's been more than twenty years," Wes concedes. "But it's not like I've never caught a tube before."

"What made you want to surf, Dad?"

"I don't know," Wes replies flatly. "What makes anyone want to surf?"

"I live for the adrenaline," Zen says. "A gnarly wave comes and goes, but the stoke lives on long after."

"Think about this. I've gone two decades without touching a surfboard," Wes puts it bluntly. "You don't think that it's too late for someone my age?"

"Too late? It's never too late," Zen responds almost immediately. "You're a strong swimmer. You've said it yourself, that's half the battle."

"Before we surf, we need to find someone to watch Fefe."

"I'll look for a local dogwalker on Facebook," Zen suggests, clicking into the app. "If they can also watch her, that should give us a few hours."

"Do you think we can find one at such short notice?"

"I already did," Zen answers, clicking onscreen to confirm. "Sarah from Capitola Village just offered to take care of Fefe. A hundred bucks for the day. Her profile says she prefers smaller dogs."

Sarah parks her silver Prius in front of Verve Coffee Roasters on Bronson Avenue. Straight away, Fefe leaps into Sarah's arms, playfully nipping at her fingers. Zen helps Fefe get comfortable in the backseat, securing her in the basket. From the café, Wes takes out a carrying tray of warm seasonal coffee creations: gingerbread, peppermint mocha, and an alcohol-free whiskey latte. Wes brings the tray to the driver side window, giving Sarah the first pick. On the return drive to Pleasure Point, Wes and Zen sip their lattes without a care in the world. But by the time they're in wetsuits with their boards on the beach, the tide changes and the shoreline shifts. Wes takes one look at the cold Pacific water tumbling ever closer the shore, and he freezes up.

"Instead of coffee, I should've asked Sarah for a joint. Or maybe a muscle relaxer," Wes says. "I'm just a little nervous."

"I'll be right by your side," Zen assures him. "I can talk you through it. Trust me on this, Dad. I know CPR."

Wes cracks a proud smile. "I went scuba diving with my dad the day before he died. We were supposed to go out again the next morning. He went. I didn't. A part of me has stayed stuck in that moment, when the tsunami hit Phuket. It's been like that for more than twenty years, Zen. I feel like it's now or never. Either I've got to face my fears, or just learn to live with them."

"So, what are you saying?" Zen asks with great concern.

"Well, what I'm saying is," Wes pauses, patting Zen's shoulder as they dash to the ocean. "See you in the surf, my beautiful son."

Together, they make their way into the breaker zone, where the swells that lift them are more forceful than what meets the eye.

"Have you ever entered through the backdoor?" Zen asks.

Wes balks at the question. "Have I ever done what?"

"Backdoor surfing. It's when you start on the other side of the peak. That sets you up to go straight into the barrel and then ride it across. But first, you've got to find the curl, and bend your knees without locking up. Be ready to move."

Wes nods in agreement, trying to replay a loop of Zen's

instructions. "I'm asking you to be honest with me, Zen. No bullshit. Do you think I can pull this off?"

"I know you can," Zen says. "Just think of the epic memories you'll always have. Being on the inside of a curl is like cutting through glass. That falling water is the most beautiful freaking sight I've ever seen. Now the waves are breaking to the right, so let's plan accordingly."

"Is this the one move you did in that video?" Wes asks.

Zen doesn't have time to respond. Paddling vigorously, he points to a clean-looking set bestowed on them by a generous groundswell. "That's the one. Go get it!"

At first, Wes balks at the six-footer cresting behind him. Springing to his feet, Wes hears the voice of his nineteen-year-old son calling for him to lock up, to bend but not too much. As the wave curls, Wes finds himself caught inside, looking through a curling, shimmering cascade. He can barely see the beach beyond the spray, and no longer hears Zen's voice guiding his moves. In that moment, Wes is on his own. On a wave. On a roll. And also, on a quest to locate Zen.

Salt water stings his eyes. Wes calls out Zen's name, panicking until he flops off the board. Wes paddles ashore and finds Zen on the beach, kneeling beside an unconscious boy in swim trunks. While humming the repetitive chorus of Pinkfong's 'Baby Shark,' Zen delivers swift compressions into the boy's chest until he's coughing out ocean water. His parents come rushing frantically, crying in Spanish while a strange young man in a wetsuit resuscitates their child. From the pier, three medical ATVs plow through the sand, arriving on the scene with aluminum oxygen tanks.

"I was catching a wave when I saw him drift with the current," Zen explains to one of the medics. "It took a minute for me to swim over and pull him out."

The emergency responders strap the boy on a long yellow backboard, deploying an oxygen mask and lifting him into the skid unit on the biggest of three ATVs.

"Mateo, Mateo!" the boy's parents cry out as medics lift their son into the ambulance.

"As soon as I saw him getting swept into the current," Zen

says to Mateo's mom. "I swam closer and got him out of the water. We were on the beach in two minutes. He's going to be fine."

"You saved a child's life today, Zen," Wes says solemnly as they walk with their boards up 41st Avenue, where joggers tread along a jagged cliffside.

"What if the HBSO ended in Huntington Beach as planned?" Zen asks. "Who would've been there for Mateo?"

"Did you hear back from the coach?"

"Let me check my messages," Zen says, reaching into the drybag for his phone. "Holy shit. The final round is in ten days! Coach Spencer says they've decided on next weekend in Nazaré."

"Where's that?" Wes asks.

"Portugal," Zen replies. "Nazaré has got some of the biggest waves anywhere in the world. By the way, I'm freaking proud of you, Dad."

"Really?" Wes asks in disbelief. "Why?"

"You just cut through that tube like a bat out of hell!"

"I thought I almost lost you there," he replies. "In that moment, I was only focused on finding you. I wasn't thinking about the wave, but I remember it was beautiful. Almost like cutting through glass."

"I wanted to ride it with you," Zen says. "But then I saw the little dude Mateo was in real trouble. Sometimes, duty calls."

Wes wraps his arm around Zen's shoulder as they stare at the sneaker waves tumbling into the low-lying shore. "Let's pick up Fefe. We've got a big trip to plan."

On the drive north from Lisbon's international airport, Wes and Zen take in the rolling hills and ridge-terraced vineyards on steep slopes. Eventually, the hills fade into a sandy coastal plain, with patches of hardy, swaying shrubs lining the road. During the ride, they rattle off their first impressions of Portugal: *ancient and rustic, gentle and tranquil, a dreamlike tapestry of color and ruins.* The coastline feels small and provincial after spending months on California's colossal coast. Zen looks out the passenger window and his expression sinks in disappointment over Nazaré, which looks nothing like the sky-high swells he remembers seeing on YouTube.

Beyond the beach, the cliffside road overlooks a dense village of quaint red terracotta rooftops. One of those red rooftops is their rental, a cottage tucked deep within a cluster of beach-facing homes. Wes steers the rental car into a stony street and parks the all-electric supermini when the shrinking path turns impassable. The cottage is a small, pet-friendly space with soft carpets and decorative padding along the white stucco walls.

"Fefe would've loved this," Wes says.

Through the dense wooden door, Zen enters the cottage carrying a black Under Armour duffel bag and long gun surfboard. "Make sure you send mom a DM reminding her to spend time with Fefe," he tells his dad. "Lately she's been living in her screenplay."

"Don't worry. We'll FaceTime them a little later," Wes says. "For now, let's check out the beach."

As they set out on a walk to *Praia de Nazaré*, Wes turns around to pluck a jacket from his suitcase. The cool, damp air smells faintly like the brink of rainfall. For all the hype about Portugal's monster waves, the barrels are shockingly unremarkable. With around twenty wetsuits paddling for swells, the lineup is crowded, but everyone on the water is bodyboarding on low rollers.

"Must be amateur hour," Zen comments. "How could anyone call this a challenge?"

"The finals round is at the North Beach, a few miles from here," Wes says, pointing in that direction. *"Praia do Norte* has an underwater canyon. It's three miles deep and twenty-five miles long."

Zen scoffs. "Ha! Don't threaten me with a good time, Dad."

Wes stares deeply into Zen's eyes. "You're my only son, and I can't bear the thought of something happening to you. Keep in mind a surfer died there last year."

Zen turns away. "Man, you really do know how to kill the mood. I don't need to hear about that kind of shit."

"Look, I'm sorry if it's my PTSD talking. But I've seen the

ocean at its best and worst. I know what I'm talking about."

"And I know what I'm doing."

"Sometimes I think surviving a tsunami is even harder than dying in one," Wes confesses. "You never forget it for as long as you live."

"I've already heard this a million times. Dad, I'm sorry for what happened to you, and for all the horrible things you had to see. But we've got lives to live."

"This is going to sound cliché," Wes says. "But one day if you become a parent, maybe you'll understand where I'm coming from."

"Hey Zen," a familiar voice beckons from the gentle foamy waters. "Are you loving Portugal or what?"

"Hillary!" Zen replies as they come together for a hug, her hair and wetsuit feeling damp and salty on his land clothes. "We're fresh off the plane."

"I've been swimming in Nazaré for a couple days," Hillary says. "But I haven't been to the North Beach yet."

"Me neither," Zen adds. "This is a good start. The waves here are pretty chill."

Hillary locks eyes with Zen, touching his arm. "I heard about the drowning child you saved in Santa Cruz. It was all over my newsfeed. You're a hero back in California."

"But what if you hadn't told me to take that CPR class? You're the real hero, Hillary."

With an inviting smile, Hillary pulls back her wet hair, accentuating her high cheekbones and deep blue eyes. "Feel like going for a swim?"

"Sure," Zen replies quickly. "Aren't you with Alex?"

"No. In fact, I'm trying to avoid him. On our connecting flight out of Atlanta, I sat a few aisles away from Alex, and heard him acting racist to a Black flight attendant."

"He wasn't acting," Zen clarifies. "That's who he is."

"Alex is at the North Beach wearing himself out on big waves," Hillary says. "Coach Spencer advised against it. That's like running twenty miles the day before a marathon."

"Good analogy," Wes chimes in. "I ran the Amsterdam Marathon last year. And get this, my time was four-twenty."

Zen winces awkwardly at his dad. "Okay. We're going to head out for a swim. Let's catch up later, yeah?"

"I'll see what's going on in town," Wes agrees. "Have fun."

"I'm glad you're here, Hillary," Zen says as they walk to the water.

"But Zen?" Hillary asks. "Aren't you with Ava?"

Zen shakes his head. "We broke up on Thanksgiving. She took down all my social media content, and now I feel like a big nobody."

"No way," Hillary calmly replies. "You made it to finals not because of your videos, but because you're a bad ass. Back in Malibu, I know plenty of serious surfers who still don't have a presence on YouTube."

"At first it was a shock seeing all my videos deleted," Zen recalls. "But then I came to realize where I went wrong. Ava spent so many hours with a camera in her hand, making it possible for me to have this self-indulgent ego trip. Guess I didn't show her how much I appreciate everything she's done for me."

Hillary smiles at him. "You're very self-aware, Zen. I love that about you."

"You're warm," Zen says to Hillary, the small of her hand gracing his shoulder. "Can I?"

Hillary leans in and they almost kiss. Before their lips touch, she tilts her head oceanward. "It's cold. You'll want a wetsuit."

"Is there a changing room along the promenade?"

"Just change on the beach. Everyone does," Hillary suggests. "See you in the water."

Zen strips down to his underwear and kicks off the board shorts, looking around in case anyone on the beach is watching him. One leg at a time, he jumps into his neoprene wetsuit and leaves his land clothes and drybag on the soft, golden sand. Zen follows Hillary into the ocean and they swim past the breakers to where surfers on the sand look like tiny seals in their black wetsuits. Paddling further still, Zen keeps his head above water, kicking his feet and having no idea what ocean depth lurks beneath his feet.

"Hey?" Hillary whispers, holding hands with Zen as they

tread water together. "How are you holding up?"

"Not bad," Zen replies. "Feeling pretty good."

"Same," she says to Zen in the moment they move close enough for their lips to align.

What starts with softness and restraint quickly slides into a faster, more succulent kiss. A sudden gust flattens a train of slow waves, but it's the onshore wind that powers their swim back to the shore. There, they hop out of the wetsuits, baring private parts on a public beach while getting dressed in their land clothes.

"I live by a simple rule," Hillary says, slipping a sports bra over her full, rounded breasts. "What anyone thinks of me is none of my business."

"Can I tell you what I think?" Zen asks earnestly. "I think you're amazing. I knew how to save a life because of you. A little boy who almost drowned in Santa Cruz is alive today because you cared enough to remind me that every surfer should know CPR. If I lose tomorrow, it'd be an honor just to have shared the final round with you. And if I win, I don't know if I could totally accept it."

"Oh, come on," Hillary nudges him, smiling playfully. "You're going to kill it tomorrow. But before either of us can win, we've got to get past Alex. He's so obnoxious."

"Together, we're stronger," Wes says confidently. "Should we plan it out?"

"It's better to see what the day brings. Mother Nature makes the plans," Hillary explains. "All we can do is make adjustments."

"So," Wes says, walking along the coastal promenade where the savory scent of fresh pizza warms the colorful windowfront walkup. "Why don't we grab a bite?"

"Tomorrow's the big day," Hillary replies. "I was thinking about laying low tonight. Let's get some takeout and unwind at my rental, which has Netflix."

"I'm game," Wes says, following Hillary through a narrow side street that opens into an alley of sea-view terraced condos.

After midnight, Zen returns to the rental cottage without a key. He knocks on the solid wood door and waits to the calming sound of waves murmuring close by. Finally, Wes opens up.

"Zen, really?" Wes says in mild irritation as Wes walks by.

"I missed your texts," Zen responds while hanging his wetsuit on the shower rod. "I was with Hillary."

"We've got to be on the beach tomorrow morning at six sharp," Wes says, stifling a yawn. "When you didn't reply, I was worried something happened."

"Sorry to make you worry, but we were having a nice time," Zen tells his dad. "Let's just say I wasn't focused on my phone."

"Don't get me wrong. I think Hillary's great. But as your manager, I'm not sure it's wise to spend so much time with your competition."

"Actually, I surf better when I like the people in the water with me," Zen answers matter-of-factly. "And besides, I like her. A lot."

"Glad you finally came back," Wes says. "Jetlag's kicking my ass, so I'm about to crash. Let's both set the alarms on our phones."

Wes wakes up to a dead phone, and his American charger doesn't fit into the double round pin socket behind the nightstand. Without an international plug adapter in his luggage, Wes powers on his laptop and connects the cable to a port. Slowly, the battery catches a charge and the phone turns on. Zen is still sound asleep when Wes knocks on the side of his bedroom door. They rush outside carrying Zen's longest board. His wetsuit is still a little damp, but it will have to do.

They touch sand on the North Beach a few minutes after seven. A couple dozen locals in festive flannels and floral dresses are on the beach, swaying with the morning breeze. Though no music is playing, most of them look ready to dance.

"Sorry I'm late," Zen says to Coach Jon Spencer, who's pacing circles on the beach.

"Glad you made it," Jon replies, tapping a pen on his clipboard. "Get warmed up fast, Zen. Trust me, you're going to need it out there."

"Hey, nice of you to show up," Alex hisses. "Can we get this show on the road, Coach? I stretched while the rest of us were waiting for this cosmopolitan poser to roll out of bed."

Zen shoots Alex an indignant scowl. "Eat a dick, Nazi."

Sneering, Alex steps into Zen's personal space and throws down a two-hand sign, two and three fingers. "Power to the White man. Surf City, U.S.A. rules!"

"Okay, how about a little sportsmanship?" Jon tells them.

"Sportsmanship?" Wes asks sharply. "This blatant bigot just flashed a white supremacist sign at my son, and that's all you've got?"

"Don't be stupid," Jon mutters when Wes steps closer to confront him. "Zen's worked too hard for you to get him disqualified."

"You take my son out of the HBSO, I'll see you in an L.A. courtroom."

"You might want to brush up on the fine print," Jon counters. "When Zen registered, he agreed to the rules like everyone else."

"It's funny to hear such a crooked sleazeball go on about rules," Wes begins calmly. "And you used to be an educator?"

"Look," Jon whispers. "I'm here to oversee the final round of the surf off. We have a lot of money tied up in this contest."

"Oh, I'm sure you do, Jon," Wes fires back. "I bet you made out real nice with all those repeat registration fees. Why are you allowed to be in charge of this event? You were convicted of stealing funds from a school for children with special needs."

Jon's face turns white as a sheet. "What did you say?"

"I looked you up, Coach. I saw how you cried for the judge to give you house arrest and probation."

"That's privileged information," Jon replies bashfully.

"Have a word with Alex," Wes warns the coach. "Or I will."

Jon glances up at the crowd gathering on the rocky platform, turning to the ocean to avoid looking Wes in the eye.

"Just give me a minute to talk to him, okay?"

With his back against the lifeguard tower, Wes watches them from a distance. He can't quite make out the words, but feels his stomach turn upside down when Jon pats Alex on the shoulder and they exchange affable grins. The competing finalists strike a straight-faced pose, holding their surfboards in a firm formation behind the coach, who welcomes the standing crowd to the international bonus round of the Huntington Beach Surf Off.

"This is no ordinary surf off," Jon announces, tapping on his bullhorn to test the mic. "It was supposed to end where it began, in my hometown of Huntington Beach, near Los Angeles. On the morning of what we thought would be the final round, the wind was not in our favor. But thanks to a unique partnership between our local surfing associations in California and Portugal, these three finalists will face off once more: Hillary Flanagan, Alex Linder, and Zen Souza. One winner will receive a quarter million U.S. dollars."

"Hey," Hillary whispers to Zen, giving him a fetching smile. "Good luck out there."

She dusts a little sand off her board and sighs at the ocean as the coach's bullhorn continues to blare at the Nazaré locals who might not grasp every word but smile politely at all the right moments. "Just stretch when you can, but don't let Coach Spencer scare you like that. Sorry I kept you up so late."

"It's all good. I had a great time," Zen says, turning up his thumb and pinky for a shaka sign. "Let's slay some tubes and celebrate after."

"I don't know," Hillary says reluctantly. "By now, I'm sure you've heard about the ocean floor. Winter's the big wave season, and I'm going into this with a lot anxiety."

"Hillary, I know you've got this," Zen whispers, his hand brushing against hers. "We've got this. I've seen you shred."

"We're standing on an underwater canyon," Hillary responds with caution.

"You'll do fine, Miss Malibu," Alex jeers at Hillary. "That's just your anxiety talking. Or maybe PMS."

Hillary recoils at the comment. "Fuck off, creep!"

"Check yourself, Alex," Zen says, measured and calm. "Who raised you?"

Alex stands aghast at the question. "What did you just say?"

"I said who the fuck raised you?" Zen repeats. "Talk to her like that again and I'll break your head."

Before Alex can snap back at Zen, the coach steps closer

and they stand up straight for an introduction by hometown.

"Venice Beach. Huntington Beach. Malibu." Jon announces into the bullhorn. "These three young surfers are California's crème de la crème."

"We've got to face the music," Hillary whispers to Zen as they clasp pinkies for one more moment of connection. "Let's come out of that water alive."

"We will," Zen replies. "Follow the wind, and ride it out."

"And now for some ground rules," Jon announces into the bullhorn. "The surfers will compete in three heats that begin and end where we're standing. May the good graces of Mother Nature be with our brave finalists today."

Coach Jon Spencer points the locals to a steep platform at the top of the nearest cliff. From the beach, they take the funicular up a cable railway. The cabin ascends to the top of the platform, where spectators are confronting the ocean head on. From the shore, Zen looks up at the cable car perched high on the cliff. There, his dad stands among a growing cluster of onlookers waiting for the event to begin. Hundreds are watching from the platform above, more people than all the California rounds combined. From below, the three HBSO finalists in black wetsuits face off with an ocean waking slowly with the sun.

Zen heads into the water, paddling ahead of Hillary and Alex. The shoulder peels off, giving Zen the power to ride the line. Alex pops up for a wave that peaks early and falls apart. Meanwhile, the lifeguards on jet skis are circling around the unpredictable forces in the ocean. Zen and Alex are back on the beach watching Hillary engage the rail with a swift and decisive backside carve, pulling off a stunning flip that wins her the first heat.

"Imagine having something like the Grand Canyon under the water," Coach Spencer tells the surfers from the sand. "This is home to the largest submarine canyon in all of Europe. That canyon becomes a funnel, causing a change in depth that amplifies the waves. Always try to be aware of which way the current is going, and take what you can handle. Good luck and godspeed."

The next wave is a massive wall of water that reaches cliffside heights, even splashing the lantern room atop the lighthouse. The swell rises way too high for anyone to see what's behind it. Eventually, the wave curls and Zen paddles hard to get out of the danger zone. He tucks himself into a ball and takes cover under the water. Once he comes up from the seafloor, he looks for Hillary in the penetrating whir of jet skis blowing circles in the water. She's on the other side of the break, pushing her board away to resist the sheer force of water and pull herself back to the surface. Ahead of the lineup, Alex is shredding to the shore.

From the rocky platform up above, the cliffside crowd goes bonkers for Alex, who skips past the coach to take the funicular to the top. He stirs up the crowd on the oceanfront platform, striking zany poses in selfies with mild-mannered onlookers around the lighthouse.

"I'm going back out," Zen says to Hillary, who at first stays behind. She watches him paddle on the weblike surface of an ocean about to exhale another monster wave, and follows Zen out.

With Hillary paddling closer, Zen faces the rugged headland separating the North Beach from the old village, *Sitio*, a cluster of red rooftops situated along a golden coastline.

"You okay?" Hillary asks Zen.

"I'm going for something mid, not a monster wave," Zen replies. "That last one really wiped me out."

"I'll ride it with you," Hillary insists. "Two of the lifeguards are stuck on the beach with broken jet skis. We can't afford to go out there alone."

"Then let's do this together," Wes says as a sudden splash of salt water stings his eyes.

"Fucking sneaky rat!" Alex yells from behind the current. "Get off my wave. You're nothing, Zen!"

Zen splashes him back. "You can't just drop in like that!"

"I'm from Huntington, and I'm winning this surf off, you foreign piece of shit!" Alex shouts.

"Have at it, mate!" Zen turns around, the nose of his board pointing to the beach. "Hillary, let's get ahead of this, now!"

Zen and Hillary split off, east and west. Once again, Hillary is inside the barrel, carving her way out. She springs for a stunning, gravity-defying aerial. But instead of cheering, the entire cliffside falls silent. Caught inside a rising swell, Alex is bleeding from his ankle with a snapped leash and a Great White tracking him from behind. Zen sees the shark fin circling on the water and shreds ahead with uncommon speed, racing against a wave looming high enough to touch the lighthouse, where spectators interface with the swell of a lifetime.

"Alex! Blood in the water!" the coach yells into his bullhorn.

A faint, blood-curling scream echoes across a monster wave that breaks on the sand bottom like an avalanche. On the shallow side of the roiling white water, Zen and Hillary find each other once again.

"Did you just save my life?" Zen asks, coughing out a mouthful of salt water.

"I don't know," Hillary gasps. "You might've saved mine."

In a daze, Zen drags his lips on Hillary's forehead. The funicular descends on the cables and the coach makes yet another indecipherable announcement on his bullhorn. Meanwhile, the judges are unanimous in their decision.

"Hil-la-ry! Hil-la-ry! Hil-la-ry!" the Nazaré locals cheer from inside the funicular carriage.

"Zen, are you okay?" Wes asks feverishly, rushing ahead of the crowd.

"I'm fine, Dad," Zen answers, catching his breath.

"Are you sure, son?" Wes turns to the coach, raising a finger to make a point. "Alex dropped in on Zen. Zen could've won."

"You're repulsive, Levine," Jon scoffs haughtily. "A shark just ate Alex for breakfast! And you got some nerve for digging up my past like that. I should kick your ass right now."

"Do me a favor, Coach," Wes replies with hands interlocked behind his head. "Take your best shot."

With a cocky grin, Jon lunges at Wes with a fist that doesn't land. The coach takes another swing. Wes returns with a quick hook and Jon wobbles, crumbling to the ground like a wet sandcastle.

"Nothing personal," Wes says to Coach Jon Spencer, a convicted felon with his face in the sand.

"Alex could've gotten us killed," Zen recalls. "Did you see him getting bashed into that rock? What if that was us? We were *this* close to being lost in the motherfuckin' surf."

"You made it," Wes tells them.

"I love you, Dad," Zen utters. "I love *you*, Hillary."

"We survived this thing together," Hillary says. "Love. Nothing but love."

12

Once again, Amsterdam is home. During the gray, wintry chill of January, Zen is spending more time indoors than he did in Los Angeles. These days, Zen and his parents live in a two-bedroom apartment with wide windows looking out at canal houses along the Damrak. He's checking his phone constantly. Hillary, nine hours behind in California, doesn't usually answer Zen's texts right away. The Palisades Fire has finally been contained after twenty-four blazing, devastating days. Hillary and her family had evacuated their Malibu Spanish villa to stay with an uncle in Riverside, over a hundred miles from the wildfire-scorched Santa Monica Mountains. Nearby houses had burned to the ground, with most homes on their street sustaining serious structural damage. But the lush, fire-resistant gardens around Hillary's house had somehow spared their beloved beachfront villa from the spreading flames. It's three o'clock in the afternoon, the final hour of daylight. Zen lays in bed with his second-place prize from the Huntington Beach Surf Off, a vintage fiberglass longboard with Hawaiian-style floral inlays pressed into the deck. His energy isn't what it had been during those endless summer days in California.

Back in Los Angeles, Hillary and her family have been navigating an unprecedented hellscape. Zen grabs his phone to immediately respond to a photo text. He sits up in bed to type another reply, but Hillary beats him to it.

Sorry it took me a minute to write back! Hillary's message to Zen begins. **I'm thinking about spending the summer teaching young surfers in Ghana, and would love it if we could go together. Portugal was magical. You made me feel right at home. Anyway, the Ghana trip comes with a stipend and free beachfront housing for the summer. I know it's a big ask, but this will be my last hurrah before law school starts in Fall. Today I woke up in my own bed for the first time in three weeks. The fire took out every other house on our street, but we were lucky. Hope you might find yourself back in California one day. Until then stay warm, and stay golden!**

"Hey!" Zen calls to his dad, who is in the living room reading the final draft of Jen's screenplay.

Wes looks up from his laptop. "What's new, bud?"

"Can you read this message and tell me what you think?" Zen asks, holding out his phone. "I really like Hillary. But how am I supposed to respond to this?"

Wes scrolls through the message quickly. "She obviously cares for you. Sounds like she wants to stay connected."

"When should I write her back?"

"Later today," Wes suggests. "She's asking you to spend the summer with her in Africa. If you reply right away, it may seem impulsive. Just take a moment to process her message, and write back before turning in tonight."

"I don't know, Dad. Would you spend a summer teaching kids to surf in Ghana?"

"If I was younger, I'd jump at the opportunity," Wes replies frankly, distracted by an incoming text message. "It's your mom. She says hi. Sounds like she's having the time of her life in Prague."

"That's why she's getting paid the big bucks," Zen says. "Maybe Amsterdam is the new Hollywood?"

"Well, Amsterdam's Red Light District has turned into a cliché," Wes observes. "At least that's what movie industry experts say. The agent who optioned out the screenplay swears it'll be a much more appealing film set in Prague instead."

"It's the bohemian capital of the East," Zen remarks. "But Prague's a pub culture, not a pot smoking haven. One of my surf buddies got pickpocketed outside the train station in Prague last summer. Do you think Mom's safe there?"

"Your mom is smart and resilient," Wes replies, swiping his winter wool overcoat from the tree rack by the door. "She seems to be finding her way around. Call her back when you have a minute. I'm going to go see Faisal and Omar off to the airport."

On a short walk to Central Station, Wes glimpses restaurants from around the world: an Italian pasta joint, an Argentinian steakhouse, and a traditional Dutch cheese shop with windowfront shelves of Gouda rounds aging in yellow casing. Across from the ornate grandeur of Amsterdam's red brick train station, Wes finds himself standing under a dazzling new Sub Shoppe logo. He scans the train station gates for Omar and Faisal, allowing himself no time to get nostalgic over the slice of the city that for so long had been his home.

Faisal stands outside the front gate with Omar, three large suitcases between the two of them. Omar is bundled in a scarf, a sweater, a thick corduroy coat. Wes notices Omar has lost a lot of weight since the heart attack. When Wes mentions it, Omar says that getting away from Sub Dude helped him get slim.

"The heart attack was a warning," Omar says. "But I think that getting out of the restaurant business was what really saved me."

"My father said the same thing about when he moved to Mexico and became a scuba diver," Wes says. "I'm thinking about starting a vegan sub shop. Any chance you might consider staying in Amsterdam to give it another go?"

"Wes, my brother, please don't even joke like that," Faisal tells him. "We're going to be very well off in Egypt. But if Dad and I stay here, our share of the buyout will be gone in a couple years."

"I hear that," Wes says. "Six months in California, and I burned up a quarter mil."

"Damn, dude!" Faisal replies. "What exactly did you do for work?"

"Nothing," Wes admits. "After twenty years of owning and operating Sub Dude, I needed a vacation. Now that I'm freezing my ass off in the Netherlands again, California seems like a dream. I didn't accomplish much in L.A., but my son became a world class surfer and Jen finished her screenplay. All I did was become a vegetarian."

"That's not nothing," Omar says. "Health is everything."

"*Barakallahu feeka*, my brother," Faisal gives Wes his blessing. "Drop me a line on Facebook when you can. I want to hear all about Hollywood, homeboy!"

"The fires in California look horrible," Omar adds. "Maybe you got out of there just in time."

"I'll always love L.A. But the truth is, I would've spent my last dollar if we'd stayed another six months."

"Good luck with the rebrand," Faisal says as they hug once more, a brief respite from the piercing cold of Amsterdam in the dead of winter. "We've got to get to Schiphol and wait for our flight."

"Is that all your bags?" Wes asks.

Faisal nods. "We sold what we could, and donated most of our winter clothes. It's a lot warmer where we're going."

"Love you guys," Wes says to Omar and Faisal. "Can I call you a driver?"

Omar waves off the suggestion. "The train is much faster. In ten minutes, we'll be checking in for our flight to Cairo."

"Travel safe," Wes says as they pass through the gate to find their train to the airport. "See you."

Wes turns around and heads back into Amsterdam's main throughfare. His phone rings. It's Jen, calling from Prague. Even after reading Jen's new script, Wes is still curious about how the Czech red light district is different from Amsterdam's. Jen explains that unlike in Amsterdam, Prague's sex industry is illegal and unregulated. The working girls she's been interviewing don't have public-facing cabins like the brightly lit windowfronts in De Wallen; to avoid the police, they change their work stations often and on the sly. Amsterdam's brothels are a tourist attraction, while hookers in Prague earn their living away from the palaces and spires that make the city's conservative façade.

"Tell me, babe," Jen asks eagerly. "Do you like this one better than the old version?"

"Definitely. Prague for the win," Wes answers straight away. "Besides, no one's more tired of hearing about red light district clichés than people who live in Amsterdam. That latest draft you sent me is a winner."

"Thanks, darling."

"How's Fefe?" Wes asks.

"Our girl is warm and happy," Jen replies. "My host family is amazing. They take care of Fefe when I go out and interview locals."

"Give Fefe a hug for me," Wes says. "I'm at the new Sub Shoppe to see what they've done. Talk soon. Love you."

Wes walks in as a few customers are walking out, their expressions dyspeptic and pinch-faced, their half-eaten cold cut subs abandoned on the table. Behind the service counter, the cashier in a Sub Shoppe uniform polo shirt also wears an odd-looking beret, flat and raised like a graduation cap.

"You look familiar," Wes says to the cashier, who has stitch tracks running across his forehead. "Aren't you?"

"I'm Robert," he begins, taking off his cap to reveal an off-color skin graft. "Sorry about what went down last summer."

"After everything happened, I took my family to California."

Robert smirks and grabs a broom. "California, huh?" he asks, pretending to sweep. "So, you're one of those."

"If by 'one of those' you mean vegetarian, then yes. Living in California showed me what real food is, and what it is not."

"Are you mad you lost the restaurant?" Robert asks.

"I would be if I did," Wes replies. "But I didn't lose the restaurant. I cashed out before you could sue me for it."

"I get mad sometimes," he says, scratching the healed suture marks across the crown of his head. "Mad at myself for letting things go that far."

"You and your little friend were way out of line for attacking

Omar," Wes says. "But that doesn't mean I wanted to slam anyone's head through a window over it."

Robert cocks a lopsided grin. "Well, I didn't press charges. I've changed since then. During my hospital stay, I was saved."

"I trust you had the best doctors. Glad you pulled through."

"So," Robert says, returning his broom to the corner. "When I said that I was saved, I didn't mean by the doctors. Now, I know you've got a Jewish name, and you're a California guy, so that's two strikes against you. But have you ever been saved?"

"Okay man," Wes says, turning to the exit. "This is getting weird. I'm out. Good luck."

"You're all going straight to hell, anyway," Robert says with a fire in his eyes that speaks for itself.

"I won't know," Wes responds, walking through a cold gust in the open doorway. "Because I'll be dead."

Within a month, the old Sub Dude sign hangs in a new window. It's the same silhouette of the same surfer dude with a board and baguette. But this time around, Wes is launching a smaller, smarter kitchen, kosher and humane by design. A local rabbi with a blowtorch spends two days heating all the metal utensils to a glow, purifying every surface in the kitchen with boiling water. It's the end of February and Amsterdam is still chilly. But gradually, the sun is putting up more of a fight against the frost and rain. Wes is developing a new menu, slowly becoming the master of his new grill. Until the summer, when he'll reconnect with Hillary in Ghana, Zen is doing what he can on social media to draw customers away from the Sub Shoppe and into the more organic, animal-friendly arms of Sub Dude 2.0.

This latest incarnation of Sub Dude is too small for a café or a dining area. In a minimalist kitchen, Wes prepares the subs and hands them off to customers who climb a short stairway to a narrow service counter. Hanging above the grill, a chalk-drawn menu is written in wavy, psychedelic letters: *Choose Your Alternative.* The new Sub Shoppe is on the same street as the vegan Sub Dude, which is now located four doors closer to the

Central Station.

It's taking time for his new venture to gain traction with customers in the dead of winter. On yet another slow day, Wes is scrubbing the grill an hour before closing time when he hears footsteps in the stairwell.

"I think I'll get the California Satan," a woman at the counter reads from the menu.

Wes pauses for a moment. *"Sigh-tan,"* he pronounces.

On her phone, she briefly looks something up. "What in the hell is that, exactly?"

"Seitan has an earthy flavor like a portobello mushroom. Tofu's closer to scrambled eggs. Jackfruit's my favorite. It's warm, hearty, and a little chewy. On a chilly day like today, I'd go for a California with jackfruit."

"Okay, I'll take that instead," she says lightly. "With all their nasty processed garbage, the Sub Shoppe isn't going to last."

Wes nods and smiles appreciatively. "Our menu is entirely free of animal products."

"This order isn't for me," she says, checking her phone for an incoming text. "Let me switch to a Philadelphia with jackfruit. Does that come with dairy-free cheese too?"

Wes nods. "The Cheese Whiz is made from natural ingredients like tofu skin, a mushroom stock, and a hint of dairy-free caramel."

"Sounds good. Could I have that with a handle bag? I'm taking it on a motorbike to my boss in De Wallen."

"Oh wow," Wes says, rolling the sub in paper wrap. "You've got a boss in the Red Light District?"

"Please stop," she responds quickly. "I work at a hash bar."

"Sorry for putting it like that. Look, if your boss might be into working out something in trade, send him my way."

She swipes the bag by the handles, recoiling from the counter. "We don't do illegal deals or laundering schemes."

"I don't do those things either," Wes says.

"Well, I didn't mean to assume," she replies, reaching into her slim handbag for twenty euro.

"I shouldn't have assumed either," Wes admits. "The Red Light District is far from just one thing."

"If he's interested, I'll let you know. I'm Jennifer, by the way."

"That's also my girlfriend's name. I'm Wes Levine."

Jennifer waves off the change Wes owes her. "Keep it," she tells him. "Next time, I'll try the California with jackfruit. Good luck with your new kitchen, Wes Levine. Cheers!"

"Come back anytime," Wes says to the customer.

Later in the evening, Jen comes home from Prague with Fefe and a suitcase full of gifts. After three months apart, Wes and Jen slip off their coats and reconnect in the warm apartment, where they look out the window at a starry Amsterdam skyline twinkling over the canal. Zen tears into the bags of wrapped boxes: ceramic Czech trinkets, sweet-smelling packets of linden tea, and an iron tea kettle so sturdy and heavy that it feels like home.

While Jen settles in, Zen gives Fefe a ceramic surfboard floor tray with built-in steel bowls for food and water. Fefe sniffs the little feeding board but quickly loses interest and leaps into Wes's arms. With a free hand, Wes feels around for the little velvet box bulging in his front pocket. At forty-six, Wes is about to make his first marriage proposal. He whispers to Zen that it'll also be his last. Cozying under a quilt on the living room sofa, Wes and Jen embrace, and at their feet Fefe is holding her head high as she springs upon the surfboard tray. Maybe she's imagining herself out in the ocean, standing on the precipice of an epic swell. In the kitchen, Zen lifts the tea kettle off the stovetop, bringing it to his parents on a bamboo tray with tiny red lotus cups and heart-shaped saucers.

Acknowledgments

Thank you to my Los Angeles-based editor Ray Lewis III, whose insights on surfing, both in California and beyond, have infused these pages with clarity, wisdom, and wit.

I'm grateful to Tova Mirvis for showing me how to evolve and grow, both in the writing game and in the human one.

Special thanks to Tamarah Benima, Norca Caicho, Lynne and Paul Channing, Marci Dawson, and Jonathan Gill.

Nothing but love and gratitude to my supportive and eclectic West Coast family: Catharine Baca, Corry Felix-Castillo, Jara Harris and his band SLAPBAK, Richard Lange, George Lauricella, James Slovak, and "Malibu" Barbara Williams.

And to my East Coast crew, this one's for you: Christian Alfonso, Nick Cellinese, Bailey Dicus, Hilary Hoagwood Eaton, Gabriel Michael Gilmore, Jeremy Konstanzer, the poet Henry Lefkowitz, Pat Renny, April N. Sanchez, Julia Simpson, and Paris Thalheimer.

Finally, I'd like to thank my mom, the artist Sara Credito, for watching *Point Break* with me in the early 1990s. At the time, I might've been a little too young and impressionable for a movie about masked surfers dressed as ex-presidents who rob banks to fund their endless summer in Southern California.

I hope my daughters Jacqui and Zoey Credito, to whom this very grown-up novel is dedicated, might one day dig into *Lost In The Surf* and dare to dream big.

About the Author

Derrick Credito graduated from Johns Hopkins University in 2010 with a Master of Arts in Fiction. Soon after, he became a popular college English professor and formed Credito, a critically-acclaimed indie rock band based in the Baltimore-Washington area. *Lost In The Surf* is his second novel.

Connect with Derrick Credito on Instagram @creditotheband or @dcreditoauthor.

Lost In The Surf

DERRICK CREDITO

A Book Club Guide

Derrick Credito's playlist for
Lost In The Surf

Soon after deciding to write a sequel to *The Year Of The Tsunami*, I started to cobble together a playlist of songs from the Baltimore-Washington area. All of them have inspired something — no matter how small or subtle — in the settings, moods, and vibes of this novel. A list of songs at the end of a book might bear all the hallmarks of a soundtrack. But this is not that. Instead, I think of the *Lost In The Surf* playlist as a companion to the novel, something more than just background music or end credits songs. I'm also sharing this playlist to elevate my hometown's music scene, and hope to turn my readers on to some new tunes.

"Empty Highway" by Pat Renny

When his first **LP** *Driven* dropped in 2023, Pat Renny released other tracks off the album as singles, and later said he wished this song had been chosen instead. So, here it is. Whether you're grinding it out on beltways, freeways, or wide-open country roads, *Empty Highway* is sure to strike a poignant chord.

"Sunset (Don't Leave Me)" by Brad William Cox ft. Niki Thunders

Brad William Cox wears many hats: rock singer and acoustic songwriter, novelist and lyricist, event host and podcaster. And on *Sunset (Don't Leave Me),* the hard-driving Skitzo Calypso frontman brings out a mellow alter ego named Niki Thunders, an indie pop wunderkind from the streets of Hollywood who also resurfaces as Neco Baal in Cox's fictional *Children Of The Program* trilogy. Equally fit for a trend-chasing night on the Sunset Strip or a subdued day at the beach, this is one sunset you won't want to miss.

"Love Will Find Its Own Way" by QueenEarth

A multi-faceted artist and beloved pillar of communities both locally and globally, QueenEarth sings about love's trials and uncertainties with a confidence and vulnerability that's sure to stir even the most hardened of hearts. As a novel about found family, *Lost In The Surf* is infused with the passion and perseverance of love. The hopeful yearning in *Love Will Find Its Own Way* might echo the tender, romantic soul of Janet Jackson in her peak years.

"Take Me Home" by Christian Alfonso

I've always thought of it as a privilege to have spent a period of my younger life traveling without putting down roots or staying in one place for too long. In a melodic moment of acoustic soul-searching, Christian Alfonso sings about home with affection, but also with longing and reluctance. Music can move someone to embark on a life-changing journey. Who knows how many road trips, red-eye flights, and backpacking adventures that the beautifully conflicted verses of *Take Me Home* might inspire?

"Everyday Screenplay" by My Useless Self

A few years before I became the bassist in My Useless Self, the modern rock powerhouse released their magnum opus, 2013's *Gifthorse.* The album's closing track was written after our East Baltimore community had been shaken by a freak accident that claimed the life of Shawn "Shlong Dog" Appel, whose memory lives on in this bone-chilling, Zeppelin-esque rocker.

Epic and elegiac, *Everyday Screenplay* is a reminder that life can unfold like a movie script, with twists and turns no one sees coming. My musical sensei Nick Cellinese is one of the hardest-working musicians in Baltimore, or anywhere else. This song is a heart-wrenching labor of love, and in My Useless Self, we rarely if ever perform it live.

"In My City" by LJR

Luke Justin Roberts (LJR) was one of the last artists added to this playlist, at the suggestion of April N. Sanchez, my band Credito's promoter. And I'm so glad to have this utterly hip and contagious track as a powerful pulse for the *Lost In The Surf* playlist. Hailing from Central Maryland, LJR is a high-energy vocalist who seeks to empower his audience to live life to the fullest. The urgency and immediacy of *In My City* makes it the perfect companion for an urban, cosmopolitan story about making moves, taking chances, and getting the most out of every moment.

"One Way Ticket" by Laura Baron

I can tell you a thing or two about how traveling one way is quite a different experience from going somewhere round trip. For many travelers, an itinerary without a return ticket might feel too final, or otherwise impractical. But not for me. And perhaps also not for Laura Baron.

At once folksy and soulful, this sweeping take on travel as a single journey is a reminder that freedom has a sound. Whether that's the sound of a train engine roaring or an airplane revving before takeoff, the connection between freedom and travel is profound and undeniable. For a big chunk of my twenties, I traveled mostly one journey at a time, bouncing around the Asia-Pacific without having a return ticket to the United States. Whenever I listen to *One Way Ticket*, it teleports me back to the planes and trains I hopped on the way to New Zealand and the Netherlands, places I'd later fictionalize in my novels.

"Man Without Skin" by Boy Hits Car

Boy Hits Car is my favorite band in L.A. right now. I'm drawn to their fierce and fearless stage presence, and to the humble connective energy of frontman Cregg Rondell. For decades,

BHC's brand of music, dubbed "LoveCore," has been bringing together people from all around the world. The intense yet zen-inspired *Man Without Skin* might be the most surfable song on this playlist.

"Coastline" by E. Joseph

My friend E. Joseph, a powerhouse performer who always seems to be on a stage somewhere, is also a stellar songwriter who knows his way around a hook. With *Coastline,* he has crafted a mellow and masterful take on life's rough edges. Rich with metaphors about the coastal edges of the Earth, this song takes a deep and meaningful dive beneath the surface. The sonic qualities remind me a little of Australia's alternative rock forerunners The Church, who, in the late eighties, had serenaded Planet Earth with *Under The Milky Way.* Fast forward to today, and my buddy from Bel Air, Maryland goes top to bottom with intoxicating melodies and haunting arrangements that bring to mind oceanic visions from the water's edge to the seafloor and back again.

"Learning To Fall" by Whalen Nash

Whalen Nash is a cowboy from Baltimore whose performing career began as a busker on the streets of Amsterdam. Later, he'd flourish as a singer-songwriter and recording artist in Austin, Texas. On this wistful acoustic tune, Whalen lulls the listener through an entire lifetime within a single verse. I happened upon *Learning To Fall* in late 2020, when I'd just found out that my estranged brother Ryan Credito had been diagnosed with an irregular heartbeat. Unfortunately, many years of hard living had taken a toll, and doctors handed Ryan a five-year life expectancy. Six months into the following year, Ryan would succumb to a deadly overdose. Blindsided and shattered as I had been, this Stephen Doster-produced folk gem comforted me when I needed it. The warm guitar licks uplift the melancholy lyrics, and the sincerity in Whalen Nash's voice always takes me back to happier times.

"Through Days" by Letterbox

This is a twenty-first century novel. To that end, the characters live a considerable portion of their lives online. Digital age trade-offs and the perils of life in a social media rubicon are topics Letterbox addresses on *Through Days*. Singer-songwriter Scott Lester is a twenty-first century music man. For Scott, there is no side hustle, fallback plan, or day job outside music. The guy lives and breathes music, and it shows in his extraordinary songwriting.

Back in 2007, Scott became my first-ever friend on *any* social media platform when I started a MySpace account. Finding Scott's profile was like a gift from the universe, and the important firsts didn't stop there. A few years later, Scott bought one of my electric guitars, making it possible for a struggling graduate school student to take the first of many trips to Amsterdam. Had Scott not been there to tip over that first domino, what would've become of my first novel, *The Year Of The Tsunami*, which is set mostly in the Netherlands?

By extension, this novel — *Tsunami's* sequel — probably wouldn't have manifested, either. Letterbox frontman Scott Lester is the reason why you're reading this. Now show the man some love and check out his music, dammit!

"Imposter Syndrome" by Black Sevens

Soothing and scathing, the introspective *Imposter Syndrome* speaks to *Lost In The Surf* protagonist Wes Levine's wildly divergent life journey. Tam Raistrick delivers impassioned vocals like a nineties grunge goddess, while Paris Thalheimer's blues-inflected guitar work — wait for the solo — elevates the song to even greater heights. And with a no-nonsense rhythm section like bassist Daniel Bradley and drummer Scott Stack, it is clear that Black Sevens are no imposters. They're the real deal.

"Like There's A Gun To My Head" by The Loss

As the hipster darlings of Baltimore's bohemian music scene, The Loss is just one or two degrees removed from music industry giants. The video for *Like There's A Gun To My Head,* an alt-rock anthem that took ten years from conception to completion, features a cameo from MTV legend Matt Pinfield. I've always thought of this song as something like *Smells Like Teen Spirit* on mood stabilizers.

In 2017, I first connected with The Loss bassist and frontman Michael Moran, when he organized a Chris Cornell tribute concert mere days after the iconic Soundgarden singer's tragic and untimely death. That night, the stars were shining bright over Charm City, when we played this special show in a packed basement bar at Joe Squared, a former pizza joint and live music venue in Baltimore's arts district. The Loss is a band you'd want to have brunch with. Musically and personally, their vibes are somewhere between trashing a hotel room on a wild night and spending a calm afternoon at an art gallery. Or, like, doing whatever child-free hipsters do in their cool, gentrified city neighborhoods with all that free time on their hands (suburban dad rant over).

"No Wrong Turns" by Eryn Michel & Eli Lev

A romantic duet about everlasting love, this uplifting genre-crossing ballad revels in the freedom that the open road can provide. As an atypical family that has only recently found each other, Wes Levine and his loved ones come to realize that what will sustain them are collaboration, compassion, and confidence in each other. Eryn Michel and Eli Lev are two of the finest singer-songwriters in the DMV, and together they are simply sensational. I could listen to *No Wrong Turns* on repeat driving all the way across Route 66, and discover something new about it each time.

"Oceans" by Ray Weaver

Maryland-born Ray Weaver is the king of Danish-American acoustic music, if there is one. A couple years ago, I met Ray at the New Deal Cafe in Greenbelt, while he was touring on this side of the Atlantic. The calming, poignant *Oceans* is a heartwarming ballad that underscores the heights and depths of love. From Copenhagen to the Chesapeake Bay, Ray Weaver proves time and again that even an ocean is no match for love's lasting power.

"Blue Sky Goodbye" by Let Go Echo

In this lifetime, Chris Henry and I have co-founded a band twice. First came Mad Tea Party, a jam-oriented college outfit that formed and fizzled out in the early 2000s. Twenty years later we reunited as suburban dads in Columbia, calling ourselves Let Go Echo, an EDM endeavor that would reignite my longtime obsession with the bass. Our partnership peaked in Amsterdam, where we traveled with some friends in 2023. Whenever I listen to the fleeting, subtle notes of this song, my mind goes back to those canal bridges and brick townhouses where Chris and I made our stand. The one Let Go Echo album I played bass on, *Hibernate,* was released that summer, and it hit streaming highs beyond all expectations. But just as things were starting to heat up, I walked away.

The following year, I went with Chris to the 2024 Maryland Music Awards with a nomination for Best EDM Band. By this time, we were musically pretty far apart, focused as we'd become on our respective repertoires. *Blue Sky Goodbye* didn't drop until a little later down the track, and it brings to mind peaceful, happy memories. For me, that "goodbye" was bittersweet, though we always seemed to end things on a high note. Back in 2001, Mad Tea Party sold out the Recher Theatre, calling it quits soon after. Leaving Let Go Echo wasn't an easy decision. Just as LGE was about to become a globally-known brand with a fast-growing catalog in a hip and emerging genre, I felt a need to center my creative energy on Credito, a more lyrically-driven indie rock experiment in which I sing, play bass, strum guitars, and write songs. Imagine that, a bass player who writes the songs! Credito has become an important part of what I consider my legacy, and I know that Chris feels the same way about the boldly innovative music he makes. To this day, Chris Henry is an EDM workhorse who releases a new album or two every year. Check it out if that's your vibe.

"Corporate Rock" by Kim Eaton

This novel depicts the impact of wealthy, overreaching organizations (read: corporations) on the restaurant and entertainment industries. Even surfing, with all its historically purist ethos, is not entirely beyond the influence of Big Money. On *Corporate Rock*, Kim Eaton pokes a stick at the same commercial powers this novel portrays as convenient and inauthentic, prolific but soulless, glitzy yet hollow. By contrast, the Washington, D.C. folk scene is down-to-earth and independent-minded, with many artists functioning — some might even be thriving — on a grassroots level. Kim's music always inspires me to break loose and cherish the true freedom that comes from standing on your own.

"20 Years" by Kaly Clauss

A two-decade gap separates the time settings of *Lost In The Surf* and its predecessor, *The Year Of The Tsunami*. One voice and one guitar, Kaly Clauss fills that vast chasm of time and space on *20 Years*. With an onstage persona and style that combines sleek East Coast fashions with western boho-chic, her bicoastal vibes could pack the hippest of venues up and down either seaboard. The longing and astonishment of this melancholy song never fails to put a lump in my throat.

Topics and Questions for Discussion

1. Describe Wes's reaction when he learns about his paternity of Zen. Does Jen's surprising disclosure change Wes suddenly or gradually?

2. Who does Wes first convince that he's cut out for fatherhood, his partner and their son, or the reader?

3. Where in this novel does the author's perspective of California come across as realistic? Romantic? Glamorous? Gritty?

4. As co-parents, what values do Wes and Jen share, and how do their value systems differ?

5. When and where is Wes most aware of his own vulnerabilities? To the reader, does it seem like Wes is going through a midlife crisis? Why or why not?

6. Why is Hollywood heavy hitter Kyle Langley so disillusioned with the entertainment industry? What might Kyle see in Jen's screenplay that her critics have missed?

7. Overall, does this novel leave the reader with a good impression of surf culture?

8. How does Zen's relationship of convenience with Ava prepare him for a deeper, more mature connection with Hillary?

9. As characters in their own right, do the animals in this novel have self-determination and autonomy?

10. Which setting would you most like to experience for yourself: Amsterdam, Southern California, Northern California, or Portugal? How does *Lost In The Surf* make that place the most desirable?

ALSO BY DERRICK CREDITO

The Year Of The Tsunami

"This is a novel of discovery, told from a unique voice at a unique time."

—Michael Chin, author of *This Year's Ghost*

"The *'Tsunami'* crashes onto your frontal lobe. It soaks you in diverse culture. A vacation for the mind and soul."

—Brad W. Cox, author of *Children of the Program* Trilogy

"In Derrick Credito's *The Year Of The Tsunami,* the journey is both literal and metaphorical. This adventurous first novel reads like a quest in itself, as though Credito had just told himself a crucial story, all while keeping the reader entertained."

—Madeleine Mysko, author of *Stone Harbor Bound*

"A beautifully written, deeply immersive novel that masterfully blends history, faith, and suspense. Credito's storytelling is both poignant and unforgettable."

—Reader's House, London's Literary Gateway